THE ACCIDENTAL MEDIUM

THE ACCIDENTAL MEDIUM

TRACY WHITWELL

MACMILLAN

First published 2022 by Macmillan
an imprint of Pan Macmillan
The Smithson, 6 Briset Street, London EC1M 5NR
EU representative: Macmillan Publishers Ireland Ltd, 1st Floor,
The Liffey Trust Centre, 117–126 Sheriff Street Upper,
Dublin 1, D01 YC43
Associated companies throughout the world
www.panmacmillan.com

ISBN 978-1-5290-8751-2

1 3 5 7 9 8 6 4 2

A CIP catalogue record for this book is available from the British Library.

Typeset in Stempel Garamond by Jouve (UK), Milton Keynes
Printed and bound by CPI Group (UK) Ltd, Croydon, CR0 4YY

Visit **www.panmacmillan.com** to read more about all our books
and to buy them. You will also find features, author interviews and
news of any author events, and you can sign up for e-newsletters
so that you're always first to hear about our new releases.

For Lee M. My legendary friend.

THE ACCIDENTAL MEDIUM

PROLOGUE: NORMAL BLOODY JOB

The phone rings six times before he picks up. When he does, there's a clunking sound and some fumbling. *Shit, I hope I didn't wake him. Surely it's too early for him to be in bed?*

'Hiya? Tanz . . . ? Hiya, sorry, I'm a bit drunk; I fell off the settee.'

Now there's a coincidence, as I'm a little tiddly myself. I don't bother with pleasantries – we phone each other too often for that malarkey.

'Milo, I have to get a normal job. I bombed in that audition and I'm really skint.'

'Oh. I'm so sorry, sweet-cheeks . . .'

His sentences are all one drawn-out word. He's mullered.

'Don't stay in that bastard London for another second. Get on that bastard train and come home and move right next door to me. Gateshead needs you!'

There's another crash. I think he's fallen off the settee again. Milo is always trying to get me to move back to the North-East. Or 'home', as it was for the first nineteen years of my life. But moving back 'home' means defeat in my career. Moving 'home' is everybody knowing my business. Moving 'home' is seeing my parents *all of the time*. Moving 'home' is not bloody happening.

'I can't move back there, Milo, all of my auditions are in London. Anyway, with your writing doing so well, you should be thinking about moving here.'

'How dare you!'

('Howairrrrooo.')

'I am a Geordie, young lady. Unlike you, I refuse to leave my roots behind. I have a laptop, I can email things. I don't have to go to London in person, and I certainly don't need to live amongst the enemy.'

The enemy being 'Southerners'. And the real reason Milo doesn't move is that he's basically agoraphobic, and he would never live more than half an hour away from his mam and her well-stocked drinks cabinet. Milo is a creature of habit, as well as a genius and my best friend. If he carries on drinking the way he does, he will also be dead by the time he's forty-five.

'I'm applying for a job in a shop,' I say.

There's a sharp intake of breath.

'A *shop*?'

'Yes. A fucking shop.'

'You are an artist, Tanz. You can't work in a shop.'

'I don't have a choice.'

Suddenly his voice is thick with tears.

'Tanz, you are a trouper. A modern-day hero.'

'I know. Thank you.'

'And, of course, a witch.'

'Don't start on this again.'

'My best friend is a witch. You *know* things.'

'I guess things, Milo. I "gather" things. I have good powers of deduction.'

'Sherlock Holmes had good powers of deduction. You have special skills, Tanz.'

He's always saying that. Other people have said that, too. But I'm a normal Geordie lass who's perceptive – and that's it.

There is one final almighty crash. Sounds like Milo sat on the back of the settee and it's fallen down on top of him. The line goes dead. He'll probably fall asleep like that.

I am not a bloody witch.

SUNDAYS ARE
SO ROTTEN

I open my eyes and it's Sunday morning. Well, it's 10 a.m. My mam would say that was nearly lunchtime. I'm still tired. I didn't go out last night but I had three buckets of Merlot, talked rubbish to Milo over the phone, then watched *The Hairdresser's Husband* again. I love that film. Right now I have a jet-black cat wrapped around my head. Inka has been licking my hair, it's streaked with damp and I'm seeping tears, the way my washing machine leaks wet foam if a sock gets stuck in the seal. I'm not sobbing; tears are simply brimming and cascading steadily onto my pillow, soaking it and me in brine.

Seconds ago I was in a field. The grass was warm and there were daisies. I was in Saltwell Park, a big sprawling place with a lake, ducks, rowing boats, greenery, swings and a fairy castle in the middle of it. I spent my childhood playing there and, just moments ago, I'd been back there with my friend Frank. Saying his name in my head is enough to make me ugly-cry. We were eating egg sandwiches by the octopus tree. We were sitting on a red tartan picnic rug and

4

Frank was laughing at me, smiling his goofy smile, because I was singing a song by The Smiths. He was joining in. It was 'What Difference Does It Make?' All we did was make the jangling sounds of the Johnny Marr guitar riff together:

'Dang-a-dang-a-dang-a-dang-danga-danga-dang-dang . . .'

Then he grabbed my hand, said 'You're mental', and I woke up.

Frank died in a stupid car crash three years ago and he was only thirty-two, so I still get a bit messed up when I see him in a dream. It happens every couple of months. It seems to be getting less frequent, but I always wake up wishing I'd given him the biggest squeezy hug in the world. Sometimes I think he's fooling with me. I never went out with him when he was alive – he was far too fickle – so now he plays hard to get with the whole cuddle thing. Sometimes I hear him talking to me in my head. I know I'm making it up, but it's still nice to hear his voice. I don't want to forget him.

I get up and mooch, then cry some more on my purple velvet chair for a good ten minutes, filter coffee in hand, sunshine piercing through the mucky brown slats. I wonder if I should run a feather duster over them. I can multitask when I weep – it's a talent. I miss Frank a lot, especially when I dream about him, but I am also a neurotic bitch and those blinds need a wipe.

Once I've mopped my face and my frog's eyes have unswollen, I pull myself out of the misery chair and let in some light. My sitting-room bay window opens onto a teensy front garden and privet hedge. After that comes my

street, East View Road, a narrow row of terraced maison-
ettes, pretty and quaint with walls like paper (I can hear my
next-door neighbours breathe) and tiny back yards opening
out onto each other, with low, lichen-covered fences separ-
ating one from the next.

I rent it on my own, since the complete bastard I used
to love moved out and left me with a huge rent to find, but
that ended all the snide comments about my 'funny shape'
and 'awful taste in mirrors'. He was actually much more
nasty than that, but that's how petty it got before I eventually told him to get lost. Now I'm wandering about in
leggings and a vest top – what passes for pyjamas these
days – and pretty much deciding that the best way to cheer
myself is to call Elsa. Elsa is my buddy, of sorts, and she's
a character. She is so pathetically trend-conscious that she
never wears a flat shoe, never gets bigger than a British size
eight and always has sunglasses worth more than my car
(bearing in mind that I've owned spoons worth more than
my old, but perfectly serviceable car).

I call Elsa and she answers on the third ring. Funnily
enough, she's another borderline alcoholic but still, most
days, gets up to go to the gym before 7 a.m. Almost all of
my friends are nut-jobs of one kind or another, but Elsa
makes me laugh, when she's not having life-sapping nervous breakdowns. She sounds groggy.

'Hi, Tanz.'

I hate my name. My mam called me Tania, barely a
millimetre behind Jane as the blandest name she could
have landed me with. Plus no middle name. My dad I've
forgiven, as men are shit with names, but my mam could

have had more imagination. Tanz is the only permutation I can stand.

'Hiya, wild night? You sound tired . . .'

'Work. A stupid article for *Woman & Home* about housework. I hate housework. And women.'

I laugh. 'You want to meet me for lunch? I'm feeling rotten.'

'What's wrong?'

'Nowt. I just fancy some chips and wine.'

'Well, if you put it that way. Half-twelve at Minnie's?'

'Yay! See you then.'

I feel better already. Warm day, and Sunday lunch covered. I will endeavour not to think about Frank being so sweet in my dream. If I don't think, I won't cry.

One good thing is that I can be summery today. It's June and it's lovely out there. As soon as it's not cold I have flip-flops welded to my feet. My latest favourites are decorated with tarnished silver sequins and butterflies. I slip on my white hippy skirt with a little top. I'm addicted to comfort, which is why I refuse to walk down to Minnie's in my best wedges, which will bring me out in blisters in 2.3 seconds. Elsa always looks glam, so I slick on a bit of gloss and layer on the mascara. What I can't do is make myself look tanned. Elsa has olive skin. Naturally I resemble a bottle of slightly pink milk. Only false tan changes this, but I'm rubbish at applying it. My legs often sport the 'giraffe effect'. Not that I like showing my legs anyway. I hate my knees.

When I open my front door I'm hit with an unexpected wave of gratitude. The warm air is only part of it. I'm grateful I'm alive, and I'm grateful my ex doesn't live here any more. I always throw up some thanks to the gods when I get this feeling. When you moan as much as I do, you have to balance the books a bit when you have a moment of clarity.

MINNIE'S
ISN'T MINI

innie's isn't mini at all. In fact it's quite roomy. It prepares lovely, locally sourced food and stocks a few choice wines, as well as other kinds of alcohol, all of which I've tried. As I walk in, a scent-wall of hot potatoes, coffee and something sweet and cinna-mony hits me bang in the face. I spot Elsa in the corner, hunching over a large Sunday broadsheet, a lemon pressé already in front of her. The tables are made of thick pine, the walls have hand-painted murals and the chairs are big school chairs. I love it in here and so does most of North London, but the sun seems to have drawn a lot of people out into the fresh air, so it isn't rammed with the usual middle-class families feeding their small children tofu and couscous. Winner!

I plonk myself in front of Elsa. She's reading a piece about fashion. I like clothes but I don't follow 'fashion'. I've always thought 'fashion' clothes are best modelled by transvestites. Models, to me, are transvestites with vaginas and don't come from Earth. Fashion clothes are rarely for five-foot-four girls with proper hips. Elsa is exactly the same height as me but has bony shoulders and perfect little boobs. I am jealous of that part of her, but couldn't be bothered to give up bread for the rest of my life to achieve her build. She has dark circles under her eyes. She has a dusky complexion and navy-blue irises. I have seen men buckle at the sight of her.

I give Elsa's arm a pat.

'Hey, handsome.'

She's wearing a lemon sundress with white rosebuds on it. I know, without looking, that it will fall slightly below the knee. She hates her knees, too.

'Hi. I look like shit, don't I?'

'Elsa, you have never looked like shit in your life.'

'I couldn't sleep again last night. I had to turn the lamp on, and the radio.'

I have an 'on–off' terror of the dark. Sometimes I have to leave on my fairy lights for comfort. I've always had an uncomfortable relationship with being alone at night. I have been addicted to old-school horror films and magazines about murderers for as long as I can remember, and yet I'm often afraid of turning off the light. Ridiculous; but I feel Elsa's pain now.

'Maybe you're stressed about something?' I suggest.

'It's my flat – it creeps me out.'

Elsa is always stressed out about something. Mostly money.

The waitress arrives. She's petite and Spanish, with a nice open smile. I think she's younger than us. I'm hitting that point where all of the waitresses in Crouch End are younger than me. I don't want to think about what this means.

I feel carnivorous. Usually I have a baked potato with hummus. Today I want gammon, egg and skin-on fries. Elsa, who's a vegetarian, tries not to look disgusted and orders a mushroom risotto. Our waitress, Maria, grins when I ask for a large glass of white. She already knows which one I'll have. If I have red, it's the Merlot, and I don't care how common that makes me; white is always Sauvignon Blanc. Minnie's stocks one from Chile, and it's bloody lovely.

Elsa orders a glass of champagne with a drop of elder-flower. She barely scrapes by after paying her rent, so much of her wages go on credit-card bills, but she still somehow manages to live like she's married to Denzel Washington. I use this example because she's completely besotted with Denzel Washington, and that's probably why she doesn't last five minutes with anyone she dates.

'Why did you move in there if it creeps you out?'

'I didn't realize until it got dark, did I? It's a nice place by day, it feels like a garret in Paris, but at night my bed-room makes me feel sick.'

She looks exhausted enough for me to feel sorry for her.

Our drinks arrive and, after a chink of glasses and a slurp, she prods me.

'So what about this new job then?'

A good-looking lad with longish hair and carefully dis-tressed jeans passes by as I shrug. He's headed for the counter. Looks like a new barman. I force my eyes back towards Elsa. I'm such a lech.

'I'm starting tomorrow. It's only part-time and, if I get that telly job, I'll be out of there within the week.'

I've been an actress for years, but jobs have been rare over the past eighteen months. I sold my flat twelve months ago and have been renting and living on the meagre profit since. My savings won't last forever, though, and a girl has to eat.

'Come on then. Tell me about it.'

'It's at Mystery Pot, up the road. I went in to get some joss sticks and saw a sign saying they needed someone to work on the till. They've got tarot readers apparently. I have to book appointments in, and all that. I asked this woman about the job: Maggie, she owns the place. She looks evil but was friendly enough. Weirdly, she offered me a trial after about five minutes. Says she wants more time with her horse.'

'And what's the telly job?'

'Oh, it's massive. Every actress in London will have her claws out for it. I don't even know why I bothered auditioning; there were six other actresses there when I arrived and every one of them was off the telly, and posh. Why would they want a broad Geordie who gets no work?'

'You never know.'

'I think I do.'

'Well, good luck for tomorrow. It might be fun.'

Acting is becoming an expensive hobby. The number of people chasing so few jobs is ridiculous. I've thought of retraining – putting my degree, and brain, to some use – but the only other job I fancy is as a forensic profiler, and that would mean another two hundred years of study. For now, shop work will have to tide me over. I glance at the long-haired bloke again. He's twenty-odd. I remind myself that is *years* younger than me. I like his mouth. I take another slug of wine.

As our food arrives, Elsa looks suddenly serious.

'If any of the tarot readers at that place are any good, give me a call, will you, and I'll book in? It might help me work out what to do next with my life.'

I'm surprised by this.

'Okay . . .'

As I raise my fork, the new lad at the bar presses a button behind him. A familiar guitar riff kicks in. Suddenly the speaker by us pumps out the slightly-too-loud intro to 'What Difference Does It Make'. And, to Elsa's utter bamboozlement, I burst into tears.

Very funny, Frank.

THE SHOP THAT
SMELLS OF HIPPIES

I used to be a goth when I was a teenager: Bauhaus and black clothes and big boots with skulls on them. Just before I graduated to being a full-on rock-chick. I love music and I also love the paranormal, so I should feel right at home in a New Age shop. And the thing is, I do quite like crystals and the smell of patchouli. I'm interested in spirituality, I'm interested in the power of thought, I'm interested in many things.

But I have a huge suspicion of anything that garners a following and generates money and claims to be 'a way of life'. As soon as something spiritual becomes a business, my palms begin to itch. It's how I feel about religion. There is something beautiful about having a faith that helps you to lead a good life and be kind to other people. But once it turns into a big gang, with rules and leaders, and money and the threat of punishment or eternal damnation if you get something *wrong*, I get very uncomfortable. Gangs always have bullies, don't they? So at five to nine, clutching a huge shop-bought coffee that I shouldn't be squandering my dwindling savings on, I approach the green door of Mystery Pot, feeling more than a little freaked out.

Maggie is waiting for me and has evidently just opened up. She wears a caramel-coloured jacket and slacks, has immaculate permed grey hair and looks like a Tory MP's mother. She hands me the keys and nods.

'I've written down all of the rules for locking up and cashing up, and the float is already in there.'

She took me through these things when she offered me a week's trial, but I'm glad she's written it all down. She has a chilly, carefully cultivated voice and a pointy face, but her eyes aren't cold. Again I wonder why on earth she owns a shop like this. With her clipped tones, you would expect her to introduce herself as an executive of the Pony Club. Still, judge not, lest ye be judged. To her credit, she doesn't hang about long and seems happy enough that I'm wearing my black polo neck, jeans and knee-high wedged boots. I thought I might be expected to wear some kind of hippy attire, as befits the shop, but obviously not. Maggie tells me that the tarot reader today will be Sheila, she'll be here by ten, and hands me a feather duster on the way out.

I'm left standing there with some God-awful, plinky-plonky hippy-shop music seeping out of the old CD player in the corner. It's not that loud, but yesterday's one glass of wine at Minnie's turned into five, as a huge debate ensued as to whether you can be obsessed by shoes and still be considered a serious person. I like Elsa, but sometimes when I'm drunk I despair of her hatred of talking about anything deep because she finds it vulgar, and of her terrified refusal to think about anything to do with death.

Death is my default subject of conversation whilst drinking. Now my head is experiencing the 'plinky-plonks' as tiny darts of glass stabbing straight into my amygdala, and I wonder if it's supposed to sound like angel tears falling from heaven or something because, if so, it's failing miserably.

As I poke the duster at a giant amethyst that looks like a magic cave, the first customer of the day floats in, like Nosferatu. He's a young man, he's wearing a cape and he stops dramatically in the middle of the shop, smiles and regards me like a museum exhibit. He's only about twenty but has a crop of thin, receding hair that eerily frames his huge domed forehead.

'Erm. Hello . . .'

He bows.

'I'm Antony. How arrrrrre you?'

He extends his hand. I tremulously offer my own and he kisses it. There's a touch of froth at the corners of his wide mouth. I really don't need this.

'And you are . . . ?'

'I'm Tanz.'

'Hellooo, Tanz, you're going to adore it here.'

He motions around the shop like it's the land of plenty. I'm not sure what to say. He has very, very wide-spaced grey eyes under that forehead.

I think on my feet, taking an almost imperceptible step back from him.

'Did you have a nice weekend, Antony?'

'Oh, yes. Yes, thank you, I did. I'm an alchemist, you see, and I took a client of mine to the Valley of the Kings.

16

We went into the great chamber of Tutankhamen's tomb and I held a quartz crystal in the air and, after several incantations, it turned into a pure diamond! It was wonderful.'

Fuckety-fuck. The hairs on the back of my neck have started to wave about like anemones. This is exactly what I expected from this kind of shop. *Nutters.* I smile encouragingly whilst wondering how I can run faster than the wind without seeming rude. I'm tempted to ask if he is jet-lagged from the flight back from Egypt, but I think he might detect my disbelief and produce some kind of ceremonial dagger from the folds of that crazy cape and jab it into my lungs.

Never has the sound of a door opening been more welcome.

The woman who's just entered is wearing a long maroon leather jacket, the kind you see in charity shops. She's got shoulder-length hair and she's wearing quite a lot of gemstone jewellery. There's a ruby on her finger (presumably fake) the size of my fist. I want to get down on the floor and kiss the soles of her golden sandals, although her toenails aren't the best I've seen. She smiles at the alchemist and nods at me.

'Hello, are you Tanz?'

I nod and wave.

'Hiya, love, I'm Sheila. Hello, Antony, are you chatting up the staff again?'

She has a cheeky London twang.

Antony giggles like a girl and puts his hand to his foamy mouth.

'God, no, Sheila. I'm behaving impeccably, aren't I,

Tanz? I was just relating some of my latest adventures. I've had a wonderful weekend in the Valley of the Kings . . .'

'Nice. Jet-lagged?'

'A little. But I have a special crystal, given to me by my godmother, that stops the exhaustion.'

He lifts his disproportionately large hand back to his face and places his finger on his lips.

'But don't go on about that, or everyone will want one.'

He turns on his heel, back towards the door.

'Must fly, my darlings – unpacking to do!'

When he's gone, I look towards Sheila, who smiles. She's late fifties, has good teeth and lots of lines around her eyes. I'll bet she smokes. I gave up a long time ago. Ageing my face, when I'm trying to get telly jobs, is a very bad idea. I like her lopsided smile. She holds out a bejewelled hand, obviously noting my anxiety.

'Don't mind Antony. He's actually a very intelligent boy. A few problems, though.'

'I noticed. He told me he turned a crystal into a diamond in King Tut's tomb. Who would leave him alone in a famous tomb to cast spells?'

Sheila shakes her head.

'He does like to embellish, but he's only a danger to himself. He's been rushed to hospital three times in the last two months, you know.'

'Oh, shit!'

'Pills and drink twice, and last time it was his wrists. His little fantasies are part of a bigger picture. I do worry about him.'

'That's awful.'

She moves towards the back room.

'Anyway, his godmother is taking him to Italy tomorrow, so he won't be bothering us for a while. Now I've just got to light my candles and take my coat off, love.'

Sheila has a much more earthy voice than I would have expected. She doesn't have the slow, deliberate speech pattern that comes straight from Victorian seances. I've always thought that if you have the 'gift' you shouldn't have to speak like you're on Mogadon. She smells of cigarette smoke (*knew it!*) and strong perfume. It's not the cheap stuff. I have a great nose for perfume, and I reckon it's Samsara. Her nail varnish is peeling. It's green.

The last time I had a reading, it was out of curiosity and it was with a young lass. She was well dressed and she came across as a frustrated performer. I left there certain she was full of shit. I fed her far too much information, and she was quite negative and I felt duped for a week. I've always believed there is 'something else'. I just don't quite know what it is.

There's a huge crash from the back room and an expletive. Inside, there's a little table, with two chairs facing each other across it. Sheila has put a pretty cloth on it, spread some gemstones about and laid down her cards. On one shelf a candle and an incense cone burn. Two holes in the wall show where the other shelf was, until about a minute ago. Now it's on the floor, with a surprisingly unscathed CD player next to it. Sheila is clutching her knee.

'Ow! The bloody shelf's loose. I caught it with my shoulder and it came out of the wall.'

We decide not to push it back in, in case it falls off again.

Her knee is bruised but not broken. I offer to make her a cup of tea, which she is very thankful for. I wonder if Sheila lives with anybody, as she seems touched by such a tiny kindness. When she's ensconced in her room with her cuppa, I check the diary. She has five readings booked already. Blimey. There's only room for two more half-hour slots; the rest are hours and are already taken. I decide I'll call Elsa later. I think I may have found her a 'good one'.

The phone rings and a nervous-sounding lady called Rita asks for a reading with Sheila. She snaps up a half-hour. I peep my head round the door and tell Sheila, who emits a big, throaty monster of a chuckle.

'Rita would come every bloody day if she was allowed. I only let her visit once a month, though. I'm not her therapist.'

She pronounces it 'ferapist'. She chuckles again.

'Well, if she's coming in, I might be up for a day of people making problems where there are none!'

'How come?'

'Rita's a lovely lady, but there's nothing actually wrong with her life, she just wants to talk. And you often find, when you're doing a whole day of readings, that they start to follow a pattern. The "problems" follow a theme. Some days you'll get six people who simply need reassurance. Another day it'll be all kinds of relationship nonsense; on another, God forbid, it'll all be odd and dark.'

My ears prick up, like nosy meerkats. Anything to do with scary stuff and I'm interested. But the door has opened behind me and I know it's time for Sheila's first customer. Blast!

The first man is short, Chinese and very quiet. He wanders into the room that's barely bigger than a stock cupboard with a blissful look on his face, and Sheila closes the door behind him. I would really like to be a fly on the wall in there. This is a good sign. Maybe I might like working here after all, despite the nutters and the hangover. I've taken some aspirin, I have a mug of coffee in front of me, a book to read between customers, and a colleague who gets 'odd and dark' people in.

Yes. This could be okay.

HOME, SWEET HOME TIME

I always like the drive up north. There are two reasons for this:

1. I passed my driving test when I was twenty-eight, so the novelty of the freedom that this fast-moving, albeit old and cranky piece of metal affords me as I pop up the motorway, howling along to my favourite CDs, still thrills me. Especially since I've been single and not answerable to anyone else.

2. Newcastle is still one of the best places in the whole world, and seeing as I travelled all over the world as an actress, before it all went tits up, I know what I'm talking about. Theatres, cinemas, museums, art installations, music venues, poetry nights, pubs with character, gorgeous old buildings, history, lovely hotels – I could be a tour guide up there. The countryside is beautiful, the nearby beaches are white and unspoiled (and, mostly, chilly) and the people are hilarious.

Like anywhere else, it has its problems, but Newcastle and its next-door neighbour Gateshead contain my family, many of my old friends and a huge barrel of nostalgia from my upbringing and teenage years. In the old days, when I couldn't drive and I went off to 'that London' to college, one of the biggest thrills of my existence would be my first sight of the Tyne Bridge from the train. As it approached Central Station I would draw an excited breath, knowing that I could soon alight and make my way to the 'night-life' – nightlife that I didn't really leave behind until I reached my thirties.

By the time my thirties came, I had a car and a man who didn't like me driving off up north to see friends all the time. I had budget restraints and worries, and confidence issues and all of the other baggage that seems to get worse instead of better if you don't handle it right. This was, of course, compounded by the fact that I was an actress, and my bloke was jealous. He didn't admit it, but in retrospect he was, and by the time we split up I had shown up at enough auditions looking haggard and argued-out for the rot to have kicked in. Now, even though we split up months and months ago, there's a feeling that acting is taking a rest from me because I let it down.

Still, being single and out of the loop means that I can drive off to my mam and dad's house whenever I've got a couple of free days, throw my diet in the air by eating white-bread fish-finger sandwiches and fall asleep in the room that I grew up in; or, better, on my mate Milo's spare futon, usually rolling drunk. My parents live in a very cute two-up, two-down; we moved there when I was eleven, and they have a fat, but lovely, dog called Zorro. Zorro has so many brands mixed up in him it's impossible to guess his lineage, although the black fur around his eyes, which makes him look masked and earned him his moniker, could well be a German-shepherd thing.

As soon as I walk through the front door, my mam looks up from her paper, lips pursed.

'Your nanna's hurt her leg. Your dad's had to go along. She's not been off the phone all day. She only banged it.'

My mam and my nanna are still vying for who gets the most attention from my dad. Primarily because he doesn't pay anyone any attention, apart from the dog. He has a shed. He really does. He goes out there and closes the door, in between tending his tomatoes in the greenhouse and walking Zorro. What with all of that, and his work hours, no one sees him much. I suffer from being in the unfortunate position of 'exactly in the middle' of the two feisty northern women in this triangle. My mam still feels aggrieved that my nanna wanted my dad to marry someone 'important' (like a secretary) and made her feel bad when they were courting. My nanna is furious that she's old and doesn't get enough visitors. Even though she gets visitors most days. I feel sorry for my nanna because she's eighty-two, but I also feel sorry for my mam because she's kind and nice really, but these two have built up such a wall of niggling grievances over the years that all approaches to the subject have to be handled with extreme caution. I hate that it's the first thing that's mentioned, so I go for the easiest riposte.

'She always moaning, you know that, Mam. Why are you letting her upset you?'

I am blatantly ignoring the fact that my mam can moan for England. She could probably represent the Earth in a Universal Grumbling Competition. Sometimes I catch myself complaining about some rubbish or other and I'm mortified. I do not want this to be what I'm remembered for: how many people I sent to sleep, miserable, from listening to my woes. I give my mam a slightly awkward hug. She's four foot six and was never really one for cuddling, but I do it anyway because I convince myself she likes it really.

She asks if I want a cup of tea. I hate tea and haven't drunk a cup since I was eight. I used to have a milky one because it was nice to dunk biscuits in. My mam knows this, but it's a Geordie default to offer a cup of tea. My parents drink about twelve mugs of Tetley a day. They even drink it with hot meals, which I find utterly perverse. That's what wine's for, isn't it? My mam is a cleaner, and my dad works in a factory. They'll retire soon. In their world, only alcoholics and unutterably well-to-do folk drink wine with their dinner.

I look at my mam, sitting there with her big eyes and tiny doll's mouth, and suddenly feel sorry for her. She had a very hard childhood, hasn't got the most romantic marriage and could probably do without continued sniping from an old lady who isn't even her own mother (who, by the way, wasn't exactly Mary Poppins, either). I go and pour her a cuppa from the pot and make myself an instant coffee. I can't bear the stuff, but I'll sip a bit of it black, just to be sociable. I perch on one of the new two-seater sofas that appear to be made of concrete and change the inflammatory subject from Nanna to Mystery Pot.

My mam is very proud of the fact that I am an actress and have been on TV, and she is still absolutely furious with my ex, Blake, on whom she totally blames my drop in confidence and waning career. The only way to avoid the inevitable diatribe when I speak of my career is to quickly convince her that I love working at the shop. For her, the work ethic is strong, so ultimately she'd rather I was at the shop than nowhere, and she listens with interest about Sheila.

'She sounds like your Nanna Lily.'

'Nanna who?'

As far as I know, I had a Great-nanna Eve, a Nanna Betty, a Great-nanna Mary and I have my current sole surviving nanna, Marge. I didn't know anything about a Lily.

'Oh, she was your Nanna Betty's mam. Your great-grandmother. She died a long time before you were born, when I was young.'

'So how does she sound like Sheila?'

'Did I not tell you? She was a well-known medium in Birtley. People used to come from all over for readings.'

Cogs whir in my head. I'm sure I have a vague recollection of hearing this before, but I don't recall any details.

'Your nanna – my mam – didn't agree with it, so we didn't talk about it. Your nanna saw some very strange things when she grew up. Shadows wandering around the house, a little girl in old-fashioned clothes standing at the top of the stairs . . . She was terrified to go out to the toilet at night. Said she wet the bed sometimes, she was so scared.'

'You never told me this before, Mam. What else did Nanna Betty say?'

'Not a lot; we weren't exactly close, were we?'

True, we didn't see much of Nanna Betty when we were growing up. You don't question it when you're young. Later on, after she'd passed away, I simply assumed she'd been a loner.

'One thing I do remember clearly, from when I was three or four, was that Lily dressed in a fitted coat and she smoked like a chimney. And she used to wear a lot of rings. I remember thinking she must be very rich to have so much jewellery. Turns out people gave her stuff in lieu of payment. Jewellery, food vouchers, all sorts. She was a right character. Well, that's what me mam said just before she died, when we were getting on a bit better.'

Funny how my mam didn't get on with her mother, but she still gets a lost look when she mentions her being dead. That's why I try hard with my mam. We're very different, but she's done her best, and I don't want her to disappear into the ether thinking I didn't like her. This is despite the fact that she once swung at my head with a packet of oven chips and only missed me by a whisker.

'Mam, have you never seen any ghosts or anything over the years? Isn't mediumship supposed to be passed down in families?'

My accent always becomes stronger when I'm with my mother. And I start murdering my grammar, just like she does. She is suddenly uncharacteristically quiet.

'What? What, Mam?'

'Nothing.'

'Nothing what?'

'I sometimes have dreams.'

'Eh?'

My little mam looks distinctly uncomfortable. I can't believe this. Nobody tells me anything. She said she 'felt' things once, but I thought she was talking about a 'mother's intuition'. I didn't believe her anyway. I was fifteen, and your parents are nothing but idiots when you're fifteen. Now I'm all ears.

'You know, when you have a dream, something will happen – and then when you wake up, it really does?'

'NO. No, I don't know. How come you're telling me this now, when I'm thirty-eight? Why haven't I always known this? What do you dream?'

'All sorts. I don't like to talk about it.'

'You don't like to *talk* about it? But you have now. You've got to give me an example.'

She looks ill at ease but eventually replies.

'I dreamed my dad phoned me at seven o'clock in the morning and said goodbye, on the day he had his stroke. The Andrews Sisters were playing in the background. He said he was going dancing.'

My little mam's eyes are filling up. I'm shocked.

'He used to love dancing with me mam when they were first married.'

'Why didn't you say you had that dream at the time? That's so sad and amazing.'

'I don't like to talk about it because I don't dream anything you can change. Like when Uncle Dave was attacked on holiday. I tried to tell him not to go, and he thought I was being difficult. So I didn't tell him what I'd dreamed, because it would only have upset him if I had. And maybe

if he wasn't attacked there, he'd have been attacked somewhere else. If you can't change anything, what's the point?'

'Wow! You dreamed it would happen?'

Incredible. And that was quite a philosophical statement
for my mam. I like her right now. The middle of my forehead feels weird, though. It feels strange when I'm talking
to Sheila, too. Talking to Sheila is an eye-opener. She
believes 100 per cent in what she does, and she doesn't give
a fuck what anyone else thinks. She worked two days this
week. I like her much better than the other reader, Martin.
He's little, with worried eyes and a nervous laugh, and his
regulars are all squirrels, like him.

Suddenly my mam tries to launch into another volley
about my selfish nanna and how she needs to make the tea
in a minute, and she doesn't want my dad to be kept late.
'Tea' is what Geordies call 'dinner', and most people have
their 'tea' before six o'clock and then have a snack later. She
doesn't really *need* to make it right now, as no one is doing
anything later, unless you count watching the TV all night
as doing something, but tradition and habit decree it as
'time to make tea' and she will not vary by even five minutes. Therefore nanna and her gammy leg are interrupting
a vital routine.

I refuse to get into this. Especially as I'm socializing at
seven o'clock and need a shower. I make my excuses and go
upstairs to get my glad rags on.

'When in doubt, go out and drink cocktails': that's my
favourite saying, apart from 'How did this bottle get so
empty?'

SLEEP?
NOT LIKELY

When I open my eyes it is pitch-black and for a moment I haven't a clue where I am. This often happens when I stay at my parents' house. I've woken up in a bit of a panic and I don't know where my phone is to check the time. I was dreaming about something scary but I've forgotten the details. I still have the vague feeling of running to try and catch up with somebody, and them getting further and further out of reach.

This is the kind of dream I have regularly. I have very vivid dreams, when I can remember them. The dream I have most, along with many actors, is the one where I'm standing in the wings of a theatre, knowing I have to go on soon and knowing I have left it too late to learn my script. Sometimes I have the script in my hand, but can't make any sense of it; and sometimes I have no idea where I've put it. It's such a relief when I wake up from that one.

I feel about on the floor, my eyes useless in the absolute darkness afforded by my mam's lime-green blackout curtains. Eventually, after plenty of fumbling, I locate my handbag and take out my phone. I groan at the time: 5 a.m. As I'm getting older I'm finding it harder to sleep the whole night through, after a night on the booze. Especially when I mix my drinks. I often wake up criminally early, my head buzzing with all sorts of worries, and it can take a good hour to doze off again.

Bits of last night flash back at me. The big-hug hello between me, Milo and Chris . . . Milo doesn't like leaving the house much, as he prefers to cocoon himself and write made-up stories for a living. Therefore he gets pie-eyed before any evening out, and this was no exception. He arrived already warmly drunk, with red-wine teeth. (Milo never stays with a boyfriend for longer than three weeks, as they always want attention and he never wants to give it. That suits me just fine, as we have world-solving chats on the phone several times a week.)

As for Chris, he's something to do with computers – I couldn't tell you what. We're not close, like I'm close to Milo, but I've known him a long time and I think Milo might still have a crush on him (Milo was two years below us at school), so I don't object to Chris coming out with us occasionally. He is single at the moment, too. He has eyes like giant chocolate buttons, and ladies love to love him. But he's very picky and extremely neurotic when it comes to girls. Sometimes I despair of him, especially when I bother to pick up one of his calls and have to listen for a good hour to his latest tale of agony with yet another weak, strange woman that he should have avoided like double VD.

Last night we'd started off in a nice pub on Pink Lane with a civilized glass of wine for me and Milo, and pints for

Chris, then eventually found our way to some kind of reggae club, where we draped ourselves over big loungy seats in the chill-out area and talked about relationships and our childhoods, and stupid stuff that you talk about with people you've known for ages. All the while they carried on with their usual drinks and I graduated to margarita glasses containing a dangerously blue liquid.

At a late point in the evening, something odd happened. I was chatting with Milo, head bent towards him so that he could hear me over the bass, which was so guttural it made my stomach vibrate, when Chris came back from the loo. As he passed, I stopped what I was saying and grabbed his hand. He looked down at me and I got closer to his ear and words began to tumble out of my mouth.

'Chris, it's all changing. You're going to get married next year. The girl you'll marry is completely the opposite of anyone you've ever had before. She's not some over-glam fool. She's got long hair, it's auburn, she's funny and her name is . . .'

I thought for a second.

'I think it's Lynn.'

Chris stared at me. I stared back. What was I bloody saying? He bent down to face me.

'Who have you been talking to?'

'No one. I . . . it just came out.'

He laughed nervously.

'No wonder Frank used to call you the White Witch.'

I felt a wrench at Frank's name, but I was drunk enough not to indulge it.

'He probably said that because I knew what he was up to before he did. He was as clear as a glass of water.'

'Frank once told me he could never get anything past you, and that you could see inside people's heads.'

'Did he?'

I misted up.

'Anyway, just so you know, I met a girl two weeks ago when they sent me to Manchester for that conference-thingy. Her name is Linda. She is exactly how you've described, she is adorable and she takes the piss out of me, and I've been having a secret affair by telephone. But I have to say, the chances of me marrying her are slim to zero. Avaunt, thee, *evil witch*!'

Milo only caught little snippets of what was going on (thank the Lord, as I don't think he'd appreciate pronouncements of Chris's upcoming nuptials), but he laughed drunkenly at Chris's last sentence and struggled to his hazy, wobbly feet.

'Can I get you another blue concoction, Fenella?'

Chris snorted at the reference.

'Haha-haha. I love Fenella . . .! *Ohhh, I hate yew, Chorlllton!*'

And thus my out-of-the-blue prediction was sidelined by a ridiculous impression of an animated Welsh witch. That's why I love having boys as friends. Uncomplicated.

And now I'm awake at 5 a.m., with a toy drum beginning to play a samba inside my cranium. I switch on the lamp, reach into my overnight bag to redeem my paracetamol and neck two down with a huge gulp of water, strategically balanced in a plastic tumbler on the Formica bedside table. Only when this is done do I warily allow myself to ponder the whole 'prophecy' business.

I have often been referred to as a 'witch' in my life, and mostly I put it down to having good old-fashioned intuition and (pre-bob) Kate Bush hair. I've always known 'things' about people. But describing someone's new and as-yet-secret girlfriend to them – even, near-as-dammit, their name? That's another level. It's made me feel uncomfortable. I want to call Milo, but he was so sozzled by the time we left the club that I put him to bed and came back to my parents'. If he'd been more alive, I would have stayed there and we'd have chatted, like we always do. It usually takes a huge amount to render Milo comatose, but tonight it was the final sambuca shot after several buckets of wine that did it for him, I reckon.

Despite my best intentions, my head is beginning to whir. For now I'll let it. I'll just lie still while the drugs kick in and hope that my spinning mind calms down. Four hours of M1 madness are not best tackled on three hours' kip and a stinking headache.

I no sooner think this than I begin to fidget and tug restlessly at the duvet. It's going to be a long night, whether I like it or not.

SEX CANNOT
BE IGNORED

I 'm wandering around Crouch End Waitrose again. I do a lot of wandering when I'm not working. I came here for some fish to steam, some salad and some broccoli. I should get these from the local fishmonger and the local fruit-and-veg shop really. I still may. I often mooch around shops then leave again – it's part of my 'walking to stay fit' drive. If I don't go swimming, I walk around for an hour or two. That's my rule.

There's a very good-looking man by the fridges comparing different pots of hummus. (I adore hummus, it features heavily in my life.) He has sandy-coloured hair and is wearing a trendy suit. I don't go for suits as a rule, but there's something rebellious about the way he wears it, like he has to put it on for work but hates to conform, so he got Charlie Brooker or Stewart Lee to make it for him. I love those two.

I'm having trouble at the moment with my hormones. I haven't had sex since I split up with Blake. Mostly because I was with him for so long, and it got so nasty, that the thought of any more than flirting fills me with terror. It's all very well fancying and being fancied, but I get myself embroiled so quickly once I've taken my clothes off, and it's just not worth the risk. That's what my head tells me anyway. But my body is rebelling against this by turning me into a caveman every time I spot someone vaguely attractive. I simply can't control my rampantly roving eye any more. Worse than that, I'm not really one for masturbation; it makes me self-conscious. Or it used to. But last week I got cheeky with myself for almost an hour in the bath, thinking of this funny bloke from a dog-food advert. Before I knew it, I was up to my chin in suds and imagining him living down the road from me, and me bumping into him in the corner shop and him unexpectedly knocking at my door after seeing where I lived, while I was taking a shower, and . . . Well, the rest is nobody's business, but I know I'm reaching critical mass when it comes to needing a shag. I have to do something about it. I'm just not sure who the victim will be yet.

It's crossed my mind that I could contact an upmarket escort agency, but let's be honest, they might send a minger – and you don't know where they've been, do you? As for vibrators, how do people use them without feeling completely stupid? I think they have a very particular sound. What if my neighbour brings all her friends round to stand with a glass against the wall and snicker at the dildo-lady?

I decide to abandon hummus-man and, indeed, to get my greens from the fruit-and-veg place three doors away, like a responsible local should. As I pass the newspaper stand near the exit I notice a missed call on my phone from Elsa. *Damn!* Suddenly, I also hear a voice as clear as crystal in my head.

'Call Sheila.'

I stop short, and a lady with a basket and a toddler holding her hand walks into me from behind. I apologize, she growls something and walks off. I reach around inside my brain.

'Sorry?'

'Call Sheila. Go round and see her.'

Fuck! This voice sounds male, but not rough or anything. Friendly. And it's not like that other voice – you know, the one you hear in your head all the time: your narrator, which is basically you, putting a spin on everything that happens. (For me, usually a paranoid spin.) This voice is removed from that; it's someone else's voice. I read about murderers all of the time. They say they hear voices. As do schizophrenics. Double-fuck. A tiny part of me thinks I may be on some kind of devilish *Candid Camera*. I look around suspiciously. No one is even glancing in my direction.

Luckily, I took Sheila's number to give to Elsa. Sheila does home readings as well as shop ones. If she reads for Elsa at home, then she'll be able to pocket all of the fee. Seems only fair. I press 'dial' before deciding what to say to Sheila. She picks up almost immediately.

'Hiya, it's Tanz . . . Er, a voice told me to come and visit you.'

There's a throaty guffaw down the line.

'Well, you'd better come round then. I just got back from the laundrette, so you called at a good time.'

Bloody hell, she took that well. The address she has given me is only around the corner. I insist on bringing her something, and show up at her front door with a cappuccino for me and a large Americano for Sheila. The building she lives in is stunning. She has a studio flat on the ground floor; she'd already told me this, but nothing had prepared me for what's inside. It's how I always imagined the interior of a Gypsy caravan would look, when I had romantic notions of running away with a man with dark curls and a hoop earring who played the fiddle. I truly have lived in a fantasy land since I was born.

The flat is, of course, bigger than the inside of a caravan, but it has the same sense of being enclosed by a person's whole being. Every wall, surface and item of furniture seems to be dressed in or covered by velvet, silk, flowers, angels, fairies or twinkly lights in gorgeous hues of purple, crimson, burnt orange, ochre, deep blue and scarlet. There is so much stuff, but it all fits, and the effect is one of being cushioned from the world. I am well aware of how soppy this makes me sound, but sometimes you have to call a spade a spade, and this place rocks.

We sit opposite each other at a table beside the French doors, which lead onto a tiny terrace edged by pots of herbs and small rose bushes. We drink our coffees and I begin to feel a bit wrong for showing up here because 'a voice told me'.

But Sheila merely says, 'I had a feeling about you.'

I am in awe of this woman, who has people queuing up

to hear her wisdom. She's a down-to-earth Londoner, she has roots showing in her lightened hair and she wears funky clothes. She is not some self-important, self-professed mystic, lining her pockets whilst scaring people into coming back to her every week. 'Dances to a different drum' is how my mam would put it. My mam is only seventeen years older than me, which means that I often look up to older women who are wise and strong. My mam was always more like a big sister, really. Frank used to say I 'collected new mams'.

'What kind of feeling?' I ask.

I'm wondering if the coffee is extra-strong, as I've started to feel dizzy. My forehead has this swimmy feeling, like I'm breathing through it, or I'm a Cyclops and I just opened my one big eye. I actually think I might faint. Sheila looks at me through cigarette smoke.

'Are you okay?'

'Yes, I'm fine. But I'm feeling a bit dizzy.'

She looks around the room, then back at me.

'The middle of your forehead, between your eyes?'

I nod and she smiles.

'That's your third eye.'

'Eh?'

'You're clairvoyant, love. Actually, if they're speaking to you, you're clairaudient. It's quite strong in you. Was that the first time you've ever heard a voice?'

'I think so. I mean, I've always had "feelings" about things, but that voice was quite distinct.'

'Well, it must be your time to learn. Some people have

those voices with them from childhood, others close off from it and open the door again later in life.'

Sceptical but excited is what I'm feeling now. Everyone wants to be 'different' don't they? But really I know it's not possible.

'When did you learn, Sheila?'

'I had it as far back as I can remember. I saw ghosts everywhere. People no one else could see. Think it kept me sane, the madhouse I was brought up in.'

I can't help laughing at the notion of being 'kept sane' by the presence of ghosts.

'I would be terrified if I saw a ghost.'

She nods.

'Probably why you hear them, love. Less scary for you. Lots of psychic people are scared of seeing spirits. Ridiculous, isn't it?'

'It was only once. How can I be psychic? I'm just . . .'

'One not enough for you?'

She laughs and drinks her coffee.

'Of course, love, it could be schizophrenia.'

My eyes goggle and she tuts.

'I'm joking! I know how mental illness affects the aura. You don't have any signs of mental illness. Well, no more than any other normal adult! When a medium or a psychic speaks to another one, or sometimes even stands next to them, there's a sensation in the forehead – sometimes in the tummy. I get that when I talk to you, and I think that's why we've met. You need to develop. You have strong presences with you. I can feel three.'

This is all madness.

'Three?'

'They're not revealing themselves to me right now, apart from an older lady. She's smiling. She's called Lily. Lots of jewellery. Do you know her?'

I feel a coldness down my spine when she says that.

'That sounds like my great-nanna. She was a medium up north.'

'Well, she's just stepped forward and given me a nod. She's letting me know that she did indeed pass her gift to you. She's widening her hands. I think she's telling me your gift is stronger than hers. She wants you to learn.'

'Tell her "thank you". But I don't really think—'

'Tell her yourself!'

'Oh.'

I fix my eyes on the carpet. I'm not sure I want to do this.

'Out loud?'

'Out loud, in your head – it doesn't matter. She's only passing through anyway. Busy, busy.'

I say, *'Thank you'* in my head to Nanna Lily. I could swear I hear, *'You're welcome.'*

It's very faint. Then it's gone. I jump a little in my seat.

Sheila smiles encouragingly at me and I get a teensy rush of excitement. All those times I heard people talking to me in the past, and I thought I was making it up. Conjuring them up in my head. Could it be?

'How come this is suddenly happen—'

I stop because I've seen a shadow. It was coming towards me and now it's halted about three feet away. There is no reason for a shadow in this room to be moving

41

about. Or for the sudden pressure on my head and chest. My throat has tightened. I just stare.

Sheila looks from the place where I see the shadow to me and back again.

'You can see him, can't you?'

I nod. This is mental.

'Him?'

'Yes. Do you see him or feel him?'

'Both. Mostly feel. He's a shadow.'

Now I'm panicking.

'Why don't you speak to him?'

'Because he's a ghost and I'm scared. Really?'

'Like I said, out loud, in your head – either works . . .'

I test it out.

'Hello!'

The shadow steps forward. It's like I'm being pushed back in my seat.

'Whoa. *Whoa!* What's happening?'

'Ask him to step back, so it's more comfortable.'

I breathe in and out slowly, then think, 'Can you step back a bit, please. I'm new to this.'

And he does. I feel him backing off, and I'm sure I can 'feel' him laugh. He seems to be excited. I can 'see' in my mind that he's older, has greying hair and he's wearing a blue cardigan and brown slippers. I take the plunge.

'What's your name?'

'*Edward.*'

I hear it clearly in my head. He has a gentle voice and is very posh.

'He says he's called Edward! I heard him. He stepped back. Thank you, Edward. I'm Tanz, nice to meet you!'

I can't help speaking out loud, I'm so delighted. I'm positive he's clapping his hands. Sheila is suddenly very bright-eyed.

'Well done, Tanz.'

'I can see what he's wearing. He's got a cardie on, he's got grey hair . . .'

'And he's wearing his favourite brown slippers?' she finishes with a flourish. The fact that Sheila is 'seeing' the same thing is mind-blowing to me.

I try speaking to him again.

'How come I can see your shadow, Edward?'

'Call me Teddy.'

I feel a thrill when he speaks to me.

'He's told me to call him—'

'Teddy?'

'Yes! Do you know him, Sheila?'

'Of course! He came with the house. It was a grand place, before it was split into flats and studios.'

'When did you . . . pass away, Teddy?'

'It was 1927. I wasn't old, but I had a nice life.'

I can see him in my mind's eye raising one of those old-fashioned champagne glasses. He is wearing a black tuxedo. Then the image is gone again.

'You were very dapper.'

Teddy steps forward. He obviously likes compliments.

'How come I can "see" him as well as feel him, Sheila? I can hardly believe it.'

'I think it's because I "see" rather than hear. You're

picking up on my way of doing it. You'll recognize it from now on, if you're on your own.'

That puts me in a flap.

'I'll have a heart attack if this happens when I'm on my own.'

I hear Teddy laugh. His voice is clear but small, like he's speaking down a telephone line. Sheila chuckles, too.

'You can close down, Tanz – I'll show you how. You don't have to "see" anything if you don't want to. But I think you're a natural. And I think you are going to attract help in your development. If you don't want to develop, you'll need to block it and hope you can push it away. It may not be easy.'

There's a disturbance in the air where Teddy has been standing. Sheila notices and raises an eyebrow.

'Oh. Our Teddy's not too happy with that thought. He likes you.'

Why am I so utterly thrilled by this? I hear his voice again.

'I can help you. There are lots of us who can help you. Just open up and have a chat. There's nothing to be afraid of. Don't block.'

As if I would, now that he's put it like that.

PETER SUTCLIFFE
AND SEXY PAT

I've got a lot to think about. The air is so warm I could be abroad. The streets are still quite busy, even though it's seven in the evening, and all I can think about is talking to a dead fella at Sheila's place. What a lovely man he was. Sheila says Teddy's still around because he likes visiting, and not because he's 'stuck'. She says she'll tell me some stories about the 'stuck' ones next time.

I can see people looking at me because I've got a stupid grin on my face that I can't wipe off. I'm shaking. I sit on a bench next to Barclays bank and call Milo. I get his voice-mail. He may be visiting his mum. There's no reception at her house and he usually stays late to watch loads of recorded episodes of *Judge Judy* and drink her good gin. I leave a message.

'Milo. I've just been talking to a *ghost*! I shit ye not. I can't believe it. My hands are sweating. I don't know what's going on. Either I've finally lost it or I'm like that bloke off the telly, with the white hair, who keeps channelling evil people with Scouse accents.'

I laugh at my own joke. I sound really manic. I've got to calm down. I'll do myself a mischief if I don't get a grip.

'Anyway. Hope the writing's going well. Let's speak soon. Don't worry if you get this late. We'll talk tomorrow. Big kiss.'

As I stop the call I see there's a voicemail from Elsa. Elsa's a bit crazy, so she'll text and call a lot, then not speak to me for six weeks. This must be one of her friendly months. I look through the window of an over-expensive boutique as I listen to the message. There's not a single damn thing in that window that I could wear or that would suit me. Supposedly beige is in fashion. I'd rather stab myself in the eye with a spatula than attempt to wear beige. What's wrong with these people? I'll bet Elsa has a whole bunch of clothes in a shade of beige that looks absolutely fucking fabulous against her tan. Elsa understands trends and would probably come out best in a tussle with a pair of stupidly expensive culottes.

She sounds fraught in her message. Says she hasn't slept properly in days and needs to talk to me. Minnie's is about fifty steps away. After everything that has happened, I need a glass of wine. I call Elsa. It goes to answerphone. She might be on the Tube with no signal, she might be in some cellar bar off Soho, getting smashed with alarmingly hip people, or she might still be at work. Who knows? I leave a message and step inside.

The warmth in Minnie's is overpowering this evening, but there's a small empty table with a fan next to it and I grab it. I don't know the smiling girl who comes to take my order, another new one, but she seems sweet enough, and I bagsy myself my usual pint of vino and some olives to pick at. I actually fancy cake, but that's not happening. Certainly not at this time of day – it's against the actress rules.

I wonder, as I wait for my drink, whose voice it was that told me to go to Sheila's in the first place. The voice in Waitrose. Maybe it was Lily? Sounded male, though. I'm working tomorrow, so maybe I can ask Sheila.

A glass, satisfyingly misted with cold, is placed in front of me. And a plate of olives in chilli oil with warm peasant-bread. I'd like to give the bread back, but I've suddenly realized how hungry I am. I bloody love bread anyway, it's my Achilles heel. As I take my first bite, a familiar face passes, bearing a tray. It's the barman who put The Smiths on the other day.

He's carrying food; he has his hair tied back, and I notice that his eyes really are the most extraordinary china-blue colour. My eyes are hazel and I have always coveted blue eyes. My dad has blue eyes. As I sneak another glance, I'm just in time to see him slide and trip. He manages to save himself the indignity of landing on his backside, but at the expense of the tray. Two bowls of fries and a pot of ketchup go flying and shatter on the wooden floor.

Without even thinking, my mouth opens.

'Sack the juggler!'

He looks at me. I have no idea why I said that. A couple of people giggle and, to my eternal relief, he breaks into a grin. I get off my chair, grab his tray and begin to pile chips and bits of crockery on there.

'No, no! Let me get that.'

He has a nice accent. Soft Irish. Dublin, I'm guessing.

'I'm the eejit who dropped it.'

He actually said 'eejit'. I look at the floor, pointing out an incriminating skid of potato.

'You slipped on a chip. Someone's been chucking them on the floor. Not your fault at all.'

A woman whose toddler is sucking on fried potatoes at the next table has the good grace to look embarrassed.

I grab the handful of napkins he'd been carrying on the tray and wipe up a gobbet of ketchup.

'Will you stop that – really, it's not your job.'

He takes them from me; he has nice strong hands and well-shaped nails. Just then the waitress shows up with a dustpan, brush and damp cloth. Not wanting to get in the way, I retake my seat as he explains to two estate-agent-looking blokes that new fries are already on their way. He smiles at me as he passes. I grab my magazine out of my bag, *Serial Killer Monthly*, and idly glance at it whilst guzzling my wine and thinking of those hands.

I am such a sucker for accents, especially Celtic ones – especially Irish. This, added to the fact that I have been dying for a shag for about two months, accelerates my drinking speed alarmingly. I have to be careful with my stereotyping. Just because someone is smiley and Irish, with twinkling eyes, doesn't mean he is naughty and up for anything. Especially with an older woman. There is no guarantee that he finds crow's feet attractive / he's single / he's any good at satisfying ravenous Geordies.

Shit, I've finished the glass. How did that happen? The waitress comes back. I now have a choice. Go home and watch the telly or stay here, on my own, and drink more, whilst not-so-surreptitiously sharking after some Irish lad with nice hair.

'Could I have a glass of champagne this time, please? Actually, make it a Kir Royale.'

The waitress smiles again.

'Celebrating tonight?'

'Actually yes, kind of.'

'Is it your birthday?'

Even I'm not sad enough to sit drinking on my own at dinnertime on my birthday. 'No. I've just had a good day.'

'Oh, that's really nice.'

I'm not sure what's really nice, but I'm glad she looks so pleased. She goes off to get my drink and I attempt to immerse myself in the story of a man who killed many, many women because he couldn't maintain an erection and hated them for it. All his sexual fantasies were about tying women up and pleasuring himself as he strangled them to death. I usually find this stuff compulsive reading, but you know what? This has been a fantastic, life-changing day and this magazine is in serious danger of bringing down the mood. I close it as the next drink arrives, just in time for Irish boy to pass, after delivering fresh chips. He stops, glances down and stoops closer to my ear.

'My uncle hitched a lift from Peter Sutcliffe's best mate once. After he'd been caught. His mate said Peter was a really nice bloke – no one could believe he did it.'

He walks off. I am so impressed. If I had the choice between having a drink with Johnny Depp's best mate or Peter Sutcliffe's, there'd be no contest, and *that* is saying something. Come to think of it, given the choice of spending a couple of hours with Johnny Depp or visiting Peter Sutcliffe, if he's not stone-cold dead now, I would be hard pushed to choose. What the hell does that say about me?

I hope it says I'm not as shallow as other actresses. But it could also mean I'm a potential killer. You read about it a lot: murderers who were obsessed by other murderers. I've been reading about this stuff since my nanna introduced me to her collection of *Crime and Punishment* magazines. She was a total rascal, my nanna; still is. Because of her, I'm obsessed with murder and expensive perfumes. It doesn't matter how full my credit card is, how much I need to find my rent, if the Coco Chanel runs out, I have to replace it or I'm all over the shop. Wearing another fragrance knocks me off-balance.

I'm painfully aware that if I stay in Minnie's much longer I'm going to look like a lonely old cow with no home to go to. Especially now that I'm not reading, just sitting here, drinking champagne like my mam drinks builders' tea. My head is a bit spinny. I've only had two drinks, but I've also only had two small pieces of bread and some olives to eat in the last six hours. I am tempted to have fries and more drink, but I am too self-conscious to do it. As I'm dithering, a text arrives. Elsa saying she's getting the Tube and will text me in twenty-five minutes if she's dropping in at Minnie's. A second later another Kir Royale arrives at the table. I'm about to protest when the waitress motions towards the bar.

'It's from Pat. He says you deserve it.'

She leans forward conspiratorially.

'I think he likes you.'

She leaves again. I am rooted. What are you supposed to do when someone hot sends a drink over and you need some food to soak it up? Will I look like a wanker if I order something? Like I'm expecting that for free, too? As if he's a mind-reader, he stops at the table and places down more olives and bread.

'I have never had a customer jump out of their seat and try to help me clear up a mess before. Thank you for that.'

I blush. I never blush. I've blushed at most five times since I was twenty. Why have I gone all blushy?

'Thought you might appreciate a little nibble with it.'

Seems that my stereotyping was bang-on. This lad is trouble. He winks and wanders off. I don't always like winks. Grandads wink. But this wink doesn't annoy me. This one is a cheeky-chappy wink and I can't help but forgive cheeky chappies.

'Erm?'

He looks back. I motion to him. He returns to the table.

'Yes, madam?'

'I can't sit here and have another drink on my own. I'll look like a prostitute.'

He stifles a snigger.

'We don't get a lot of prostitutes in here, as far as I know, madam, and they usually show a bit more cleavage than you are right now.'

I am wearing a little sparkly purple jumper with a denim skirt, leggings and my trusty flip-flops. I see his point.

'I have come here in my daywear. Casual is all the rage.'

'It's nice.'

'I wasn't fishing. I . . . Can't you come and sit here for a bit, so I don't look so pathetic? The murder magazine isn't cutting it tonight, and my mate might be on her way, so I can't leave yet.'

'Much as I'd like to, I'd get the sack. But they can't sack me for chatting at the bar.'

He motions to a high stool at the little bar. He picks up the olives and my drink. I follow him with my jacket and bag. Usually I would be self-conscious, but I've had a giant glass of white and I'm onto my second Kir Royale. Sod it! I feel a little less stupid now; people drinking on their own should prop up the bar.

'I'm Pat, by the way.'

I don't bother telling him I already know this, and I hold out my hand.

'I'm Tanz. Nice to meet you, Pat. Thank you for . . . this.'

I dip some bread in the spicy oil and take a bite. I'm famished.

'I can't believe your uncle met Peter Sutcliffe's best mate!'

'Yeah. He was a lorry driver, same as Sutcliffe. My uncle told me Jim reckoned Sutcliffe was a good bloke. Said he was really shocked, like. Said you wouldn't meet a more mild-mannered man.'

'You find that a lot. Those blokes who are the most dis-turbed are the best at seeming unassuming and nice. Funnily enough, though, where men see another bloke being agreeable, women know better. Female neighbours and colleagues, and suchlike, often say that they were a bit disconcerted by the killer. They say he made them feel uncomfortable, but they couldn't say why. Something about the way he'd look at them.'

'Jeez, you know a worrying amount about murderers. My mum's like that about blood and guts. She watches everything she can on TV about accidents and the ambulance service. I prefer a nice film myself.'

He pronounces it 'filum'. Where I come from, the pronunciation is very similar but not half as sexy. He's tall, he's quick to smile and I doubt bar work is his final calling.

'How come you've ended up in London with that accent?'

He shrugs and wipes the bar.

'I realized I didn't like my career choice, so I'm starting again. Fancied bumming around the world. I started here to get more money together. My sister lives up the road, so I decided to stay in her spare room and save up a couple more hundred, then go travelling for a year.'

'Wow! When are you off?'

'Jeez, are you trying to get rid of me already?'

'You're kidding me – not if I'm getting free champagne.'

'What do you do?'

I hate that question. If I say 'actress', they immediately ask what I've done. As soon as I tell them it's TV, some people turn into idiots. I know how horrid that sounds, but you do definitely become interesting in the wrong way if there's the remotest possibility that you might be a 'celebrity'.

'I'm sometimes an actress. Right now I work in a shop.'

'Crouch End is full of actresses, isn't it? There was one

in here the other night. Supposed to be famous but I don't watch TV, so I'd never seen her before in my life. She started off a right snobby cow, then got sozzled, and Maria over there had to prise her off me with a crowbar. What shop is it?'

I think I wanted him to be more impressed. I'm a mass of contradictions, I'm well aware of this.

'It's Mystery Pot; it's just up at—'

'Oh, I know it. My sister loves that place. There's this woman there does the cards, gets it bang on every time, apparently. My sister keeps trying to persuade me to get them done, but I'm scared.'

'Scared?'

'I'm not sure I wanna know – you know? Does it help to know something awful is going to happen before it happens?'

'Why on earth would it be something awful?'

I look at him and suddenly something clicks in my head. A little ball of fire ignites. He's drying a glass. I touch his hand.

'You've lost someone, haven't you? Someone close? It's a man. He says you needed to get away from the sadness at home. You've done the right thing.'

He is standing stock-still and staring at me. *Fuck, I've blown it now.*

'Sorry? How did you . . . ?'

'I'm so sorry. I should keep my gob muzzled.'

I now feel like crying. There's such sadness there, I can feel it, and I've gone and poked a stick at it. He looks like a lost puppy.

'No, it's . . . Jeez, my dad died last year.'

'Oh, that's terrible. I'm sorry to bring it up.'

'It *was* terrible. Especially for Mum. I've escaped and she's trapped there with the memories. But how could you know that?'

'I didn't. I don't. I just said what I felt.'

I don't want to say any more, but I know I have to. It's there, pushing at me.

'I have to tell you – press upon you – that you've done the right thing. Your mum was worried sick that you'd lost your dad so suddenly. I feel you're the youngest in the family. You could have reacted very badly. But now you're doing something positive. And he approves as well, I can feel it so strongly.'

Pat's staring at me still, but he doesn't look as sceptical as I thought he might.

'I'm not that young.'

I get up off the seat.

'Can you guard my drink while I go to the loo?'

SOME ARE 'STUCK'
AND SOME ARE VISITING

I need to hide for a minute. Pat's bound to think I'm a crackpot now. Men do not take kindly to spooky shenanigans; I don't know many males who believe in that kind of thing, and I don't want everyone to think I'm one of those eccentric mentalists who wear billowing kaftans and coloured Birkenstocks and claim to know where Grandma Olivia hid her wedding ring before she died. Why couldn't I simply have had a nice flirt and gone home?

Still, I got it right, didn't I? I 'felt' something and I was right. I sense a buzz in the pit of my stomach, like a couple of hawk-moths are dancing in there. A small part of me, which I'm trying to repress, keeps saying the same thing: *You've always felt you were different and cut off and 'apart', and now you know why.* And I can't help breathing the tiniest exhalation of relief.

I comb my hair, replace my lip-gloss and decide to take myself off home and tell Elsa to meet me there if she still wants to see me. This has been one hell of a day.

As I push open the door I find myself blocked by the

waiting frame of Pat. He takes my arm and guides me towards another door. Suddenly I'm outside in a tiny yard. The sky is darkening and a wall lamp is casting watery light down the painted white bricks and onto a couple of plastic chairs. He motions me to one seat and takes the other beside me. He pulls out cigarettes and gestures around.

'The smoking room.'

He offers me one. They're Marlboro Menthols. I like a menthol, especially when I've had a drink.

'I started smoking when Dad died. I'm such a wuss – I only like the mint ones.'

'Me, too.'

'Good. We can be wusses together.'

He lights mine first, his hand shaking a little. He lights his and leaves it in his mouth as he takes the band out of his hair, which falls in waves around his face, then pushes it back again and reties it. He then takes a long drag and slowly blows out the smoke.

'I have no idea how you did that. I've been thinking about my dad all day. I don't like to tell my sister, because it makes her cry. You've totally spaced me out. How did you . . . know?'

'I don't know how I knew. This is all new to me. I don't really "know" anything. I suddenly get a feeling and I say it aloud. My friend does that stuff for a living. She says it's called "being a vessel".'

The cigarette is making me fuzzy. I look at Pat again. He is shaken up, I can see it. My gob opens again.

'You're doing the right thing, you know. Your sister is comforted by you staying with her. Your mam has other family and friends, and she will find a light at the end of the tunnel.'

I smoke, feeling a strange beating in my chest. There's one more thing to say . . .

'Your dad always knew you were going to travel, and now you're on your way. He's very proud. Did he used to call you Pat Cat, or Pat the Cat?'

His intake of breath is sharp. Again I wonder if I should just shut up.

'That's what he called me all right. Pat the Cat. I was always sneaking in and out of my window. I'm glad he's proud.'

'Why wouldn't he be?'

I hear his dad clapping. That's all he wanted to say. I immediately feel his presence less strongly. He's made his point.

Pat stares into space. There's something very personal about sharing these things with a stranger. It makes me feel protective of him. I want to wrap my arms around him like I'm his mam. I'm sure that's very wrong.

'I didn't know witches drank cocktails.'

'I'm no ordinary witch.'

'I'm not being funny, but can we go for a drink some-where when I finish my shift? I reckon I'm too stirred up to go home straight away.'

As he asks, my mobile goes off. I remember Elsa. I grab it out of my bag. Sure enough, it's her.

'Sorry, Pat, just a sec.'

A very uptight voice greets me.

'Where are you? I'm in Minnie's. You're not here?'

'Sorry, Elsa. Give me a minute – I'll be right out. I thought you were going to text from the station?'

'I did! Then I jumped in a cab. I hate buses.'

She clicks off.

I check my phone. There's a text. I didn't hear it arrive.

'Pat, I'm so sorry. My friend is out there, and she's upset about something. I've got to go and talk to her. Maybe we can chat later?'

'You're a proper Agony Aunt, aren't you?' Before I can think, he's got his arms around me and is giving me the sweetest hug. 'Thank you. You have no idea.'

He smells divine. Cologne, fresh cigarette smoke and man. It's been a long time since I've been this close to a hottie. Plus, I just saw him at his most vulnerable. I breathe him in, like a filthy old perv. This hug is lasting too long now. I don't want to take advantage of a situation that's stacked so majorly in my favour. I simply gave him something he desperately needed. I think about pulling away.

All at once Pat puts his lips on mine. Lovely, warm, juicy lips. Grateful or attracted? I don't bloody care. I absolutely should not be doing this. If he opens his mouth, I am toast. I have to gather myself and get to Elsa or she'll kick off. I stop, pull away gently and smile.

'You're welcome.'

When I walk back into Minnie's, I am physically shaking. Even my jaw is trembling. Christ almighty, talk about a conflict of interests. I don't think giving messages to strangers is supposed to make me horny, but then I doubt if everyone I give a message to will be like Pat.

THERE'S A GHOST
IN MY HOUSE

Elsa is sitting by the bar. I have never seen such dark bags under her eyes. She's effortlessly rocking a floor-length black maxi-dress with flat, strappy sandals and tasteful silver jewellery, but she looks ill at ease and miserable. I go to her and give her a hug. So very different from the one I just broke away from. This one is testy and her energy feels as dark as her eye-bags.

'Have you ordered a drink?'

She scowls.

'No, I haven't. There's no one bloody serving.'

Right then Pat appears and Elsa moodily orders the biggest glass they have of Pouilly-Fumé. As I said, nothing cheap for this girl.

'Another Kir Royale?'

Her shocked eyes whip across to meet mine.

'You've been drinking champagne?'

'I fancied a change.'

'How long have you been here?'

'I don't know. An hour or two.'

'Hmm. Lady of leisure.'

I don't think she means to be a cow, but she knows I miss my career and the money that came with it. Criticizing me because I haven't been working today is like criticizing a bloke with a broken leg for not joining in his usual football game. I decide to let it pass this once, but next time . . .

Pat puts the drinks in front of us pronto, and I thank him as he casts a disapproving eye over Elsa.

We sit at the table I was at in the first place and, in a role reversal of last time we were here, Elsa starts to cry. I'm not sure I've ever seen her weep. I've seen her eyes filled with tears of rage, and I've seen her at her weakest when she was mugged by some low-life who punched her for good measure. But this – this is tired crying. This is the crying you did when you were five and you had been running about in the park for hours and you suddenly felt emotional and drained and didn't know why. My mam used to call it 'tired temper'. My dad didn't call it anything. He'd just scoop me up and put me on his knee with his arm around me until it stopped.

'What's going on, mate? Has something happened?'

Elsa nods, then dabs the tears with a tissue from her bag. Her mascara remains perfect.

'Don't laugh. There's something going on in my flat.'

'The oppressive thing, still?'

She takes a huge slug of her drink.

'I haven't slept properly since I moved in. The only good night's sleep I have is when I've had a full bottle of wine before bed. But I can't do that all the time, I'll be a bloody barrel. Anyway, not even that works sometimes. If I do nod off, I get woken up at three fifty-five a.m., no matter what. Every single day. It's bloody killing me. Tanz, there's something in my bedroom and it won't go away.'

The hairs go up on the back of my neck. Sheila taught me this thing for 'protection' tonight. I attempt to do it now. I imagine an orangey light rushing through me, expelling any negativity, then surround myself with brightness, like the Ready Brek kid. I can almost see the dark fog around Elsa.

'Are you talking about a ghost, Elsa?'

She slumps and shrugs.

'I know that makes me sound like an idiot, but I don't know what else to call it.'

'You don't sound like an idiot. What's it doing?'

She looks pitifully grateful that I'm not mocking her.

'It's not so bad in the daytime. The flat just feels a bit claustrophobic, like I'm not the only one there. It's not threatening really, though I don't write there on my day off any more, I go to Costa round the corner with my laptop. But at night, when I get in, I feel positively unwelcome. I go into the bedroom and it feels cold, even with the heating on. I keep the light on and put on the TV in there for company, but it still feels awful, like something bad is going to happen. Most nights I start feeling like I can't breathe. I can't get comfy at all and I feel like I'm being watched. Then if I eventually do nod off, at three fifty-five a.m. – almost to the second – I jump out of my skin and wake up scared. Then I wind up lying on the sofa, which is too lumpy to sleep on.'

She takes another gulp of wine and I ignore my Kir. I really have had enough to drink now.

'I'm sorry to whinge, Tanz, but I'm terrified of going to

bed. I don't like being there any more and I signed a year's lease. What can I do? Can your friend at the shop help? Does she know anything about ghosts?'

I don't know if Sheila can help. I don't see why not, though. She was about to tell me about spirits that are 'stuck'. I wonder . . .

'Let me call her right now.'

I scroll through for Sheila's number. I am so interested in ghostly happenings, but never in my life did I think I'd talk to a 'spirit'. I still think I'd have an embolism if I properly saw one, but I certainly don't mind hearing them. A lifetime of watching Hammer movies and idolizing Vincent Price, Peter Cushing and Christopher Lee has definitely left an impression on me. This kind of thing really over-excites me.

Sheila picks up eventually.

'Sorry, love, I was having a fag and watching a Cary Grant film, *Arsenic and Old Lace*, do you know it?'

'Oh my God, are you kidding me? It's one of the best films *ever made*. Plus it's got Peter Lorre in it.'

'I know. Well, I couldn't find the pause button, it took me a while.'

'That's okay, I'm sorry to disturb you.'

'You're not. That was great today. I've never met such a natural.'

I'm over the moon she thinks so. In other circumstances I'd tell her about Pat and his dad. The edited version, of course, without the thoroughly inappropriate lust at the end. But I don't want Elsa to know. It's my little secret for now.

'Look, Sheila, I'll be quick. I'm with Elsa – you know, the friend I told you about, the one who wanted to call you for a reading?'

'Oh, yes. The one who puts make-up on to go to the gym?'

'Hmm. Anyway, she's got a bit of a problem with her flat. There's something – probably *someone* – in there and they're stopping her from sleeping. They're making the whole atmosphere rotten basically, and she gets woken up at the same time in the middle of the night, every night.'

'Right. Well, first off, have you protected yourself?'

'Me? Yeah. A few minutes ago.'

'Okay, have a delve.'

'A what?'

'You're sitting with her now, are you?'

'Yep.'

Elsa is drinking the rest of her wine, looking intrigued.

'When you put down the telephone, have a delve. Think about her flat and feel about for any kind of energy that you can pick up through Elsa. You'll get an idea of who's in there. We can pop over there after work tomorrow, if she wants? We should be able to sort it, unless it turns out to be "complicated". I reckon you'll be a dab hand at ghost-busting!'

I can't help laughing. Suddenly I'm visualizing Bill Murray with his backpack on and a laser beam coming out of his spook gun.

'Wow! Thanks, Sheila. How exciting is this? Just a sec.'

I look to Elsa, who's dying to know what's going on.

'Are you around tomorrow evening at six-ish?'

'I can be.'

'Good. Sheila, that's fine. Let's do it!'

'Good girl. See you tomorrow.'

I grin at Elsa.

'What? What did she say?'

'We're going to come and ghost-bust your house tomorrow.'

'Really? I mean, how can you help? Isn't it a specialized thing?'

'Sheila's going to teach me. Just a second, I want to try something. Sit still.'

I sit still myself, look at Elsa, then 'feel about' with my mind, looking for a clue. Two things come to me. It's an old lady in Elsa's flat and she is angry and confused. Plus, she's not evil, she's scared. Interesting.

'You're being haunted by an old lady. She's terrified and she's angry.'

Elsa almost jumps out of the seat. She glares at me with absolute alarm.

'Please don't – I have to go back there tonight. How can you possibly know that? That's the last thing I want to hear. I'm bricking it, as it is.'

'Elsa, I have a very nice sofa bed. Don't go back there. Stay at mine. Even if you have to get a cab to yours early in the morning for clothes and stuff for work, you'll still get more sleep at mine than yours.'

I've never seen her look more grateful.

'You are a lifesaver.'

'Shut up.'

'No, really. Who the hell else could I go to with a

65

"haunting" problem and they'd know what to do? How exactly do you *know* that about the old lady, though? I mean, anyone else would think I was a loon.'

'You *are* a loon. A lovely loon, obviously. And to be honest, I'm not sure what's going to happen. I may be awful at the whole spirit-clearing thing.'

'Well, whatever happens, you'll be less scared than I am.'

Elsa glances at the bar.

'That surfy-looking barman keeps looking over here. Do you know him?'

'Oh, not really, we were just having a chat earlier. Nice lad.'

Her eyes narrow.

'Nice lad? He can't take his eyes off you. Is there something you want to tell me?'

'No.'

'He's quite handsome, isn't he?'

'Yeah. He's cute, I suppose.'

'Cute, my arse. He's gorgeous. Isn't it time you dipped your toe back in the water?'

'Erm, no. You know I can't keep a level head. I can't be bothered with it all.'

Elsa yawns like a lion.

'Tanz, I'm sorry to be a pain but I'm dying on my feet here, that wine's gone straight to my head. Could we maybe . . .'

'Of course.'

I wave Elsa's tenner away when Maria brings the bill. I pay with my groaning credit card and, as I'm slipping on my jacket, Pat approaches and hands me a square of paper.

'Let's go for that drink sometime, if you fancy it?'

Then the cheeky blighter kisses me on the cheek. I want him to kiss me on the mouth, but that's not prudent. Elsa is looking at me smugly, not without a little envy. Like many pretty women, she's used to being the centre of attention with attractive blokes. My looks are interesting, rather than beautiful, and I'm not as skinny as Elsa, so I always feel like her ungainly chubby sister when we go out. This is a new situation.

We use her tenner to get a cab. We should walk, it's not that far, but both of us are tired. Once inside, I rustle up crudités and hummus, which I quickly realize is not mopping up the drink sufficiently, so I add a few rounds of toast.

After I put the duvet on the pull-out sofa bed and Elsa gratefully curls up under it, she peeks out and smiles.

'You've got to call him, Tanz. Or I will.'

'Stop it. Let's just concentrate on sorting your flat. God knows what's going to happen there.'

She's almost asleep before I finish my sentence. It's probably the carbs. Usually Elsa treats bread the same way she treats tramps and beggars – like their existence makes her sick. She doesn't mean to be horrible to tramps and beggars, incidentally, she is simply mortified by uncleanliness and assumes they are filthy. I leave on my cherub lights and put a glass of water on the table next to her. I think of leaving on the TV, but I reckon she'll be fine.

I can't believe it's only ten-thirty. It feels like I have lived a forty-hour day. It should be at least 6 a.m. I programme Pat's number into my phone, not because I think I'll call him, but because at least I won't lose it if it's in there. I'm always losing things. It amazes me that, after a day of revelation like today, I can still be thinking with my loins. I push thoughts of his lovely mouth out of my mind. Nightmare!

As I clamber into bed my phone rings. I pick up.

'Hello, is this Rent-a-Ghost?'

'Hiya, Milo.'

'*Hiya, Milo*, Mrs "I-have-no-powers, I-am-not-a-witch"? Spill the beans. I want details of the undead, and I want them now . . .'

I laugh. Obviously my day isn't over yet.

FIND THE LOVE

I don't get to talk to Sheila much at work because she's booked out the whole day. Talk about Mrs Popular. Today's theme seems to be rude, toffee-nosed idiots who want to be told their lives have meaning when they don't. Sheila slaps my hand when I tell her this.

'We're all looking for meaning, love. Some people are rude because they're scared.'

'So what! They're still rude. Wankers . . .'

Just then another leather-faced rich woman troops in, in ill-advised spike-heeled boots, white skinnies and obvious hair extensions. I'd usually think this rocked on a sixty-odd-year-old, if she didn't look at me like dog poo. I always wonder where well-off people get this idea that they can be as horrible as they want? It always seems to be worse in people who used to be poor, then acquired money. Anyway this one has a huge stain on her aerobicized old arse, and I'm not telling her. She is also the colour of beef gravy. She doesn't look tanned, she looks barbecued.

As the door closes on her grubby bottom, I happily

recall Elsa leaving my place by taxi at 7 a.m. with a smile on her face. She slept like a baby and she was feeling relieved that someone was going to (try to) help.

At lunchtime Sheila manages to explain quickly about spirits who come back to visit as and when they please, as opposed to poor lost souls who don't, or won't, leave for whatever reason. The latter need guidance and help, whereas the former may have a lot to teach us. God, I love all of this.

Turns out she's done a few 'clearings', or 'ghost-busts' as she prefers to call them. I've noticed that Sheila finds the humour in spiritual stuff, which is probably why so many people come back to her for readings. She doesn't take herself too seriously and she's down-to-earth and truthful. When I ask how she got into this business, she just repeats that her childhood was shocking and if she hadn't had her 'other friends', she might not have survived it mentally. When I ask about her mam, she spins her finger next to her temple and chirps, 'Cuckoo, cuckoo, cuckoo!'

And now we're in my car, which is looking more sorry for itself than usual, as some idiot knocked a dent in the door while I was parked outside my house and drove off without leaving a note. This is the norm for London, but it still riles me. When you're already skint, you can do without people knocking lumps out of your car and not owning up to it.

'What if I can't feel anything?'

Sheila snorts.

'How can you *not* feel anything? You only had to concentrate a tiny bit last night to discover it was an old woman, and what her state of mind was. I think you're more likely to need to protect yourself from feeling too much. You're obviously very sensitive.'

'If I'm so sensitive, how come I only found out about all this now? Why haven't I been doing it for years?'

'You have.'

I think back to all of the times in my life when I've 'known' something and called it 'instinct'. The most glaring was the day I turned up for school when I was eight years old and my form teacher wasn't in class. He was a funny, clever man, we all adored him, and I'd never known him not to be there before the students arrived. My instinct was that it was too cold in the room, unearthly cold. There was a stillness; an absence that I couldn't vocalize. Basically, as soon as I walked into that classroom I knew that our teacher was dead. Ten minutes later it was announced in assembly that he'd died of a heart attack the night before.

Afterwards I told myself it was a conclusion I'd come to because he wasn't in the classroom when he should have been. But that's quite a leap: teacher late, therefore dead. Things like that have always happened to me and I've put it down to educated guesses. Now I'm not so sure. It seems to be the truth that if you're not looking for something, you don't see it. Maybe I always 'knew' stuff. I just didn't recognize what was happening.

The traffic on the way to Elsa's is shocking. The roads of London always jam up with cars around teatime. I ask Sheila to pick some music and she rifles through my little leather CD case. I am chuffed when she hands me *Led Zeppelin II*.

We pass the journey happily enough, singing at the tops of our voices and making inappropriately sexual comments about the members of various rock bands who were *gorgeous* in the seventies, and that Sheila was old enough to see live in their heyday.

It's only as we get a couple of streets away from Elsa's flat that the merriment suddenly dries up and the atmosphere becomes a lot more sober in my Peugeot. I switch off the music.

'Why do I suddenly feel like shit? Do you feel queasy?'

'You're picking up on the energy in the flat. You're picking up on the lady we've come to meet.'

Fucking hell! It's all very well loving the concept of all this, but now it's real and I'm going to have to face a troublesome, possibly angry spectre.

When we knock, nobody comes. We've been there a couple of minutes when Elsa comes haring around the corner, scattering apologies like shotgun pellets. She's been working in a coffee shop, as she didn't want to be in the flat on her own. She shakes Sheila's hand as she's unlocking the door, and starts gabbling what she already told me last night. As we mount the stairs she throws a smile my way.

'I'm not feeling so messed up today, because Tanz took good care of me last night. After taking care of the barman at Minnie's, of course.'

Sheila raises an eyebrow and I roll my eyes and shake my head.

Soon we're on the top floor and the door is open. Elsa switches on the light, then holds back. She really is scared. Eventually she enters cautiously behind us.

'I'm sorry it's a bit messy. I wasn't around to clear up today.'

I have been in this flat once before. I found it pretty, but quite oppressive. It was sunny and light enough, but I couldn't wait to get out. Now I know why. As I walk through the front door it feels okay, but entering the living/dining area is like walking into an invisible wall. The air is so heavy, it's almost viscous. Sheila nods at me and smiles.

'Feel that?'

'How could I miss it?'

Elsa is standing in the kitchen doorframe watching us, not quite sure what to do with herself. Sheila notices her discomfort.

'Why don't you boil the kettle, love, whilst we feel about a bit? The good news is that you're not going mad. There's someone here and they're not too happy. We'll have to see what we can do about it.'

'Ohhh . . . Okay.'

Elsa does as she's told. Which is a distinct novelty.

'Tanz, concentrate on what you feel. I usually walk about until they make themselves known.'

Sheila goes to the wall with the shabby-chic sofa against it, rests one hand on the faux-antique wallpaper and closes her eyes. I'm drawn to the window overlooking the street, where Elsa keeps her big, old-fashioned school desk. As soon as I reach it I feel completely dreadful. I close my eyes and I can hear a voice. A raspy, breathless lady. She has longish, wild grey hair and must be quite old. I can see her in my mind's eye, trying to pin her hair up in a bun. I recover from the initial shock, closing my mouth with a snap. I decide to speak to her with my mind, so as not to shock Elsa. Again I feel a little self-conscious.

'Hello, there. What's your name?'

'What are you doing in here? Get out. Why are you sitting there? You can't be here. Get out. Get out NOW.'

She sounds very panicked as well as angry. In my mind, it looks like she's waving an umbrella. I know it sounds strange, but I can visualize her, rather than see her. Like I have new eyes that are turned inwards. I feel terrible for her. She's angry, but so tiny and frail.

'We're leaving really soon, honest. Is this your place?'

'Of course it is. Why won't you all just leave me alone? Have you seen the walls? Have you seen the state of my bathroom? This is private property.'

Her energy abates as if she's stormed off.

I open my eyes. Sheila is watching me. Elsa is standing quietly in the doorway.

'What did she say, love? I could see her standing over you. She's a spunky little thing, I'll give her that!'

'She says it's private property. She was threatening me with her umbrella.'

'I saw it. It was bigger than her!'

'Elsa, you've messed up her bathroom, apparently?'

Elsa moved in with me for a couple of months about five years ago, and I can categorically confirm that she's one of the most untidy women I've ever met. My bathroom looked like an explosion in TK Maxx every time she took a shower. She only tidies up when there's a possibility she's bringing a man home, and then she's like the House Doctor on roller-skates. It's bizarre. Why sell yourself as a super-housewife if they're only going to find out imminently that you're a total slob?

At this moment Elsa looks mortified and scared. She doesn't like being told she's untidy anyway, but it's a hundred times worse when it's a dead old lady telling her. I try to give her a reassuring glance. Sheila walks towards the door.

'Let's have a neb in the bedroom now, Tanz. I think that's where we might get some answers.'

Elsa looks at us.

'Should I just stay in here? I've made a pot of coffee . . .'

'Yes, love. You start without us, we'll be as quick as we can.'

BLUE PETEY

The bedroom is an absolute tip, even by Elsa's standards. There are clothes, belts, shoes, deodorants, a damp towel and half-empty water bottles all over the place. The bed is unmade and the blinds are half-shut. There's also a feeling of confusion and sadness in this room. I look to Sheila, who blows out a puff of air.

'Bingo.'

'This is horrendous. It's a miracle Elsa's slept at all. I'd have nightmares sleeping in here.'

'Me, too. It makes me want a fag.'

For a second she looks longingly towards the door, beyond which is her packet of Regals. Instead she taps my arm and points to the unkempt double bed.

We both go to it and sit down. I close my eyes. Within seconds I am feeling absolute panic and my breathing is short. There's such a desperate feeling here that I want to move. Sheila stands. I pat the mattress.

'I think this is where her bed was, when she lived here. It may even be the same bed.'

Sheila stares at it in disgust.

'Christ, I hope not, love.'

Suddenly I can feel the lady beside me, standing to my right. She doesn't like anyone being in this (her) room. But there's something else. I seize on it and speak to her pale shadow-self.

'Please tell me your name. We really want to chat with you. Then we'll go. I promise.'

She pauses a second, then can't help herself.

'Sarah.'

She's so lonely. It's underneath all the panic and the anger. Hollow, desperate, awful loneliness. I speak aloud now, so that Sheila can be part of the conversation.

'Sarah. Hello, I'm Tanz and this is Sheila. We just wanted to check on you, that's all. Do you live on your own?'

'Since Len died. Yes, since Len.'

'Your husband?'

'My Len, yes.'

'Do you know when he died?'

She is indignant, and the tone changes.

'Of course I know. I'm not batty. The first of April 1962. Ten years he's been gone. Still miss him like it was yesterday.'

My heart goes out to her. I look at Sheila.

'She thinks it's 1972.'

'Of course it's 1972, silly girl.'

She must have been a pocket-rocket in her time, this one. But her voice is wispy and I guess that she has suffered from chest problems of some sort.

'Can you feel the disturbance when she gets mad, Tanz? The air shakes.'

I nod.

'Her breathing doesn't sound so good.'

'Bad chest. I always have a bad chest. Asthma 'n' all. No kids, no one to look after me. It's murder.'

As soon as she says 'asthma', I link in. Tiny old lady in a single bed by the window in the dark. She's trying to breathe and she can't. She's coughing and wheezing and her face is changing colour. Now I know what happened. She caught a chill, got a chest infection, then died from asphyxiation, fighting to get some oxygen in. Poor lady. As I'm thinking it, Sheila puts her hand to her chest. She's obviously picked up on it, too. Suddenly I feel tearful.

'What a terrible way to go.'

'It feels like she had emphysema or a really bad chest infection, love. She definitely couldn't breathe.'

'She says she had asthma.'

'Bloody hell. Can't imagine that's much fun, Sarah?'

'No, it isn't.'

'Does this mean she still has a chest infection now, even though she's—' I begin.

'Oh yes. If she was lonely for ten years and this place was her only reality, maybe she couldn't let go of it. If she didn't let go, then she's stayed here in exactly the same state as she was when she passed. She only needs a nudge and she'll suddenly realize she doesn't have a bad chest at all.'

The air begins to vibrate as Sheila speaks. Sarah's not having any of this.

'Of course I've got a bad chest – listen to it! It's rattling like my Petey's cage. How can she say I haven't got a bad chest, the stupid woman?'

I'm intrigued.

'Who's Petey, Sarah?'

'My budgie. That blue budgie out there in the cage. My little baby. Who did you think? I'm all he's got, the poor sweet lamb.'

Oh, my goodness.

'Sheila. She stayed for her budgie. She's been here forty years because of her bird!'

Even Sheila looks surprised. Something else occurs to me.

'And I'm going to bet she died at five to four on the dot. That's why Elsa wakes up terrified. Oh, Sarah. Sarah, listen to me, we have to tell you something . . .'

I'm not quite sure how to put it. I glance at Sheila, who looks back expectantly.

'Do I just explain the situation?'

She nods.

'Sarah, you have to go into the living room and look. Look properly. Look around you. It's not only the new wallpaper and furniture. Look where Petey's cage was. It's not there. Really it's not. Petey died many years ago. Petey's gone . . . and you should be going, too. Going to see him.'

I feel the vibration in the air again. Sarah doesn't like this one bit.

'Don't be ridiculous. Petey's through there. Petey's fine. Petey's my little lamb . . . he's—'

I speak as gently as I can.

'Sarah, you have to listen. This is horrible for you. You are living a lonely life in this place. You feel ill and angry, and strangers keep coming in that you don't want. The girl who messed up your bathroom lives here now. And there's somewhere much nicer you could be. Where you'd feel well and strong and happy. You deserve to feel wonderful, Sarah, and you could, easily.'

'What do you mean?'

She sounds hesitant, but at least she's listening. Suddenly Sheila speaks.

'Sarah, love, look to your left. Go on, look to your left. There's a door opening, isn't there? Who do you see? Who's there?'

All goes still. Faint but clearly, I hear it. I hear the anger and the pain drain away from Sarah's voice as she says just one word.

'*Len?*'

'That's right, Sarah. Your Len's here and he'll take you to Petey. Walk towards him.'

I feel her leave. It's nothing dramatic or showy. There's no massive flash of light or crash of thunder. It's like something was here – an energy – and now it's gone. An absence. I look around the room. It's lighter. The oppression has lifted and now it merely looks like a messy room. I can't believe it. *Is that it?*

I turn to Sheila, who smiles at me.

'Well, that went all right, didn't it? Well done, you. All that stuff about a better place where she could be. That's so right. And kind. Being kind was exactly right. They're so used to being confused by all the comings and goings over the years that they don't understand. They can't see the wonder that's waiting for them right in front of their faces.

You simply have to introduce some doubt and they're suddenly open to the possibility that they don't have to stay trapped. That's when I jumped in. Well done, girl. Took to it like a bloody fish to water.'

I am awestruck once again. Is that truly it?

'Sheila. That was un-be-lievable. Has she really gone?'

'Looks like it.'

I move to leave, but she stops me. Lowers her voice.

'Your friend out there. Is she a depressive? She must be, to have chosen this place. Or to have let this place choose her. And this kind of mess – you find it a lot in "disturbed" rooms. Troubled spirits thrive in mess. She needs to tidy up; it'll help to tidy her head up.'

'Okay.'

We go back through to Elsa and tell her the good news. She doesn't look as if she knows whether to believe us or not. We explain about the old lady, and how she didn't want to move on because of her bird. I decide not to tell her that Sarah died at 3.55 a.m. precisely in the bedroom, as that might do more harm than good. We promise that we saw her move on. I accept a coffee and a biscuit. Ghost-busting has left me gagging for sugar. I adopt my most serious voice.

'Elsa, we're going to drink our coffee and eat most of your expensive biscuits. You are going to get in that bedroom and tidy up. Put all the bottles and cans, and used-up creams and whatnot, in a black bin liner. Shove the dirty clothes in your wash basket, and the clean ones in a drawer or the wardrobe or in another bag – I don't care, just do it quickly. By the time we leave, in about twenty-five minutes,

I want you to have a tidy room. Sheila says it'll help to keep the place "clear".'

I have to bring Sheila into it. Elsa won't do it solely for me. She's so shocked that she doesn't speak, then she jumps up.

Sheila chimes in.

'Open the window and burn a nice smelly candle, if you have one, 'n' all. Can I smoke in here?'

Elsa looks like she might say no, then shrugs.

'How can I refuse, after what you just did? Smoke by the open window, if you don't mind.'

She throws open the window to the street, goes to the kitchen, then tentatively enters her bedroom with bin bags and a box of matches. She runs back in for a second.

'Thank you so much. Both of you . . .'

Then she's off again.

I can't believe Elsa did as I told her. Nobody ever does what I tell them. Sheila goes to the window, her face thoughtful. We hear a lot of rummaging from Elsa's room.

'That was impressive, love. What you did in there. I hardly had to say a thing. Your first time – you got it.'

'I don't know about that. I simply felt awful for Sarah, being so unhappy. She was in the kind of trap you see living people in all of the time. Still, at least she was dead and could move on.'

Sheila emits one of her dirty laughs.

'True enough.' She looks like she's sucking on a stick of nectar right now.

'Just so you know, you can't talk them all down that easily. You get some right buggers. Evil so-and-sos in life, and still evil so-and-sos in death. But Sarah wasn't evil, she was merely a lonely old lady who was worried about her bird. God bless her. Best not to talk about her right now, though. Or think too much about it. She's only just gone over, and we don't want to bring her back.'

I wonder if my admiration is too apparent? I'm buzzing again. What happened was awesome, and Sheila is my new hero. Still, I do have one unanswered question.

'How did you know that she should look to her left? When it was time to go?'

She sucks again on her nectar stick.

'When you know you've got to them – made them doubt or hope – close your eyes and visualize where they're standing. You'll see a pinprick of light somewhere, or a door opening, whatever attracts them in. In Sarah's case, maybe she imagined she would "go to heaven" through a door when she was a child. Sometimes you see someone waiting to accompany them; sometimes they spot someone through the porthole and tell you who it is. They usually sound happy about it, and they almost always go through. We simply help them by soothing their fears beforehand. What a lovely job, eh?'

'Sure is.'

And it really is. When I go and check on Elsa twenty minutes later, it's a different room. She has piled her dirty clothes into one bag and her clean clothes into another and wedged them into the wardrobe. The shoes have gone in their shoe rack and the rubbish has left the room in another bag. Now the floor is cleared, the room looks bigger. She has switched on the make-up lights around her mirror, lit a

Jo Malone candle (probably a freebie from one of her free-lance jobs) and she's straightened the duvet. The open window has let in fresh air and the candle smells great. I call in Sheila. Neither of us can believe how different a room can look in such a short time. Elsa's cheeks are pink.

'It feels different.'

Sheila nods and hands her some crystals from her bag.

'Wash these under the cold tap, and don't carry them next to coins. They should help with any negativity. Don't dwell too much on what just happened – we want to let Sarah get settled, wherever she is. The chances are she'd not want to return here in a month of Sundays, but you don't want to call any unwanted energy back. Keep the windows open for a bit. And I'd get some sage tomorrow, light it and take it around the house, carry it into each room and waft the smoke around. This should be a new start for you and your flat.'

'Do you want to come back to mine again tonight, Elsa? You can, if you're not ready to stay here.'

'No. Actually, I'd like to tidy up the rest of the flat. Doing the bedroom has got me in the mood. Plus, if I run off again, I might be too scared to come back. I need to see if I can sleep here now.'

I admire her spirit. *Spirit. Geddit?*

As we walk down to the car, Sheila grins.

'If she wasn't your friend, we'd have had a little wage for that.'

I can't believe anybody gets paid for doing something so gratifying. I send a little wish up to Sarah. I hope she's having a lovely time. I visualize her cuddling her husband and feeding her bird. It makes me feel warm.

That night in my dreams there are no nightmares. I see a quiet wood filled with bluebells. I love bluebells.

THE PHONE CALL
OF FORTUNE

Inka, so called because she's the blackest, shiniest cat you'll ever see, is sitting on my lap, purring like a truck. It is noon and I've only been up an hour, as I was reading my book. It's a tarot-card book that I picked up in a charity shop. Talk about God providing (if you believe in any of the gods). Fifty pence it was. The brand-new ones in Mystery Pot cost eleven quid.

I can't be spending that kind of money right now, as my savings are dwindling fast. In fact in another week or two I will have reached the end of the wire when it comes to cashflow, so I am now limiting myself to one crushingly expensive shop-bought coffee a day when I'm at work, and I stick to home-brewed coffee on the days I'm not working. Today I'm not working. I'm also shockingly bored by this tarot book. Sheila says I should check how good I am with the cards. She recommended the Rider-Waite cards, but they didn't inspire me. I've seen the deck I want. They're called the Medieval Scapini and they cost a bomb. I'm not sure I can justify the expense.

I'm toying with putting on a repeat of *Homes Under the Hammer* when my phone pings. It's a major novel of a text from Elsa. She usually texts rather than phones, if she's freelancing from an office instead of from home. She says the last few nights she's slept like a baby, one of them on no alcohol at all. She's followed instructions and has also set out more candles around the place, dusted and cleaned the whole flat and added flowers. (I can't help wondering if we gave her a personality transplant by accident. I mean, Elsa, buying flowers? Really?) She says it feels much more comfy now and she's less stressed. I text back that I'm happy for her and would love to see her for a catch-up sometime soon.

Just as I'm sending it, my home phone rings. I usually wait for the answerphone to kick in, in case some idiot is trying to sell me double-flamin'-glazing, but I take a chance and pick it up.

'Tanz! All right?'

The booming tones of Bill. Six-foot-four, blond, piercing green eyes, Glaswegian, funny, my agent and, crucially, gay. (So many of my friends are gay. One blessing of being in the entertainment industry.) He is engaged to my other agent, handsome, sensitive, equally hilarious Jo, who stands a foot shorter than his man, but has the spirit of a tiger.

Even though I've had only one audition in the past three months, I would never leave them (probably). I know how horrid the acting world is at the moment, and I know my past victories in the 'business' are now as nothing, compared to the pouting, frivolous females who are younger, still considered up-and-coming and manage to get a few of their lines right in *Hollyoaks*.

I really cannot compete in a world of vacuous celebrity consumerism. I could now prove myself as an actress a million times over and it would make no difference. I have an 'interesting' face, I am not a lover of schmoozing, and I live in a universe where sporting massive plastic tits and selling every aspect of your life to the tabloids is pretty much expected. I will never fit into this new world order.

'Hiya, Bill, how are you?'

'Not as good as you're about to be. You know the Snow-bar ad?'

How could I forget? A fortnight ago they had me pretending to be a liberated housewife in the imaginary snow, doing a silly dance to some awful song about their new chocolate bar. To be fair, they let me taste one and it wasn't appalling. Then they kept me hanging on until three days ago, when they announced that unfortunately I'd got down to the last two but they'd gone in a 'different direction' – that is, away from me towards some other lucky cow.

'Of course. The bastards.'

'Not so fast! "The bastards" would now like to offer you the part, as their first choice just broke her foot in a pothole. Apparently she thought it was a little puddle. Compound fracture – can't walk. So now they need to go back to their other and, of course, superior choice.'

'Oh my God! Oh my God, Bill. When?'

'Flying to Spain tomorrow. Is your passport in order, darlin'?'

'Of course.'

'Money's three hundred a day for two days, plus travel; plus they're offering you a three-grand buyout. It's pretty rubbish compared to the old days, but deals are getting tighter and it's better than some. Good news is they'll pay it as soon as the ad is showing, and they expect to have the first burst out in four weeks.'

'Aaaaggghhhh!'

'Well done, darlin', I'll email all the details now and speak to you later. Bon voyage!'

I cannot believe it. I hug Inka and kiss the top of her head. Her purring now sounds like rain thrumming on a tin roof. She would sit on me all day, if I let her.

I have been completely bricking it as to how to pay my credit-card bill along with everything else and still afford my rent. That job has bought me a few months' grace, if I rein in the spending, keep doing shifts in the shop and stop treating myself to enormous vases of wine at Minnie's.

Minnie's! I still haven't called Patrick. I assume he's Patrick, if he's Pat.

I decide to have a bath to celebrate getting my job. I will shave my legs and armpits, put some super-strength conditioner in my hair and slather myself in cocoa-butter cream. Then I'll go for a big walk in the drizzle with my ladybird umbrella up.

But before all that, I shall send a little text. Today I landed a job. Tomorrow I will be on an aeroplane. I will do a minimal amount of work and will return knowing I will not have to scrape for pennies, for the time being. That deserves a little treat. I shall text Pat and ask how he's feeling after our chat the other night. Maybe he'll text me back. That would be nice.

As I turn on the bath taps, not four minutes after texting him, Pat calls. I was not expecting that.

'Hello, is that the Wicked Witch of the West?'

'No, it's not. I'm the Lovely Witch of the North-East, thank you very much.'

'Oh, forget it then. I prefer bad witches.'

'Ha.'

'How are you, Geordie girl?'

'I'm okay, thanks – better than okay actually. I've just been saved from being shoved in the workhouse.'

'How come?'

'I got a job. One of those humiliating adverts that make you look an absolute twat in front of the nation. But beggars can't be choosers, and now I can keep my Skybox for another fortnight!'

He doesn't so much laugh as 'rumble'. His laugh is like a rockfall.

'Well, I've got the night off. Are you coming for a wee drinkie to celebrate?'

God, his accent is delicious.

'Are you old enough to drink, Pat?'

'You cheeky mare. I'm nearly twenty-seven – I'm positively ancient. Have you still got your own teeth?'

'*Hoy!*'

He rumbles again.

'How old are you? Please don't ask me to guess. I'm rubbish at ages.'

I am surprisingly reticent about my age. I still have to

tell casting agents I'm thirty-three. Well, I don't have to, but I do so anyway because they have no imagination. The closer you are to thirty, the closer you are to still being young. The further away you are, the more fucked-up it all is. Forty is supposedly a desert for actresses.

'I'm at the back end of my thirties. I am officially ancient.'

'You're officially sexy. Where should we meet, and what time?'

I ignore the compliment.

'I'm flying tomorrow and I have to pack and stuff, so how about six-thirtyish, so I can get home early? I really need a proper night's sleep.'

'Okayyyy. I know a nice cocktail place on the way up to Muswell Hill. It opened a fortnight ago. It's called Purple Haze. It's relaxed, it's got sofas, the drinks are ace and it's not Minnie's. What do you think?'

I like the fact that he didn't leave the choice to me.

'Yeah, cool. Purple Haze, six-thirty.'

'See ya then.'

I can't believe how easy that was. What a thoroughly nice bloke he is. I can imagine Pat travelling the world, making friends wherever he goes, having women falling in love with him, and him barely noticing. Young persons' malarkey. Even at this juncture, with no ties and no kids, I've started to feel time ticking. Getting too old to do 'young' things.

My cousin Kel is my age and she has a daughter. She loves her and she loves her husband, but she says the ticking is even worse when you give birth because suddenly your life is mapped out – as a carer for another person. Until her daughter's old enough to fly the nest, Kel can't go out when she feels like it and she can't just take off on holiday when the mood seizes her. She can't go dancing and sleep in till noon, or go to music festivals or pop down the pub for a chat, without thinking of the welfare of her child. The babysitters, the finances, the preparation, and the worry while she's out that something might go wrong . . .

Kel says she'll be going on fifty by the time the responsibility is less, and that terrifies her. At one point she was as adventure-loving as me. Now she says she's making her new adventure with her family, but sometimes she feels trapped. She reckons that's why parents become alcoholics. A bottle of Chardonnay a night lessens the burden. She's only half joking. But I'm also an alcoholic, and I am child-free and will probably stay that way.

A DIRTY MARTINI

There is no way I should be taking so long to get ready. I'm going for a drink with a good-looking lad, yes, but last time he saw me I was not dressed up, so I don't see why I'm making such a song and dance about it now. There are clothes all over my bed like I'm in a chick flick. I don't like chick flicks, and I don't want to be a flamin' girl about this. I'm only going for a cocktail.

'Bollocks!'

That is not me. That is a voice in my head. These days it's hard to tell what is the voice of paranoia and what is the voice of 'another'. But this sounds suspiciously like 'another'. One that starts to laugh.

'*You don't want to go just for a drink – nor should you. Get back in the saddle, lass, and enjoy. You take things far too seriously.*'

I'm not sure about voices in my head taking the piss out of me.

'Who is this?'

'*Someone who wants you to have fun. Wear something*

that makes you feel happy, put a comb through your hair and get yourself out there. If you don't at least kiss him, you'll have me to answer to. Byeeee.'

The voice has gone. Actually what it said was quite right. I am not auditioning to be Pat's wife, I'm going to have a chat and exercise my flirt muscle. I pick out a little black dress with red roses on it, team it with black leggings, shiny red flip-flops and a slash of lip-gloss. Done.

My hair is actually my favourite thing about myself. It's a simple bob and if I blow-dry it with my round brush, or give it a little straighten with my ceramics, it goes shiny and behaves itself. It's dark brown, but I'm sprouting the odd white hair now. It's one of the only things I'm not worried about. You categorically cannot stop your hair going grey. And so far I've only got about three of the wriggly albino buggers, so I refuse to be bothered. That's what hair-dye's for. I'll probably grow it really long when I'm older and be an eccentric bohemian. I'll wear lilac flowers in my white hair and chic long shirts with well-cut trousers and comfy but pretty shoes. (Old people have terrifying feet, but if mine stay nice I'll wear flip-flops till I die.)

I think about death and getting older more than anyone else I know. I wonder how I'll feel as my family peels away. I wonder how I'll be when I'm effectively an orphan and have to grow up. When my friends and acquaintances become full stops. Will I have to stay here on this planet, becoming more and more alone, every new death like a grandfather clock clanging a funeral march in my heart? Or, perish the thought, will I be one of the first ones to go?

It's morbid, I know, and I really wish I could forget

about it. Wine helps. Music helps. But I have to learn to live my life without suddenly being brought up short in Tesco behind an ancient old biddy who's struggling along, my eyes brimming with tears at the thought that my world is about to become a series of horrible losses.

Life has already started the process, with the disappearance of most of my grandparents and Frank, lovely Frank, who should still be here. That's probably why I'm so delighted by this latest development. A curveball. Completely inexplicable vibrations in my world. It's occurred to me that I have accepted this ghostly stuff very easily; maybe because I need it more than most.

I grab a red pashmina that I picked up in Bangkok, which looks much more expensive than it was, and give myself a spray of Chanel. I glance in the mirror. I look colourful and not try-too-hard. That'll do.

I arrive at Purple Haze feeling pleasantly warmed up after a fifteen-minute stroll. I've not really looked at the place before, but they've made it nice. It has huge windows and Mediterranean-blue paintwork and, to my delight, the window frames are rimmed with multicoloured tube lighting, like at Christmas. I brace myself for the inevitable sixty-second shyness of entering a bar alone, which is ridiculous, considering how many countries I have visited on my own. I walk in and glance around at the pleasant mosaic and harlequin-tiled bar, with a funky cocktail counter and a little stage, presumably for live performances. Small ones. There's a guitar and a microphone stand already set up. We're in for a treat later.

Pat is at the bar. He turns as I walk in. I am exactly on

time, which is a fluke as I'm always late. He's got on this linen shirt, sort of off-white. His hair is coming out of its binding and he's grinning his head off, as is the barman. They must have been sharing a joke. He looks very happy and relaxed. I can't help but smile back. He waves. I head over to the bar. He puts his hand on my back, kisses me on the cheek and gives me a cocktail list.

'You look great.'

'Thanks.'

'Now . . . I'm starting with a Brazilian Mojito, and I'm paying tonight. No arguments. What would you like?'

I glance down. Spot two of my favourite things (raspberries and vodka).

'I'll have a Raspberry Mint Martini.'

'Cool.'

My concoction looks like a stabbed dinosaur. The green stuff is apparently peppermint liqueur. This place opens at six, so it's just us and a man in a tricorne hat so far. This is Crouch End, so people in interesting apparel aren't unusual. The barman is in a very expensive T-shirt with carefully ruffled hair. North London contains a lot of people who try not to look like they've tried very hard, when they patently have. And there's nothing wrong with that. I have always lacked the knack of looking effortlessly expensive but cool. There's too much of a geek fighting to get out.

I am led to a big brown sofa near the window. We both sit, but not too close. When he kissed my cheek, Pat smelled of washing powder and whatever that great cologne is that he has. Amber and musk. I love smells. They remind me of people as much as songs. Because my dad would give us a hug when he came home from the pub when we were really young, I've also always adored the smell of beer and cigarette smoke on a man's breath, which must put me in a fan club of one.

Our drinks are icy and clinky.

'So how have you been since I went all "I see dead people" on you?' I ask.

Pat laughs into his Mojito and has to wipe his mouth with the back of his hand.

'I have to say, you completely and utterly freaked me out.'

'Oh no!'

'In a good way. I was really looking forward to carrying on the conversation. Until your snobby friend showed up . . .'

'Snobby? She's not snobby.'

'Oh, she so is. She snapped her fingers at Maria the other week; she's lucky they didn't get broken off!'

This doesn't surprise me as much as it should. Elsa has a streak of Princess Margaret in her. She can be a bit grand. Her dad is a hotshot artist, big on praise but short on money. She was brought up in Edinburgh in a nice house, but he spent more than he made on impressing people, so they had to sell it. He treats her mother like shit and cheats on her constantly. Elsa hasn't got a clue how to be normal. Her dad taught her she's a cut above everyone else and she finds it very hard to see otherwise. Sometimes being her friend is a pain in the arse.

'I so wanted to talk to you more. But in a way it was good, because I went back to my sister's instead and we talked about dad and it was great. It's lifted something that had been eating at me.'

'That's brilliant.'

'Yes, it is. It turns out I'm the one they've all been worried about – Mum included. They all seem to think I'm fourteen.'

'Aren't you?'

'Shut up! What about you? Did you sort your friend out? She was looking very sorry for herself.'

'She's fine now. There was an old-lady ghost in her house. I went round with my friend Sheila the next night and we had a chat with her and she moved on.'

Pat literally gawps.

'You had a chat with a ghost and she moved on . . .'

I nod.

'I tell you, you're certainly not a boring conversationalist. Last time I went for a drink with a girl she gave me her full manicure history. I tried to strangle myself to death with my scarf and she didn't even notice. Do you want another drink? You seem to have inhaled the first one!'

'Ooops. So I have. Sorry.'

'Don't be sorry, I've done the same. I was a bit nervous.'

I cannot imagine this lad being nervous, *ever*.

'You're not paying all night.'

I take out my purse with my 'don't mess with me' look, and Pat takes it straight off me and puts it back in my bag.

'I got paid today. Plus, you did me a big favour the other night, you know? Please. Let me get a few in. Same again or new one?'

'I think I want another one of these, even if it does look like a car crash on the moon. Thank you.'

It occurs to me that I'm not the slightest bit jumpy now. He's interested and interesting, this place is cool and I don't have any fatal diseases that I know of. That is enough for anyone, isn't it?

When he gets back, Pat listens with rapt attention to the whole saga of Sarah and her budgie and laughs his head off at the messy bathroom and the umbrella-waving. When I finish he shakes his head.

'You do know, don't you, that there are many people you could tell this story to and they would immediately have you committed?'

'Yup. Including my mam. Even though it's in her blood, she still thinks it's dangerous nonsense. When anything like that happens to her, she pretends it hasn't, apparently. And that's my own mother. Other people might think I'm trying to be one of that lot . . .'

'Who?'

'You know, those mediums on the telly, saying to people what they need to hear to feel better. And those ones who are suddenly overtaken by murderous ghosts, on camera. They look like mentalists. Vaudeville acts. I don't even know what it is that I'm doing. I'm channelling something, but I don't like the word "psychic" and I'm not sure what the right word should be.'

'Well, whatever it is, you're very good. My sister will probably accost you in the shop soon. She's absolutely gagging to hear if Dad's got anything to say to her. I told her to leave you alone, but I'm not sure I can stop her as she *loves* all of that stuff.'

This scares me. I think it would be too much pressure to *try* to get a message for someone. I hope she comes in on one of my days off.

'So how are the travel plans going?'

His eyes light up.

'Not long now.'

Turns out he's starting his trip in Thailand, one of my favourite places in the world. I feel a stab of jealousy, as I miss it with all my heart, but simply can't afford to go back right now. In an attempt to smother my envy, I tell him beaches and islands to visit and the best huts to stay in. After Thailand he's going to Australia, then he'll 'work backwards', whatever that means. He really is an intrepid little soul. He pats my knee, moving in a little closer.

'And what about you – jumping on a plane tomorrow to go to your glamorous job, like a Geordie Taylor Swift or something?'

'Hardly! I'm off to shoot an awful advert. The money's a bloody godsend, though, and I'm going to be in a nice hotel for a night, so I'm quite excited. There's a lovely pool there, so I can have a swim and a sauna.'

'You do know, now you've sold it to me like that, it's going to be a fucking nightmare, don't you?'

He's made me laugh again. Pat has the same bleak sense of superstition that I have. Geordies are remarkably superstitious. My mam once said we had Irish in our blood. It would make sense.

'Well, I will be dancing around in fake snow in a warm

place, pretending it's chilly, which might be weird, but I doubt you could call it a "fucking nightmare". What might be more of a nightmare is remembering the crazy dance I did at the audition and replicating it in high heels and a dress, in snow made of polystyrene or whatever.'

'Jeez. I would pay to see that!'

He glances towards the bar and nods, then looks back at me.

'I just did something a bit James Bond. The barman asked if we wanted another and I nodded yes, without asking you. Sorry, am I a presumptuous wanker?'

'Not if you're paying.'

'Good. Oh, look.'

I follow his eyes to the tiny stage. The man in the tricorne hat, whom I admire greatly for the selection of highwayman frock coats that he wears to do his shopping in Budgens, is working on his laptop a table away. Pat is out of his seat and heading for the stage. I'm a music fan, but I really don't want to be serenaded on the guitar. There's something a bit pre-planned about gestures like that. But he doesn't pick up the guitar. He goes to the mic stand and takes up a . . . what is it? Next thing I know, I'm hearing the harmonica solo from 'Isn't She Lovely?' Stevie bloody Wonder. I'm a bit embarrassed but also really impressed. It doesn't last very long, but it's fantastic. Mr Tricorne smiles mysteriously to himself, then gets on with his computer business. Pat puts the harmonica back where he found it and runs up to the bar to get the drinks.

I watch him as he approaches the table once more. He is basically a big, beautiful kid. Everything he does has energy.

I am not eyeing him up as a potential boyfriend, I don't want one of those, but I like how much fun he is. He didn't get up there to show off, he got up there because he felt like it. As he places the cocktails down, I am full of admiration.

'You are very talented.'

'My uncle taught me the harmonica. I've got a couple of them. Did I look like a massive eejit up there?'

Before I have time to think about it, I bend forward and kiss him quickly on the lips.

'No, you did not. You looked great.'

He obviously doesn't need any more encouragement, as he puts his glass down, takes my face in both of his hands and kisses me for rather longer than I kissed him. The fact that he's so at ease about everything is very refreshing. The fact that I have been longing to get it on with someone for ages immediately wreaks havoc with my body. I want him to push me down on this sofa, right this minute, and crush me into the cushions. He certainly knows how to kiss. The confidence of youth.

I wish I didn't keep thinking about his age. But the stress of my last relationship and the intermittent worry about money have taken the sheen off my once devil-may-care attitude. Also, ever since I passed thirty-five I've felt different, like I've crossed a line into new territory. My friends with kids tell me that I will feel like I've gone up a generation if / when I have a child. I will feel older and I will feel tired. Another reason I don't want one. My own mother told me not to have a child unless I really, really want to. It's one of the only progressive opinions she has ever voiced. In most other ways she's like a maidservant from

1764 who accidentally wandered into the future and is still slightly shell-shocked by what's going on.

Every time I come up for air from kissing Pat, I want to kiss him again. The teenage joy of snogging someone passionately, and not having to think or talk, is a heady one. Eventually it's Pat who stops, heaves a huge theatrical sigh and picks up his drink.

'Is it me, or did it someone switch the heating up *very high*?'

'No. I think it's quite cool in here.'

'So that's what it's like kissing a witch . . .'

He reaches forward, gives me another peck and grins.

'I like it.'

'Well, that's a relief.'

He looks at his hands for a minute. Ohhh, that must be Pat being serious or shy, or something. When he looks at me again, his eyes are more bold than shy.

'I'm going away soon.'

'I know.'

'We met under extraordinary circumstances.'

'I know. I was there.'

'I don't want to insult you or anything . . .'

'Go on?'

Why the bloody hell is he going to insult me?

'Do you live alone?'

'I live with my cat. I am a cat lady.'

'Makes sense. I'll bet it's a black cat.'

'All right, Inka happens to be black. It means nothing.'

'Do you have a boyfriend?'

I snigger. The word 'boyfriend' sounds so old-fashioned in his accent.

'No. I wouldn't have kissed you if I did.'

'Very commendable. And a great relief.'

'A relief?'

I'm now knocking back my third cocktail, I have just shared a hot-as-jalapeño kiss with this vision before me and I love a bit of badinage.

'Tanz, I'm well aware you are a good person. I don't think you're a pushover or a girl of ill repute, but I was wondering if you'd take me home? Like soon. Like after this drink? I can get us some vodka or something on the way. I'm not always so pushy, but life is literally too fucking short, and you are literally too tasty.'

Another time I would be self-righteously furious at being asked, less than an hour into a date, to take someone home, like a hooker. I have a definite chronology to how I do things, and what Pat's hinting at is *at least* a month in. Or it was the last time I dated. But these circumstances are extraordinary. He has taken my breath away, inasmuch as I'm now scared to death whilst being speechless with desire. He's laid his cards on the table and it's up to me. Any doubt either way is eradicated when he kisses me softly, then puts his forehead to mine.

'Please don't be insulted. Say no, if I've made you uncomfortable.'

I pick up my Martini and drain it. Offer him a small wink.

'There's an off-licence two doors away. I like Żubrówka.'

I drape my pashmina and lead him out. The vodka is

purchased within three minutes. As if Providence herself is following our every move, a cab with a yellow light shows up and is immediately hailed by Pat.

'It's only a fifteen-minute walk!'

'Which means it's an even shorter drive. Good.'

The journey passes in a blink as we kiss like sixteen-year-olds all the way home. The time between his request at Purple Haze and me fumbling my key into the wonky front-door lock is at most twelve minutes.

I take him to the living room and leave him with my iPod while I run to the loo. I am actually quivering. For a second or two I want to climb out of the window and run off. What the hell am I playing at?

'*Good girl.*'

It's the voice. There, then gone. Like permission. Maybe I really am imagining it. Who cares?

I grab two glasses and some orange juice 'from concentrate' out of my fridge and go to the living room, where Pat has lit my reading lamp and put on some nice background tunes from a collection on my iPod called 'Kick back and breathe it out'.

'Great room. Welcoming.'

I look round, glad I tidied up today. It's small, but the walls are clean white and the carpet is that hemp stuff, with a nice Indian rug on top. I have things from my travels dotted around: a Buddha here, a silk wall hanging there, a bodhrán hanging over the fireplace and a blue Tanglewood guitar on a stand. I don't play the guitar very well, but I like to have it around. I also have a banjo in my bedroom that I can play a bit better, but not much.

I pour us both a large vodka, then add the cold juice. Pat takes my drink from me and puts it down on the reading table with his own. This time when he kisses me, it's more dangerous, as there are no witnesses to behave in front of. This, however, does not render him a fumbling idiot. He pulls me towards him on my futon settee with the cheap woollen throw and kisses my mouth, then buries his face in my hair, so I can feel his breath on my neck. Those dextrous hands with the clean nails cradle my ribcage as he whispers in my ear.

'I've not really liked anyone for ages. Now I'm feeling very, very naughty.'

'You are very, very naughty.'

I can't believe how much I want to bypass ceremony and rip off his clothes. Seven months of being a nun has rendered me an animal.

'You wanted an early night, didn't you?'

'Yes, I did, but it doesn't seem quite so important now.'

'That's good.'

We do not, in any way shape or form, have an early night.

GHOST PERVERT

Half an hour into my flight, the plane has risen above the grey clouds and it's all blue with wisps of white candyfloss. I have a gin-and-slim in front of me and I am running on two hours' sleep. If that. My eyes keep closing of their own accord, then popping open again like broken blinds.

Every time they close, I have flashbacks to last night and have to stifle another embarrassed, yet smug smile. It just didn't stop. That Mills & Boon bullshit about melting into each other and 'making love all night' has suddenly taken on a whole new perspective. Except that it was more like 'eating each other alive, like starving kids with a vat of Ben & Jerry's all night'.

After the first time, we were like naughty children for hours. Every time it seemed we were sated and needed to sleep, something would set us off again and another hour would be gone. Eventually, at about 5 a.m., we managed to snatch our meagre sleep ration, and then it was 7 a.m. and I had packing to do.

Were it not for the fact I had loads of stuff to do, I think Pat would have tried for another cheeky one before he left, but I begged for mercy as I would be late and I needed a bath. With no real other option, we embraced and he trooped off home with a spring in his step, like he'd had an early night and ten hours' kip. He's a bloody machine.

At this moment I am torn between being a bit loved up and a bit excited that there are so many males (and females, come to think of it) out there, many of whom could be as good as or – perish the thought – even better at it than Pat.

That sounds greedy, doesn't it? Before I was with Blake, last night would not have been possible. I would have written myself off as a grade-one slut for capitulating too easily and would have needed to hear that Pat was in love with me soon after our first time, to justify it. Looking back, fuck that! What an idiot I was. An ocean of need. Now I'm well aware that Pat's an Irish dynamo and he's going away, and that's probably why I'm happy to have fun. And contemplate fun with others. Slut-schmut.

I'm very thankful that the seat next to me is empty. I pull up the armrest to give myself more room and snuggle into my cushion. I begin to doze. As I fall into a deeper sleep, the steady roar of the aeroplane's engines and the air-con mingle and become the sound of the sea. I open my eyes . . .

I'm in a verdant garden outside one of those villas with white-washed walls and tropical flowers growing up a trellis that you see on holiday. Ahead, over a low stone wall, are a beach and the sea. Miles of it. It is perfect. I'm sitting on a canvas seat by a metal-and-glass table. The sky is bluer than blue and I feel utterly peaceful. Suddenly I can hear music. Ridiculous music. 'Ernie (the Fastest Milkman in the West)' by Benny Hill. What the—

That's when I notice the seat opposite me is not empty.

Frank. Of course it's bloody Frank.

'Frank! What's with the soundtrack? Is this your theme tune?'

He's sniggering his head off. What a clown.

Frank always liked the sunshine, that's why I always dream about him in the sun. His brown eyes with the green flecks are bright with mirth. His hair is sticking up all over the place, as usual. He's wearing cut-off jeans just above his tanned knees and a bright Hawaiian shirt that is only half buttoned up. He looks well. Unlike other times, I know this is a dream.

'How are you, Frank?'

'How are you, you mad cow?'

'Same as usual.'

He picks up his seat, brings it over and places it next to mine. He takes my hand.

'I need to tell you something, witchy woman.'

I glory in the fact that I can feel his warm hand in mine. I can really feel it.

'What's happening now – what you're doing with your life – it's the right thing.'

Did Frank just say something serious?

'What – talking to dead people or having sex with young Irish men?'

'*Both! Look, you always had great instincts about other people, but you were ridiculously shit when it came to yourself. I'm going to help you.*'

'How?'

'*None of your beeswax. All you need to know is: there are certain people who only a girl like you is qualified to help. I'll help you to help them! You're going to have a ball.*'

I can feel myself getting tearful. I know it's a dream, but it feels more 'real' than all the others put together. And I feel I'm going to wake up soon. *Boo!*

'You've never told me – how you are . . . what it was like to die?'

He wrinkles his nose.

'*Tanz. I didn't die. It only looks like it, from where you're standing. I'm good. I'm fine. I only ever feel sad when I see my mam or my mates upset.*'

'We miss you. A bit.'

He laughs.

'*Well, stop it. I'm here. I'm always here. Just give me a shout.*'

'That's easy for you to say.'

'*I've been trying to get through to you, Tanz. I'm always talking to you. You have to open your ears – the ones inside! Anyway, congratulations on your latest piece of high art. Dancing like a fool in front of a TV crew and a sex maniac.*'

'A *what*? What does that even mean?'

Frank sniggers again and puts his finger to his lips.

'You can take the piss out of my rubbish acting jobs all you like, but I'm going to need to make money somehow whilst I'm helping all of your dead mates "transition", or whatever it is.'

'*Still so touchy! I've been talking to you for ages, you know, you just didn't know it was me.*'

I'm rather indignant at this.

'Was that you, telling me to grab Pat?'

'*What of it? Didn't it do you good?*'

'That's not the point, you massive pervert.'

Right now I'm not in a dream with a dead bloke; I'm in a nice holiday garden with my mate, Frank. Who's irritating me, like he always did. And before you know it, he hugs me. The first hug since he died. We hug like we used to, and he smells the same. That's when I burst into tears.

'*This crying for me has to stop, Tanz. I don't know what you're bleating for anyway – you were a total bitch to me when I was alive.*'

I slap him, and I sob and I hug.

'*Listen, you've got some interesting days ahead. I'll be about, okay? Oh, and shag Pat again before he leaves; that lad has stamina.*'

'You were *watching*?'

Frank's laughter is infectious.

'*I have better things to do, thank you very much.*'

I hug him again, just because I can.

A siren goes off. My head whips round to find out where it's coming from, and suddenly it's dark and I'm opening my eyes, and I'm on an aeroplane with the seatbelt light flashing and an alarm telling me to buckle up.

For the first time in a long time I haven't woken up crying from a 'Frank' dream. I've woken up thinking of him as my friend – not my dead friend. I feel stronger. But my arms feel empty again.

APPARENTLY I NEED
A BROOMSTICK

The hotel is lovely. Not that I do much exploring. I have a costume fitting at 4 p.m., so I lie down on the big bed with the whiter-than-white sheets and catch another (dreamless) hour of sleep. As I drift, I can hear people swimming in the outside pool. Laughing and splashing and enjoying the heat. It's a night-shoot tonight, so I get to stay until noon tomorrow. I will definitely have a swim and a little sunbathe if it's like this in the morning.

It feels like I've only blinked when the alarm goes off on my phone and I have to meet the driver downstairs. This is one of those modern hotels, all glass and chrome and marble, that let in a lot of light. Some people say they're impersonal, but I love the space and the cleanliness. Everything is just so, which is quite different from how I usually live. *How can anyone not love another human being cleaning for them?* Despite my own grungy flat, I do worship a spotless bathroom.

The driver is a very tanned older man with distinguished grey hair, white at the temples, who flashes glistening

Mister Ed teeth at me as he opens the back door of his air-conditioned silver car. It looks like a Granada, but I'm not sure. The air-conditioning purrs as we drive and I marvel at how refreshed and calm I feel. *Boy, I must have needed that sex.* Usually I need my sleep or I'm a monster. Not today. Though of course the two super-naps must have helped. This place is stunning. I like its greenery – it's lush but exotic. There's a sweet smell in the air, and I wonder if it's some kind of herb that grows here? It smells like a sweet shop, as opposed to London, which often smells like a sweat shop.

Soon we pull into a villa. This, my driver informs me, is where the first advert is already shooting. The ad is in two parts: the first in glorious holiday sunshine and the second at night in the snow. That's because there are two new choc-olate bars: Sun-bars and Snow-bars. Both coconut-based. I think the only difference between the two sweets is that the sun one is covered in milk chocolate and has bits of candied fruit in the coconut, and the snow one has darker chocolate and is creamier and tastes of cinnamon or something more Christmassy. The creator's imaginative powers were obvi-ously boundless.

Because they secured this place to shoot the sunshine scenes today, they decided, almost definitely on financial grounds, to hire next door's garden, which doesn't have a pool, and to fill it with fake snow for the night-shoot. This suits me down to the ground, as I don't have to shiver my tits off in a dress and shoes in the Pyrenees. But I don't envy the prop department, which has to deck the garden out and make it look like flamin' Lapland.

The living room is open-plan, with Swedish furniture and a large carved wooden statue of an Indian brave with full headdress in the corner. I like him very much. The costume lady is called Zannah, is about fifty and has died her curls an orangey-red that I find very funky, and tell her so. She's smiley, with rabbity front teeth, and her English is perfect. She shows me the wraparound dress and shoes that I have to wear. So far, so bland, as it always is with adverts. I try the dress on in the bathroom and it fits. Thank God.

There's nothing more annoying to wardrobe mistresses than actresses who underestimate their dress size. It happens all the time, especially with women who aren't twenty any longer and refuse to acknowledge their expanding waistline and widening hips. I found out myself the hard way; it's easier to stay skinny at twenty than at thirty, and I can imagine it's even worse at forty-five.

As I'm chatting to Zannah about today's shoot, and cheekily gleaning titbits of gossip about the gorgeous but hopelessly hysterical blonde actress playing one half of the sunshine couple, I spot someone approaching us in my peripheral vision. And out of nowhere, I feel a stab of fear. I turn my head a little, whilst still chatting, to get a better idea of who it is. I can make out a mass of long, dark bushy hair with grey streaks and black clothes, but not much else, as the sun streaming through the window behind her is strong. As she reaches us, Zannah touches her arm and nods towards me.

'Tanz, this is Bayana. She's your make-up artist. She speaks very little English, but I can translate anything important that she has to say to you.'

Bayana has very prominent eyes with black irises. Her skin is dark and she has a large, well-formed mouth. She isn't slim, but she suits her size, and she is staring at me. Really gazing intently. I think she was looking at me like this all the way across the room, which is why she freaked me out. Never have I seen anyone who looks more like a witch. A real in-your-face witch, who knows what you're thinking. She doesn't look very friendly. I don't like it.

She reaches out her hand and I go to shake it with my right hand, but she shakes her head.

'Other one, please.'

Her voice is deep and heavily accented. I glance at Zannah, who smiles encouragingly, and I hold out my left hand. Bayana takes it and looks at my palm. When she smiles, she looks like she might eat me. Or maybe I'm only thinking this because she scares me. She points at a line on the right-hand side of my palm, beneath the gap between my pinkie and my wedding (ha!) finger. It runs pretty much to my wrist. She says something to Zannah in Spanish, who gabbles something back. *Damn, my French A-level is useless in this situation.* I make a mental note to learn Spanish pronto. Zannah raises an eyebrow.

'Bayana says you are Romany.'

'Sorry?'

'Your bloodline, Romany Gypsy – that's where you get your gift from. You're a medium, no?'

Those hairs on the back of my neck are waving again. Bayana speaks more, whilst Zannah listens and nods a lot. Bayana traces the line with her index finger, pointing out little crosses on the main track. I have never looked at my hand in this way before, never noticed these crosses, faint but not invisible.

'She says you are frightened of your gift, and these crosses are the times you have avoided it, and maybe will again. But eventually you will accept it, and it will be a great time of learning for you. This is your "medium" line. Not everyone has one. She knew, as soon as she saw you, that you had it. She is also Romany.'

Bayana nods at me. She's not so much evil-looking as full-on. English people do not stare at strangers this intently. Her smile is seeming less sinister now. I look back at my hand, amazed.

'How does she know all of this?'

'You . . . are very good – you help people.'

Bayana speaks so falteringly in English compared with her machine-gun Spanish. Her voice is rich, masculine. Again she speaks to Zannah, who translates.

'She says you have a teacher on Earth, which is good, but you have even better teachers in spirit. You need to trust yourself. She says you have interesting times ahead. She also says you should get the cards you wanted to buy. Play with them. It will help you connect.'

I look at Bayana in amazement. The centre of my forehead has gone haywire. She is the real deal. More than me, more than Sheila even. I bet she's never been scared of her gift. And if she's to be believed, I am a *Romany*. The joy!

I thank her. Zannah then tells me that Bayana will be giving me natural make-up and a little coral lippy to complement the dress, which is navy.

Just then a man walks in. He is good-looking, in that

plastic 'actor who looks after himself' way, and he's about fifty. He has sun-bleached red hair and a smattering of freckles. He's as posh as hell and uses it to comedic effect.

'Hello, Tanz. I'm Rog. Flew in yesterday and paid for an extra night, so I could get a bit of sun.'

He ignores my proffered hand and kisses me lavishly on both cheeks.

'Coco Chanel. Very nice.'

'Thank you. Are redheads supposed to sunbathe?'

'Oh, I'm not one of those blue-skinned gingers. I'm more of a bronze really! I like your accent. Reminds me of college. The Geordie girls were always a lot of fun.'

'I'll bet they were.'

He looks around him towards the garden doors, on the other side of which stand the crew, about to go for another take. I can't see the actors, but I know they're out there. Something akin to fear crosses Rog's face. I wonder if he's nervous about shooting the ad later on. He doesn't seem the nervous type.

Roger is an old-school womanizer – you can tell from a mile off. I find this kind of man quite amusing. Mostly because they're as clear as tap water and they love hanging out with the ladies. The trick with the Rogers of this world is to have a laugh with them, but never, *ever* fall for their patter. They are incorrigible and they shift their favours around like pieces on a chequerboard. Their stories are great, but if you actually get in any way sucked in, they will run like hares and leave you weeping into your brandy. So many of my friends have been fooled by this kind of man and I've had to delve deep to find any reserve of polite sympathy, because mostly I could see it coming from the millisecond they met.

When Rog stands next to Zannah and gives her a squeeze, they look like a pair of Duracell batteries. Two copper-tops. I've always fancied redheads, but this one I'll be giving a miss. Zannah smiles indulgently at him. Bayana looks him up and down once, then dismisses him and looks back to me. She leads me off towards her make-up table. When we're out of earshot she takes my hand again but doesn't examine it. She frowns, then smiles straight at me. It's like the weather suddenly brightening after grey skies. She nods.

'Not worry. Protected.'

I seem to recall hearing this kind of thing before, in about two hundred horror films, just before something terrible happened.

'You will have a lot of new experiences when you back in England. Romany witch. Very nice. Now, try this . . .'

And that's the last Bayana says about it. She slaps a coat of lippy on me. It doesn't look terrible.

'Yes, good.'

I like her better now. But I'll have to do that protection thingy that Sheila taught me, because I'm feeling a little dizzy from the force of nature that is Bayana. I want to ask her more questions, but her English is pretty terrible. So instead I surreptitiously watch her out of the corner of my eye when she's not gawping at me. I wonder what she sees that makes her stare? I do hope it's not the evil eye floating above my head. Though, to be fair, she did say I was protected.

Soon I'm back in the purring silver car with Mr Suave, the driver, and Mr Flirt, the actor. Rog is determined that, as we're not being called until nine-thirty, we should dine together. I would have liked to have gone for a little wander on my own, maybe pick up some grilled fish somewhere, but he wants us to go 'à deux', and that's that. And it's not like he's unpleasant; he's fine. It's just that I have things to think about: Spanish Gypsy witches, ghost-protectors and all-night sex with an Irish sex god being but three.

Anyway, good as my word, I meet Rog in front of the hotel after a shower and a change of clothes. He's scrubbed and shiny in a black T-shirt and cargo pants. I get the feeling he's been craving company, as he chatters away about the champagne in the hotel and the holiday he had last year, where the pool was so big you could swim to a bar on an island in the middle. His stories seem to be peppered with bars. I'm pretty sure he's already partaken of at least one bar today. We walk down the street, alongside the beach, and actually it is wonderful to breathe sweet air whilst the sea blithely swooshes beside us. It's been a crazy week. It's great to unwind.

Rog takes us to the place he went to the night before. Open-plan, open-air, good wine list and a waiter who looks like Ryan Gosling. *Woof!* What is it with me and serving staff? Rog asks if I mind him ordering the wine. I do mind and I order him to order Sauvignon Blanc. Because we're on the coast, I indulge my fetish for seafood. He goes for a large steak. Men always go for steak; it's something to do with their penis and needing to seem manly, I'm sure of it. The wine is too delicious. I ask Ryan to get us some tap water to stop me getting squiffy. He smiles and I slip slightly down the chair. Rog is oblivious as he tells the twelfth story about his theatre exploits.

Surprisingly, Roger admits to having a wife. She is a renowned TV actress and a little younger than him. They have three young children.

'But, Tanz, she goes to bed by nine o'clock most nights. We live in the bloody back of beyond. What am I supposed to do after nine? I tell you, I bloody miss Hampstead. She said to me this week, "Rog, why are you doing that stupid advert? We're not that skint!" And I said, "Darling, a few grand never goes amiss." But the truth is, there is only so much fun to be had from mopping up milky vomit and goo-goo-gooing all day long.'

'So why the hell did you have three, then?'

'It was her. She had our first, Aimee, and it was quite good fun and it made her feel all womanly, so she got the bug. Then she went all Mother Earth, making chocolate brownies and organic butternut-squash sandwiches and all that. But I can see she's getting bored now. I give her until our youngest, Harry, is two and she'll be "Fuck all the voiceovers, I want to be Mrs Famous again." She's on that rowing machine two hours a day as it is, to keep her figure. It's only a matter of time before our nanny gets completely lumbered. But you can't stand in the way of a woman and her ticking womb!'

I can't work out why actors ever have kids. They're the most easily bored, fidgety-minded juveniles on the planet.

'Rog, you need to be supportive. You were evidently bored today, showing up on set early, so being away from home obviously isn't as enthralling as you thought it would be.'

'No, it was great. I could float about being the man I was before: posho pain-in-the-arse on tour! It's not like I'm ever going to leave them for good, you know – I'm not a total bastard. I just like to remember what it was like years ago, when I was free. There's nothing wrong with that, is there? I didn't ask for three sprogs. I was happy with one.'

'*Roger!* You can't say that. Well, you can, but it's best not to.'

'I know, I know – I'm a shit. But a charming one, don't you think?'

'You're all right.'

'I'm starting to worry that you're impervious to my charms.'

'Worry no more, I absolutely am. Ohhh, look at the time! I need to clean my teeth and check on my cat-sitter.'

'Come on then, let's get the bill, you Teflon-hearted Geordie wench.'

NIGHT GAMES

After a thank-you to the director, Tom – the wiry chap from Walsall, who has provided me with a night in Spain and enough money to settle my stomach for a couple of months – the actual shoot passes painlessly enough. Obviously I have to dance like a loon, with jazz hands and can-can legs, which tickles Rog and the crew no end, but instead of taking hours and hours, like other ads I've shot, this one takes a wondrously brief eighty-seven minutes. Rog's close-up takes an extra ten minutes, and then we're done.

I'm cock-a-hoop. Last night's exploits are finally taking their toll. I look forward to a glass of wine on my balcony as a sleep-balm. Then I shall collapse on my lily-white sheets and snooze to my heart's content. As we sweep into the bar, Rog asks if I'd like a nightcap. I tell him I'm bushed and get a glass of vino to take to my room.

'Fair do's, my lady. Pleasant dreams.'

I wonder who he'll chat up in the bar tonight. Probably anyone and everyone until about 6 a.m. I'm so tired I take the lift. I put on my black lounging trousers and saggy vest and immediately feel comfy. I open my balcony door and sit down on a cosy seat overlooking the pool, which is lit from below and looks like the Blue Lagoon. I can hear crickets and soft chatter. To think that last night I was in sex heaven, and tonight I am in peace heaven. I offer up my usual little prayer of thanks as my head begins to nod.

I am just drifting off when I hear a tapping. I have no idea what it is. Dazedly I wonder if someone is doing DIY in the hotel. Tap-tap-tap. Is it coming from my room? Tap-tap-tap. What the hell? I get up and wander inside. There is silence, then the tapping again . . . Someone is knocking at my door. I open it a crack. And there stands a half-sheepish, half-beseeching red-haired man brandishing a champagne bucket with a bottle of Perrier-Jouët in it and two crystal flutes.

'Rog?'

'I'm so sorry, darling, I know you said you were tired, but you only have one night here and, well . . . downstairs is a bit of a no-no for me at the mo. Can I join you on the balcony for a little glass of shampoo and then I'll leave you be? Scouts honour.'

Oh God. I don't want company, but I actually feel sorry for him. Rog looks like a chastened schoolboy. I open the door.

'Oh, you're an angel!'

He heads for the balcony as I wrap an electric-blue pashmina around my shoulders. I refuse to put on a bra when I feel so comfy, but I'm not really a show-off-my-nipples kind of gal, either, so this will do the trick nicely.

Rog is already uncorking the champagne when I get out there. Luckily there are two balcony seats and he's making himself very comfy in the other one. He pours the champagne like an expert, remembering to tip the glass. Perrier-Jouët is not exactly the cheapest champagne and I dread to think how much it cost at the hotel bar. But judging by the number of telly programmes his wife has starred in over the past ten years, I'm sure he can afford it. I wonder what she'd say if she could see him now?

The bubbles tickle the back of my throat as I receive the first sparkly hit. It immediately takes the edge off my sleepiness.

'Why was the bar downstairs a no-no?'

He fingers the stem of his champagne flute for a second or two.

'Erm. Do you promise you'll still love me if I tell you?'

He is *such* an actor. I sigh.

'Yes, Rog, I promise.'

'The actress – the one playing Mrs Sun-bar?'

'Yes, I met her briefly this afternoon. Gorgeous-looking blonde with tiny hips and sink-plunger lips.'

'Yes. Her.'

'Well?'

'She's staying at this hotel with Mr Sun-bar. Who looks a nice enough chap. Not long out of drama school, apparently; still has that sheen of hopeful enthusiasm that gets kicked off you and trodden on by the time you're thirty . . .'

'Right!'

This business is rife with bitterness. I wonder how Rog feels working in the theatre and doing bit-parts in adverts while his wife garners TV fame, and probably fabulous pay packets. I don't know many men who like to be 'kept' by women. Apart from my ex, of course, but I'm not going there right now. I'm far too happy this week to hark back to that bullshit—

'Anyway the actress, she's called Ruth. I worked with her on a thing at The Bush about a year back. It was one of those progressive little plays that look like they might be rather profound, then turn out to be fucking awful. Our director seemed a nice enough chap, until we started rehearsing and it became abundantly clear he didn't know what he was doing. The only upside was Ruth wandering around in the altogether for half of the show every night. I played her lover; she played an obsessed woman. You know how it is when things go a bit tits up at work . . . the Dunkirk spirit and all that – we got close.'

'You had an *affair*?'

'An affair? God, no. That's not what it was at all. Harry had just been born, and my wife hated my guts. Partly because of the hormones, and partly because I'd decided to do the play instead of staying at home. But I always feel so helpless in those first months; it's her and the baby, and I'm the spare prick at a wedding. I mean, she's got a nanny to help her, so what does she need me for?'

This is why actors shouldn't have kids. But the thing is, in twenty years I'll bet he's the one who'll be proudly speaking of his brood, embarrassing them by showing up when they go clubbing, and probably attempting to steal his son's girlfriends.

'Your wife probably felt fat and vulnerable, Rog. She probably wanted you to want to be at home.'

'But she's not usually the clingy type, so how was I supposed to know that?'

'You could have asked her?'

'I did. She told me not to do the play.'

He refills both of our glasses. Rog is a hilarious car-crash. I wonder if he's aware of how contentious he is. I reckon he milks it. I think he loves his wife a lot, but wants to be the centre of attention, like an adopted toddler.

'So what about big-lips Bertha then? Why are you hiding on my balcony?'

'Oh God. Well, as I said, I played her lover and after she indicated that she rather liked being naked in front of me, we took it somewhere a little more private in the last week of the show. Places like the theatre cleaning cupboard, the pub loos, the back of her Mini Cooper – that one was interesting; then finally against a wall down an alley by some rather potent West London bins.'

'*All right*! I don't need all the details.'

'Sorry – yes, sorry. You're quite prudish for a Northerner, aren't you?'

He guffaws.

'Anyway, when the show finished and I went back to domestic bliss, I found out that life had quite horrendously mirrored art. Ruth was indeed a young nutter. Spoiled rotten, and not used to anyone saying no to her – especially a forty-odd-year-old ginger – and totally incapable of taking a bloody hint. Even a hint involving a threatened police protection order.'

'Jesus Christ! You're joking?'

'No. In the fortnight after the show finished Ruth texted me four hundred and twelve times. We were soulmates; we were going to love each other forever; she was going to be with me, whether I liked it or not. By the end of the second week she was going to tell the *Daily Mail* if I didn't come to her flat and "fuck her into next week". By that point I'd pretended to lose my phone and got a new number. I was shitting it, and my wife was plunging into despair, due to post-natal thingamabob. If she'd found out, it would have finished us. That's when I dropped my old phone in the local duck pond and called my agent. He took Ruth's number and said to leave it with him. Turns out that he called her, made himself out to be more important than he was, and told her that if she breathed a word to anyone about me or my family she would never act in this country again. Her ambition won over her determination to ruin my fucking life, and I never heard hide nor hair of her again until I walked into that villa today and saw her through the window, being Mrs bloody Sunshine!'

'That must have been a great moment for you!'

'It was pant-fillingly scary.'

'Did she see you?'

'No, she had her back to me. I very quickly checked my costume, then ran off to a little tapas place with my book and kept out of the way. I only wandered back when you were due in, as I knew they'd be taking you to the hotel soon afterwards and I wanted a lift. Thank God they were still in the thick of it out there.'

'I hope you've learned your lesson.'

'I don't know. It's all quite exciting really.'

'Roger, if you really think that, you're an idiot.'

'I like your pashmina, by the way. Isn't it a little warm, though? Don't you think you should let the air get to your lovely arms?'

'Fuck off. Don't start with me. I told you, I'm impervious.'

'I can't help myself. I'm a sex maniac.'

He winks. Suddenly I remember my dream on the plane: Frank telling me I would spend my time with a sex maniac. I stare at Rog.

'Don't look like that, darling. I said a sex maniac, not a bloody rapist.'

'Sorry, no – slipped off there for a minute. Anyway, I'd kung-fu-kick you right off this balcony if you tried anything with me.'

Rog guffaws again. I reach over and refill my glass. I think I deserve it, after listening to his ridiculous and, let's not forget, self-inflicted miseries.

'Anyway, what happened in the bar, you Class A fool?'

'Well, here's the thing. I'd just bought the champagne. I was going to call up to your room and try to force you to come back down again.'

'Presumptuous!'

'And that's when I turned and saw Little Miss Sunshine, sitting outside on the lap of Little Mr Sunshine, her pre-pubescent co-star. Looks like she fancied a bit of younger meat this time.'

This phrase tumbles me back onto the rug with Pat last

129

night. I blink hard to get rid of the pictures that flood my mind. Boy, was he vigorous.

'To avoid embarrassment, I briskly made for the lift. I have no idea if she saw me, but I wasn't hanging around to find out.'

He laughs and, as he does so, there is a furious hammering at my hotel-room door. My back stiffens.

'Oh, lawks, I think I've been hunted down.'

He makes to climb over the balcony. We are five floors up and Rog is pissed. I grab him and make him sit back down.

'Stay!'

The pounding continues relentlessly.

I stand and, like a condemned witch heading to the ducking stool, trudge warily towards the rattling door.

THE PAIN OF
BEING ALIVE

I glance back at Rog's owl-eyes peeping fearfully over the back of his chair out on the balcony, before I steady myself and open the door. Ruth is in a sarong, tied halter-style around her neck to make a slinky dress. (She's one of those girls who doesn't need a bra, the cow.) It's silk, it's fuchsia and yellow and it shows off her bony shoulders and toned arms to perfection. Her golden hair is swept up and her tawny eyes would be enchanting, were it not for the crazed look and the flustered red nervous patches on both cheeks and her neck.

The moment the door is moving she is hopping around, trying to see past me into the room. She attempts to barge past and, in a move that is entirely out of character for me, I grab her arm and push her. She almost falls backwards and grabs the doorframe to steady herself.

'Excuse me, what the fuck do you think you're doing?'

I always lay on my accent more thickly when I am trying to sound hard.

Ruth's mouth opens and closes like a guppy. Then she lets out a cry.

'Rog! Roger, I know you're in there, you bastard.'

She has a soft Yorkshire burr. She is radiating energy – it's coming off her like heat. She glares at me, bile and spittle flying.

'You wait, you stupid old cow. You think you're special because he came to you? Well, it won't last. He'll dump you and make you feel like shit. Anyway, what kind of slut bangs someone they only just met on a job?'

This girl is priceless. Plus, she pouts even when she's apoplectic. I can't help it. I begin to laugh at the absolute cheek of it.

'What are you laughing at? Are you laughing at me?'

She lifts her hand as if to hit me. Suddenly Roger is sweeping up from behind, as I land a good kick to Ruth's left ankle. I am not a violent person and I'm only wearing flip-flops, but she *really* shouldn't make assumptions.

'Whoa! *Whoa there.*'

Roger grabs her arm as Ruth dramatically falls sideways, after hopping about in agony. What a total cry-baby. I can hear approaching voices. I don't want the management, or indeed anyone, being party to this fiasco, so I drag them both inside my room and close the door. Ruth slumps on the bed, cradling her ankle. I look at my foot – I've split my big toenail. Damn!

Rog stands a little away, afraid she might attack. Her eyes dart viper-venom.

'You prick!'

'Now come on.'

'You complete shit. We had something so amazing and you dumped me out of nowhere. Wouldn't answer my texts, wouldn't speak to me.'

'I'm married, Ruth, I have three kids.'

'You weren't thinking about them much in the back of my car, were you? And it doesn't look like you've been thinking much about them tonight.'

She glances towards the balcony and spies the empty champagne bottle.

'Oh, lovely, a little romantic drinkie before the big deed, is it?'

She turns on me, her lip curling.

'Well, just so you know, he's not exactly as big in the pants department as he is in the *mouth* department.'

'Oh, you know what: can I just fucking clarify? Rog was in here hiding from a mentalist and wasn't on a romantic mission. You might think he's God's gift, but some of us don't get our rocks off shagging married men.'

Her face contorts.

'A mentalist?'

'So you don't think it's a teensy bit mental that you pounded on the door of a stranger and tried to push your way in, screaming and shouting at a man who may or may not be there, and who you haven't seen in a year?'

Her anger now seems to be melting into self-pity.

'You told her? About . . . us?'

Rog rolls his eyes.

'There was no "us". We had a few jolly little bunk-ups at the end of a job. Why is that an "us"?'

Well, I have to hand it to him: Rog has a way with

words. He might as well have punched her. Ruth begins to sob.

'I'm not a . . . I'm not a bunk-up. Men love me, they fall at my feet. *Why?* Why wouldn't you answer me?'

'I did bloody answer you. I told you it couldn't happen. There was nothing else to say.'

'And then you got that gangster agent to call me – you tried to destroy my career.'

I am horribly tempted to point out that a fringe show and the odd advert is hardly a 'career' to break, but that would simply be cruel. Roger is moving from one foot to the other. Obviously Ruth's emotions are freaking him out. I am feeling more respect for his wife by the minute. She must really have to treat him like a big child. I wonder if I should boot them both out of my room and let them fight it out in the corridor.

'Help her, Tanz.'

A bloody voice in my head. Why should I help Ruth? She's been curling her lip at me since she came to the door. She called me an old cow. Fuck her!

'Speak to her. She needs you. We'll help.'

I don't know who 'we' is, but I can't say no. It makes me feel very harrumphy, though. I heave a tiny sigh, then turn to Rog.

'Can you do me a favour? I'd like a word with . . . erm, Ruth, on my own please. Stay by the bar downstairs and I'll call down if we need you for anything, okay?'

I don't take his mobile number as it might make things even stickier with Ruth. The relief on Rog's face is farcical.

I just hope he doesn't kiss me, as that will not help matters in the slightest. Ruth is confused and reluctant.

'But, Rog, I want to talk to yoooouuu!'

She is still snuffling, and her beseeching tone is wrenchingly pathetic. Sometimes I truly wonder what made me want to be an actress. Am I as messed up as these people? Crikey, I hope not.

Rog can't get out of the room quickly enough. Ruth sits on the bed, cradling her ankle. I try to sneak a peek at it and, through her fingers, I spy blood. Ooops! I must have cracked her right on the bone. That'll be how I ripped my nail then. I go to my suitcase and produce the Żubrówka vodka I purchased from Duty Free on the way here. I then go to the minibar and fish out my stash of apple juice. In the ice bucket I find a few solitary blocks floating in mostly melt-water. I put them in the flutes, pour generous measures of the vod and top them up with apple juice. I hand one to Ruth and she takes it. I hold mine aloft.

'Here's to your ankle.'

'You kicked me.'

'To be fair, you were about to hit me, and I hadn't done anything.'

She takes a tentative sip, then a swig.

'What on earth is this?'

'Bison-grass vodka with apple. It's total heaven.'

'It is actually.'

Her amber peepers regard me over her considerably less-full glass.

'Were you really sheltering him from me?'

''Fraid so. He's not the bravest of blokes, and I think

you scare the shit out of him. I don't know Rog from Adam.'

'I loved him.'

I remember falling helplessly in love with people I worked with, when I first became an actress. I soon learned. Ruth is downing her drink like it's water. She seems to be fighting back tears. I grab her glass and top it up, then sit next to her.

'Can you really love someone you shagged for a week?'

'Yes. I can.'

Peace and stillness. I feel them descending. I put down my drink and look at her. Suddenly I don't see a pouty, slim, spoiled bitch with all the advantages I didn't have. I 'feel' something else coming out of her, and I see a person who is struggling.

'There's something wrong with your neck, isn't there?'

'Sorry?'

I steady myself and let the words come.

'Two years ago, maybe a little more, something . . . something happened to your neck and shoulder, and your confidence was shot to pieces. Did you have a crash? You crashed the car. Your boyfriend was with you. You split up not long after.'

She is gaping. I feel bad for her. I feel warmth towards her.

'Then you got the job. A long time later. It was your first proper gig since . . . your neck. Roger put a smile back on your face, didn't he? And then he ran off. I'm so sorry. You wanted to die, didn't you? Oh, you're too young and beautiful to die. Please tell me you'd never do that now.'

I sense her sadness acutely. She grabs my hand; in shock, I think.

'I did have a car crash. I did. I was with my ex and he was being horrible to me, and I lost concentration and crashed into a lamp post. He was okay, but I got whiplash and I hurt my shoulder. I couldn't move properly for ages and I didn't know if I would act again. When I got that shitty play, I was over the moon. Then I met Roger and he was so-o-o funny. And I know it's horrible, but because he was older, I thought he'd adore me. I thought he'd help me stop feeling so sad. We were so connected when we . . . you know. I thought we had a future. I know he's got a wife, but when he spoke to me, it was like I was the only person in the world. I could only assume he wasn't happy in his marriage. Why else would he behave like he was single?'

She stops to draw breath and glugs down another third of a flute of rocket fuel. She is a bit googly-eyed now.

'How did you know about me? Are you, like, a witch?'

'Yup.'

I push a straggly strand of hair behind her ear.

'Can I tell you something, Ruth?'

'Okay.'

'What happened with Roger – it was horrible for you. It's understandable that you were upset. But I promise you, if you hadn't been in such a vulnerable place, you wouldn't have lost it so badly over him.'

'Wouldn't I?'

'He's a handsome, funny bloke, Ruth. But lots of creative blokes are attractive and charismatic. They play with it, like a cat plays with a mouse. It wouldn't matter how gorgeous you were, how sexy, how great the shags were – he wasn't looking for a relationship. He has one of those. He was having an adventure and he wanted to feel good about himself. He picked you because you were the best-looking girl there. If you really want a shot at happiness, you need to resist these fellas who offer you the moon and hand you a pebble. When you get older you'll recognize them from a mile off.'

'You're so clever.'

She's slurring ever so slightly now.

'Bitter experience, that's all. Rog is not going to leave his wife and, if he did, he would expect you to wash his underpants, be a stepmother to his kids and turn a blind eye to his cheating. You are worth a *lot* more than that. And you're too young. Do you understand?'

'Funny. I was only thinking tonight, when I saw him, how much more knackered he looks than I remember.'

I give a little laugh.

'Believe me, that will only get worse. Roger will be selfish for the whole of his life, and he will only get more knackered-looking!'

Ruth smiles, she can't help herself. I top her up again, much more apple juice than vodka this time.

'I shouldn't have called you an "old cow". I'm sorry about that. You're actually quite pretty. I just wanted to make you feel shit. That's horrible, isn't it?'

'Oh, don't give yourself a hard time. I hated you on sight.'

Ruth really giggles now.

'What happened to your co-star?? The lovely boy with the quiff?'

The giggling stops abruptly as she remembers.

'Oh God, poor Freddie. We were getting on so well, then I spotted Rog and I flipped.'

'Right. Hang on a tick.'

I pick up my room phone and call the bar. Within seconds I have Roger on the line. He sounds more pissed than before. He is horribly grateful. I ask if Freddie is with him. He says not. I bid him good night and tell him he is now free to wander off.

Ruth is in the loo, so she misses the last exchange, which can only be good.

'He must be in his room, Ruth. Do you know the number?'

'Six-one-two.'

The phone hardly gets the chance to ring before he picks it up.

'Hello, Freddie, my name is Tanz and I'm in room five-one-four. Could you possibly come and pick up Ruth? She would like to see you and thinks she might have upset you? She needed to speak to me urgently, but it's all ironed out now and she'd like some company.'

I'm surprised Freddie doesn't knock at the door the minute I put the phone down, he sounds so breathlessly eager. Already enraptured, obviously.

When Ruth returns, I give her some water from my bottle and tidy up her mascara.

'Have some fun, Ruth. You don't need to settle down. Shag everyone or shag no one; just don't upset yourself. If it makes you feel any better, I know two things. You have a *big* job coming in the next six months, and you won't look back.'

She gasps.

'Really?'

'Yes. Absolutely. And the other thing. Your mum? She's sorry. Okay? She's sorry. You're all she cares about.'

When the knock comes, I let Freddie in and offer him a Żubrówka-and-apple. He accepts it, his noble brow creasing at the sight of his lady-love, her face like a collapsing balloon, as she sobs again.

Luckily, this time Ruth's tears are not crazy tears. And she's wiping furiously at her eyes.

'I'm so sorry, Freddie, I shouldn't have run off. Don't look at me – I'm like a swollen lizard.'

Freddie wipes her eyes for her.

'You're beautiful, Ruth, laughing or crying. Like an angel.'

A bit frilly for me, but she's pleased enough. Soon they leave, arm-in-arm and clutching the rest of my vodka. Hey-ho, it went to a good cause. Before she goes, Ruth writes my phone number on her arm. I don't refuse her, because actually she's quite sweet when she's not trying to smash down my door.

As she hugs me tight, I whisper in her ear, 'Call me when you're in London. We can talk about your mum.'

She hugs me even harder, then they leave.

I jump on my bed like a starfish and lie face-down on the cool sheets. *Thank Christ for that. I can now go to sleep.* My phone is in my bag beside my head. I check it to make sure it's not running out of juice. I've hardly used it, so it's fine. There's a text:

You have destroyed me. I am a shell of a man . . .
Same time next week? Pat

I fall asleep within two seconds.

And once more I dream of bluebells, this time growing on a grave. The gravestone is blank where the name should be. It makes me sad, but it's not scary. What is with these weird dreams?

THE HUMAN
WEASEL

I have to work at the shop three days running to make up for my day off. Today Martin is the reader. Martin is basically a small field animal or, actually, a weasel – he has a feral look in his eye and I think he might be holding down a maelstrom of resentments within his meek, veiny exterior. The people who trickle in for readings from him seem to be the most odd and damaged of our customers.

I don't really know what I think of Martin. I have many gay friends; they usually love me. Milo says it's because I'm more than a little tragic, the cheeky so-and-so. But Martin is so weird. I think he dislikes being gay. That must be awful, and how can you possibly be understanding towards the people you are reading for, if you hate yourself and everything you stand for? He doesn't wear aftershave or deodorant, either. I've got close to him a couple of times and he smells a bit musty. What kind of self-respecting gay man doesn't smell fabulous?

On the subject of smelling nice, yesterday when I got

back from the airport Inka had left me a lovely gift on the bed. When I go away for more than a day, Steve – my neighbour, and the only ninety-year-old man I ever met who introduced himself as 'Steve' – keeps an eye out for Inka and lets her come into his house if she's lonely. I don't go away that much these days and, when I do, Inka has the cat flap and the cat feeder with three days' worth of food. Steve provides extras. He used to be a chef in the army. He has a massive old tabby called Compo, which Inka tolerates, and they hang out in Steve's yard while he potters with his begonias. Despite this, Inka has seen the need to lodge a complaint that I went away overnight. Cat-shit on my white duvet cover. *Perfect.* She's no witch's cat; she's merely a mardy bitch.

When Martin rolls in, he's an hour late and he eyeballs me suspiciously from a chair near the door as he consumes a limp-looking corned-beef sandwich and a packet of plain crisps. He's drinking supermarket-brand, full-fat Coke. No wonder he's so sallow. He notices that I have a sealed pack of tarot cards in front of me. This morning I took the plunge and bought the Medieval Scapini deck, as my favourite Spanish Gypsy instructed me to. I'm excited. The first sale of the day was mine, on my poor, overloaded credit card. Luckily I know my wages are coming, so I'm allowed to treat myself.

'What are you doing with those?'

Martin's very softly spoken. He told me a couple of weeks ago that he was born in Luton, though he doesn't have much of an accent. I ask you: who would want to be born in Luton? His mam should be ashamed.

'Oh. I thought I'd get myself a deck – check them out. They're such beautiful cards.'

'It's a lot of money to pay, merely because you like the look of them. You're not a reader, are you?'

He smiles. So far, so passive-aggressive. Does he think I'm after his job?

'Well, no. Actually my great-nanna was a well-known medium back in Gateshead in the old days. She sometimes used the cards, and I decided to get a deck for myself, have a little go. Just to see . . .'

'Well, people presume that anyone can read the cards, and they can't. It takes time and natural ability. But then, with you being an actress, you might be able to blag it, eh?'

Oooh, get her! Well, that's made my mind up; after wavering on the subject, it is now certain: Martin is a prick. When I talk to him I don't get the middle-of-the-head feeling as strongly as I do when I'm with Sheila. What I do get is slight dizziness and a touch of nausea. Is this how Martin feels all the time? Churned up and threatened? *Ooof!* Well, I wouldn't want to live in his head. And I certainly wouldn't want a reading from him. Richard Dawkins would have a field day with Martin.

I am saved from any more of his sniping by a female dormouse in an anorak and specs who comes in for Martin's first (and so far only) reading of the day. He wipes his margarine hands on his dark-green cable-knit cardigan and leads her through, having not lit any candles or put a cloth on the table. Horses for courses, I suppose.

When the door is safely shut, I strip off the cellophane and take out the deck. The cards run smoothly through my hands. They are so beautiful. There are many tarot decks and each reader has a different preference, but every time I've looked through the catalogue, this deck has jumped out at me. I also adore the Russian St Petersburg deck to look at, but it's very black and stylized, so even though it's pretty, I'm fairly sure I wouldn't be able to 'read' with it. I'd simply want to stare at it, like I would a book of ornate fairy tales in Urdu. Sheila told me I'd be attracted to the 'right' deck for me and, looking at these gold-embossed beauties, I feel a stirring in the pit of my stomach. I want to give them a go.

I call Sheila. She's in her house, smoking a fag. She loves her fags. I'm not sure that 'smoking fags' should be a hobby, though.

'I'm glad you bought them, love. I think it's always good to explore the different avenues.'

'As soon as I felt them in my hands I got all excited. The book seems so technical, but—'

'Throw the bloody book away, Tanz. You don't need it. You're very intuitive, and studying the book will hinder you. There's nothing wrong with knowing the traditional meanings of the cards, but it's not the first thing you should do. You feel excited because you're exercising a new muscle. Every time there's a new chance to "play", your subconscious is going to jump up and celebrate. You should get every customer who comes in the shop to draw a card. Tell them it's a little freebie reading. Get them to turn it, and say the first thing that you "see". I don't mean look at a card with a king on it and say, "You're going to be King of bloody England", but say what you "feel". You'll be surprised, darlin'. You know you're ready, so enjoy yourself.'

Actually, if it's for free, then I think I am ready. It's not like customers will be losing anything by taking a card from me.

'But Martin's here – he might get all arsey.'

'Oh, him. Has he got no readings again?'

'He's got one. She's in there now. Really small woman with massive jam-jar glasses and a crew-cut.'

'Oh, I know the one. Nice enough, shy, looks like a miniature Rose West?'

I can't help a little snigger. I always appreciate a murderer-gag.

'She does actually. But without the excessive pie-eating. Anyway, Martin seemed to be hinting that I was after his job. If I start pulling cards out, left, right and centre, he's going to have a cow.'

'If he doesn't pull his socks up, he won't have a job there anyway. Maggie's furious with him. He's supposed to show up at ten, in case people "drop in" for readings. He usually wanders in casually at noon, gets bored and disappears at three. He did that the other day and missed out on two late readings. She doesn't actually make that much from the shop and she doesn't take a huge amount of our fee, either, but she likes things just so, does Maggie, and Martin is going to blow it big-time if he doesn't buck up his ideas. He's lucky to be there at all.'

'Do you think he hates women?'

'I think he hates everybody, bless him. What he needs is a boyfriend and a personality transplant.'

Sheila's so right.

'Look, he'll be finished in a minute so, I'd better go. Thanks, Sheils, I'll give it a bash. I'll call you tonight.'

'Okay, darlin' . . . Oh, wait, before you go. I think we've got another "bust", if you fancy it? Sounds like a lively one. Angry ghost throwing things about.'

'Holy-moly, you're kidding me? Throwing things? How exciting. Ring you later.'

Two or three minutes pass as I leaf through the cards, marvelling at the detail on them. Suddenly I hear the squeak of the door and look up, to see Martin's head poking out.

'We'll be in there another thirty minutes. She's decided she wants the full hour, okay?'

He's less unfriendly when he's pleased.

'Brilliant. Okay, Martin.'

When he's gone, the front door pings and a girl walks in. I say girl; she's around twenty-eight. *Is that a girl or a woman?* Anyway she's younger than me, with striking caramel skin and eyes like a saucy panther. She heads straight over to the counter to look at the gemstone jewellery that Maggie stocks behind glass. A lot of it is that generic 'magic crystal hanging from black leather thong' kind of stuff, but certain people seem to love it. There are also leather bracelets with runes on them, in a basket next to me. She starts to look through them. I nod.

'Would you like to pick a card? To see what today's got in store for you?'

She regards me, looking for the hard sell.

'Don't worry, there's no charge – I'm only practising.'

'Okay then.'

She reaches for a card and hands it to me. I turn it over. The Queen of Swords. A clever woman who looks very lonely to me. Private.

'You've got to stop waiting for this David bloke. He has hurt you one too many times. You're hanging on to your pain, so that you don't have to let anyone else in.'

Blimey. Where did that come from? The girl blinks. I blink. I hope to God there is a David or I'm going to look such an idiot.

'How did you do that?'

I shrug. I'm as confused as she is. There's a seat by the till and she sits on it, staring at me like I'm an alien. People do tend to stare at me much more since I started doing this. It's disconcerting.

'I just felt it.'

Tears spring to the corners of her eyes, but she quickly quells them.

'You're right. He's been a nightmare. It's taken me ages to believe he's wrong for me, but he is. He rang this morning, being nice, to confuse me again. I almost fell for it. I almost invited him over. Instead I came out of the house for a walk to clear my head. I've never been in this shop in my life. How did you know his name?'

She's very well spoken. A nice, sensible woman.

'I have no idea how I knew. I think you'd have thought I was only reaching otherwise, so I was given his name. You don't usually believe in this stuff, I reckon. Oh, and another thing: the man from abroad . . . the one who bought you flowers. You don't fancy him, so don't encourage it. There's someone else on the horizon – be patient.'

She honks a laugh.

'Oh my days! How do you *do* that? You're right, I don't fancy him. But he's so persistent. I was thinking of having a date with him . . . just to be nice.'

'I think he may be a bit unstable. Be polite, tell him you're not ready. Let him fade out. If you kiss him or give him any other green light, you will never get rid of him.'

She touches my arm.

'That's amazing. He has been very over-keen.'

'If you have to, tell him you and this David got back together. But of course don't actually do it. You already know what David's about; you've simply been scared of having no one. Well, that won't happen. Go on holiday or something, have a rest and come back ready to conquer the world! Right, reading over.'

She shakes her head. She has short Afro hair and, now that she's relaxed, a ready smile.

'I never heard of a fortune-teller knowing *names*.'

'Oh, I'm not a fortune-teller. I'm a *Romany*.'

I can't help saying it – it makes me so proud.

'I couldn't tell you your fortune if you offered me a million quid.'

'Well, you are amazing. Thank you so much. I feel like I should give you something.'

'Don't be daft, I was only practising.'

She stands up, then takes a card from the counter with the shop number on it.

'Who do I ask for, if I want a reading?'

'I'm Tanz, but I'm not a reader here. I simply work on the till.'

'Well, that's ridiculous. I'm Juliette, by the way.'

'Lovely to meet you, Juliette. Now go forth and book a holiday.'

'You know what: I might just do that. I've wanted a weekend spa break for*ever*. I'll be seeing you again. Thank you so much.'

'No bother.'

As soon as she's gone I send a text:

Milo, I have become a friggin' JEDI. Call you later x

I'm in shock. It's getting easier. I don't know how, but I open my gob and this information pours through. There's a pressure in my chest and I have to let it spill out. It's actually a great, if dizzying, feeling. Only thing is: I didn't read from the card; I looked at it and said the first thing that came into my head. Oh well, it worked out okay.

As I'm musing, out jumps teeny Rose West, followed by Martin. She seems fairly alarmed. But she pays and thanks Martin in her dormouse voice, before beating a retreat. He's looking very pleased with himself.

'I'm off for a coffee – do you want anything?'

I delve into my purse and hand him a few coins.

'Yes, please, I want a bottle of water and a banana.'

He heads off and I sit down. As Sheila taught me, I do a closing-off exercise, so that I can 'come down'. I'm hoping the banana and water will help. What I really want is cake, but I always want cake and that is not a good thing. I made some wheat-free damp ginger-bread this week and I've had a big chunk with a coffee every day for breakfast. My hips can't afford any more cushioning, so a banana it must be. I'd like to call Sheila and tell her what happened, but then the door opens again. I jump a bit when I look up. It's Pat.

He's wearing a slim-fitting grey sweater with a pale-blue shirt underneath. He looks stunning. He is with a woman. She is thirty-two or three and looks exactly like him, so I'm assuming it's his sister, unless he's one of those freaks who fancies people who look like him. He raises an eyebrow at me and mouths 'Sorry' as she approaches. Her smile is as big as a cheese. She dresses conservatively, but is wearing a magic crystal thong-necklace. A rose quartz, it looks like. I really hope she hasn't come here for some amazing psychic experience, because I'm not a performing monkey and I don't do well under pressure. Well, I don't think I do; this has only been happening for a matter of weeks.

I smile back, because it's only polite. She actually looks crackers.

'Hello, Tanz. I'm Pat's sister, Caitlin. Nice to meet you.'

I put out my hand to shake hers. It's damp. She's nervous. Oh God, she is expecting something. Just then Martin returns and passes me the water and banana. He goes through the back to the loo. I am trapped like a whale on a beach. I am flailing here. I have no idea what she knows about me and Pat. The sex. Fuck!

'Hey, Caitlin, how are you? Hey, Pat.'

'Hello, Tanz. My insane sister decided she wanted to come and disturb you, so I thought I'd come along with her. As a buffer of some sort.'

'Pat!'

Her voice and accent are sharper than his.

'Tanz, I wanted to thank you for what you did . . . for Pat. It's really made a difference for him, hasn't it?'

I'm ready to shout out hysterically, 'What, my best blow-job?', but I am completely sure it won't be as funny if I say it out loud. Pat has composed a face of pure innocence, so he is probably on the same filthy track as me.

'Yes, you cheered me up no end.'

I bite my bottom lip.

'Thank you, but really it was nothing to do with me – I just said it! Bless your dad; he's the one to thank.'

Caitlin looks extremely vulnerable as soon as I mention her dad. I feel so bad that I can't tune into people as and when. I'm sure if she had walked into this shop as a stranger, it might have been different, but now I'm nervous.

'He was a great man, our dad, wasn't he, Pat?'

'He had his moments.' Pat puts a protective arm around her.

'Anyway, Tanz, I was hoping – well, wondering – if you do readings or meetings? You know, for that kind of stuff? I would love to get some kind of idea of . . . how he is.'

Oh Christ!

'Erm. Well, the thing is, it seems to come to me quite randomly. I'm new to this, so I'm not sure how much I can force it.'

Martin is now hovering near the kitchen door, bobbing his head around. Is he expecting me to recommend him? What a knob he is. I point down at the deck in front of me.

'See these? I only bought them today and I'm getting people to pull a card out from the deck, so I can give them a mini-overview. Would you like to choose a card anyway? Just to see how your day is going to pan out? Then another time, in private, we can have a glass of vino and see what happens?'

You don't have to be psychic to see how much this girl is still grieving for her dad. God help me, the day I lose a parent. I sincerely hope, if I get Caitlin alone, I'll be able to tune in. Pat steps back and inspects some amethyst 'caves', to give us a bit of space. He's such a canny lad. Martin gives me the evils for not mentioning him. I ignore him.

'That would be wonderful. Thank you. I didn't really think you'd be able to do it now, while you're working.'

She sounds disappointed. She thought exactly that.

'Here, I'll shuffle these, then you can pull one out and turn it over for me.'

She does, and it's the Eight of Cups. I lean forward so that this information is between me and her. It isn't about her dad, but I say it anyway.

'This is about your relationships.'

Caitlin's face falls a little bit more.

'You've always, I feel, handed out too much. Always giving too much love, with not enough return. Now that's changing. The change has gone on these past six months and there's someone who wants to be by your side all the time. But you've not been sure . . .'

She nods uncertainly. Looks at the counter in front of me.

'There *is* someone. I've not been in the best shape. He says he wants us to move in together, but I don't know. Sometimes he's too nice.'

'It feels like a good move, Caitlin. If you're ready, of course. He's being nice because he understands. Madly enough, I can hear a song playing in my head as I think about him. Is he a funny bloke?'

'He is quite funny! What's the song?'

I laugh because it's so daft, I hardly want to say it.

'Erm, I don't know if you know it – it's by a guy called Joe Dolce, "Shaddap You Face"? I can hear it playing in my head: "La-la-la-la-laaa, HEY, la-la-la-la-la?" The whole chorus actually.'

I know I'm not the best singer on the planet, but I'm not prepared for Caitlin's reaction at all. Or Pat's. She bursts into tears, and he gives a whoop and starts to laugh. She then starts to laugh while she's crying. Martin looks at us all like we're dangerous lunatics.

'What? *What?*'

She wipes her nose on some raggy tissue.

'It's just that's – that was . . .'

Pat wraps his arm around her.

'My dad used to sing that to Caitlin every time she got moody. It was a running gag in the house. Eventually we all sang it. She found it really annoying, didn't you, Sis?'

Caitlin still can't get words out – she's a mess.

'Did he have a laugh like a foghorn?'

Pat nods.

'Jeez, he certainly did.'

'Well, I can hear it.'

And I can. How amazing. Pat shakes his head at me, eyes twinkling, and looks to his sister, who is attempting to rally.

'He does . . . did. Laugh like a klaxon going off! When Pat told me what you'd said to him, about Dad, I was so, so happy for him. But, God forgive me, I was also jealous. I wanted to know he was watching over me, too. I've felt so lost.'

I lay my hand over hers, I can't help it.

'Of course he's watching over you. He's still laughing, incidentally. He finds himself hilarious. He approves of this bloke, Caitlin, that's all I can tell you. He wants you to be happy. He's sorry you're sad.'

'Is he? Oh God. I'll try . . . it's so hard when I miss him so much.'

'He's around all of you. You can do that, it seems: be in lots of places at once when you . . . pass over. You want to talk to him – just talk. He'll always hear.'

She needs to go home. I'm not sure how good it'll be for business if people come in and find a sobbing woman by the till. Pat squeezes her.

'You see! Now come on, let's go home and have a nice whisky.'

'I can't. I promised to go into work.'

'Sis, you look like you got pounded by the Mutant Ninja Turtles. Phone in, take some time off. They take the piss anyway.'

As he's speaking, the door opens and in marches Juliette, my other card-turner. She's brandishing a huge bunch of flowers.

'If you won't let me pay you, then I shall give you a gift.'

'Oh my gosh, these are gorgeous. You didn't have to do this!'

155

'I most certainly did.'

She catches sight of the tear-stained, blotchy face of Caitlin.

'You, too?'

Juliette shakes her head at me.

'Do you make everyone who comes in here cry?'

She turns back to Caitlin.

'Are you okay? She's great, isn't she?'

Caitlin nods, clutching her tissue. Pat answers for her.

'She certainly is!'

Juliette looks at him for precisely three seconds longer than necessary, then gathers herself.

'Anyway, this is not the last you've heard of me. You made my day. I've booked a spa. I'm running back to get a bag together. Fuck men!'

'Thank you, Juliette.'

She's already gone. Never a dull moment.

Pat takes his sister's arm.

'Right, this one needs to go home.'

'I'm not a child.'

But Caitlin's weeping again. She'll need to cry this one out for the rest of the day probably. I am so relieved that I had something to tell her.

'Thank you so much, Tanz. I didn't even know how much I needed to hear that.'

'You're so welcome, Cait. I'm sure I'll bump into you on the high street, now that I know who you are.'

Pat crosses to my side of the counter and kisses my cheek. I react immediately to the smell of him. He whispers, 'Call you later, after my shift.'

Then he's off with his sister, who leans into him like the walking wounded. I sit back down on my seat and open my water. I am now knackered, but also buzzing. I take a swig and peel back my banana. I am so hungry. A voice shocks me.

'Well, somebody's popular.'

I'd forgotten about Martin. He is sitting in the reading room with the door open, so that he can spy on me. He is a glaring, malevolent weasel-man.

ANGRY
SPOOKS 'R' US

After a swiftly bolted plate of salad and steamed cod at home, I have a quick conversation with Milo, who is climbing the walls with anxiety because he has a scriptwriting deadline – one that will prove he can write for a TV show that he detests, God bless him.

'My head's exploding, Tanz. I hate every single character in the show, and the producer is a massive knobhead.'

'You're not a knobhead, though, Milo – you are a total genius. You can do it. Think of the money; think of the fact that once you get that job, you can finance your own plays.'

'I know you're right, but I'm eating my own feet here.'

'Have a glass of wine, clear your head of everything else, then write the first thing you think of. That's what you said works best.'

'I know, I know. I'm just panicking.'

'I have every faith in you.'

'Stop it, you'll have me sobbing here.'

Twenty minutes later I've surrendered into the arms of Purple Haze and a Raspberry Mint Martini with Sheila.

Tonight she has outdone herself in a multicoloured shirt, black dress pants, a long gothic cardigan and rings on most of her fingers. The scent of Samsara greets me before she does. She opts for an Espresso Martini. I love them, too, but the caffeine sends me doolally at night. We sit at a high table with bar stools, and I'm amused to see that tricorne man is there in a different frock coat, once more beavering away at his laptop. He gives me the tiniest of nods as I look his way. I nod back.

I fill Sheila in on the day's adventures.

'Bloody hell. If you didn't believe you were made for this before, then you must do now, love.'

'I'm not a natural reader, though. I turn over a card and then I just say stuff.'

'That *is* a natural reader! The cards basically help your "connection". Cards, and their placing on the table, can be consulted if someone is shut off or blocking you. Then you can take clues from the spread itself. The cards are a conduit – it's you "tuning in" that really does the trick. And you did brilliantly today. You couldn't have asked spirit for more.'

It's funny; Sheila says 'spirit', but I don't define it in my head like that. I think of it simply as people I'm chatting to. If I go all airy-fairy about it, I don't believe it myself. I don't know what else to call it, though. 'Spirit', 'angels', 'guides'? I usually go for silly terms like 'spooks' instead. I wonder if that's me making the whole situation manageable by taking the piss? Whichever way I look at it, something *very* weird happened again today. Sheila sips her Martini and gets a creamy moustache.

'You know, Tanz, you could try other stuff – see what you're most comfortable with. I like the cards, I'm at home with them. But if they don't rock your boat . . .'

'It's not that they don't rock my boat; they're beautiful. It's just that I seem to get the information in my head anyway, and if I then look at the card, it's a bit distracting. I start looking at the pictures for extra stuff. It sort of makes it less pure.'

'Then try psychometry.'

'Huh?'

'Holding an object in your hand belonging to the subject, like a ring or a watch. It helps you tune into them better, but you're not "reading" the object, you're using it to get closer to the subject because it's filled with their energy.'

This seems rather exciting.

'Don't get me wrong; it sounds as if the cards worked fine for you today, but if they don't make you totally comfortable, then find something else. You know you've got the ability, so it's trial and error to find what helps you to hone it. Some people use runes, others use crystals.'

'Some are simply lying and are totally rubbish!'

'Are you talking about Martin, by any chance?'

'Might be. To be fair, I have no idea if he's any good, as I've not had a reading from him. And midget Rose West had a whole hour today instead of half an hour.'

'Yes, but she may have felt she had to. Or she might fancy him. You know how crazy some people are. She may have missed the fact that he's as gay as the hills.'

'Ew! And the fact he's totally creepy. Why did Maggie employ him?'

'Martin can be a laugh when he's not depressed. But his readings have completely died off because he's stopped bothering to charm the customers. I actually think he's potentially good, if he would try harder to care.'

'Look, I know people are depressed – half of my mates are, most of my family are – but it doesn't mean you need to be a wanker, does it?'

'No, it doesn't, love.'

Suddenly I remember the other cause of my excitement.

'Oh, I forgot. The ghost-bust! Spill, spill!'

A bald man walks onto the little stage and begins to play the acoustic guitar. Luckily he's not too loud, but he does have a voice disconcertingly like Demis Roussos, which sets me off giggling. We are sitting on the other side of a large mirrored pillar, so he doesn't see, thank God.

'Oooh, yes. One of those fluke recommendations. Friend of a friend. A woman who's having problems in her bungalow. She rang and she sounded bloody awful. Really beaten down. She said she'd explain properly when we got there. I said yes, provisionally, depending on you. Obviously she's supposed to pay us, but . . . she didn't sound well off, put it that way. It's usually sixty quid an hour, plus a forty-pound consultation fee. Do you think that's bad?'

I'm not sure what to say. I don't like charging people for a natural gift, but ghost-busting is exhausting. And Sheila knows better than me about these things.

'If that's the going rate . . . And it is a specialist job,

I suppose. I've heard of people doing "exorcisms" who charge thousands.'

'Tanz, they're leeches. But you've got to stop with this "I don't like taking a fee" nonsense. It's meant to be an exchange of energies. That's where that girl who gave you the flowers had it right. You can't do it for nothing, especially if you've got nothing in the first place. It's still a job, at the end of the day.'

Sheila's husband was a grade-one abuser. She has a permanently damaged knee because of one of his beatings. He was a handsome, rich crackpot from the same kind of background as her. He made his money through dubious means and, after a year together, he became more and more possessive and turned violent. When she 'escaped' and divorced him, she didn't even try for the big house they shared or the cars, or anything. There was no point. All she wanted was enough to buy her studio flat and even he couldn't say no to that, as it was so piffling compared to what she was entitled to. Everything else – bills, council tax, food, little luxuries – they all come out of what she earns as a tarot reader and sometime 'ghost-buster'. She doesn't claim anything, she doesn't bother anybody and she'd rather have her fags, her films and her tipple than any bloke. That's what she told me, and I believe her. Sheila doesn't even bother looking at men now; she says she's had her fill, and I don't blame her. It is a shame, though, because she's smokin'. And I don't just mean the ciggies.

'Anyway, I was thinking of this weekend – Saturday, if possible, because I'm at the shop on Sunday.'

'Cool. I'm in.'

'Goody. I'll call her later.'

I don't intend to stay out late tonight, as I'm in the shop with Sheila tomorrow, so I'll be up vaguely early. But I do want another one of these cocktails. I get hooked on things so easily. Sheila gets another Espresso Martini. I have no idea how she'll sleep, she must be impervious to caffeine. We settle into a different couple of seats right at the back of Purple Haze, close to the exit and as far as you can get from the music. I am very curious about ghost-busting. It is depicted in such a sinister way in films, but last time we did it, it felt kind. I want to know if it's ever sinister.

Sheila thinks.

'It's always for the best, when I do it. I don't think people call me in when there's no problem. Some people rub along fine with whoever is sharing their building. But if there's a disturbance, you usually find that the spirit really does need to move on. The ones that aren't so much fun are the ones that are staying in one place, reliving something awful. I found one of those when I was asked by a guard at Pentonville Prison to come and look at the flat he lived in. He was feeling ill in there and it was affecting his well-being. He was also getting scared. A big thing for such a tough bloke to admit.

'The flat linked to the jail, and as soon as I walked in I felt sick. The horrible feeling was coming from the bedroom. That directly linked to a part of the prison where prisoners were hanged, before it was abolished. I went into the bedroom and the first thing I noticed was how bloody messy it was. I mean a total tip. The bloke in question said afterwards he hadn't noticed what a tip it had become. That happens a lot with disturbed entities – you find them in grossly messy rooms. It makes them feel comfortable.'

The hairs on the back of my neck are waving. This often happens when I'm around Sheila. I wipe my hand over them and sup my cocktail.

'So I put the feelers out in the bedroom and I found someone all right, but he was very difficult to pin down. He was faceless. It was as if, as a personality, he didn't exist. All he was – and I saw this because for a short while it was like I became him – was an ignorant soul who would empty his mind of who he was and let in a much darker and colder force when he killed. I saw my own hands around a young girl's neck, then that vision disappeared and I saw a large knife in my hand, coming down towards an older woman in a kitchen. It was the most awful, chilling feeling, to have emptied all humanity from myself for those moments, and I soon blocked what I was getting from him. It was too poisonous. He had been hanged, that much was certain. And his spirit was very difficult to get rid of. He eventually left, but I was bloody sickened for days. That wasn't nice.'

'Oh. I'm not so sure about that kind of ghost-bust.'

'I thought you were obsessed with murderers?'

'Not dead ones who won't fuck off.'

I decide it might be home time.

A LITTLE BIT OF WHAT YOU FANCY . . .

When I get home I make myself a camomile tea and run a bath. Inka is all over me as soon as I get through the door. Because she virtually never gets out her claws, I sometimes drape her around my neck when I'm moving about the flat. She loves this. The funniest thing about my closeness with Inka is that I'm actually allergic to cats. Only slightly now, as I've got more used to her, but I still sometimes wake up with a wheezy cough, and I get the odd rash on my inner wrist too. But it's a very small price to pay for so much love. And make no bones: animals know their stuff when it comes to love.

My bath, complete with bubbles, a smelly candle that I pilfered from Elsa's stash and my big white shower cap with red dots on it, to protect my already-clean hair, is the stuff of legend. I breathe out the day and go quiet for ten minutes. Today's shenanigans were quite mind-blowing, in retrospect. I send out some thanks for what I was able to do. I'm not sure who I'm thanking, so I thank 'The Universe', which pretty much covers all bases. Of course, being a dark-minded Geordie lass, there's a part of my brain that keeps reminding me: *If you don't know how you do it, then you could just as easily lose it.* I ignore the voice of my own paranoia. Right now it hasn't disappeared and I am so happy.

I am dried, balmed, pyjamaed and under my clean duvet with a serial-killer book when my telephone rings. It's exactly 11 p.m.

'Are you in the house, favourite witch?'

That accent.

'How many witches do you know?'

'Loads. Oh, sorry, no, wait a minute, that's *bitches*. I only know one *witch*!'

'Bloody misogynist.'

'Can I call round for a cup of tea, please?'

I panic a little. Am I now going to have to get back up and put some bloody foundation on?

'I'm already in bed, with no make-up, in my PJs.'

'Last time I was at your flat I left you with no make-up and your hair standing on end, wearing an old Super Furry Animals T-shirt with holes in it.'

That is true.

'And I liked it.'

'Pervert.'

'You've got two minutes to make me a cup of tea. I'm nearly there.'

Oh, shit!

The milk smells a bit suspicious, so I make Pat a vanilla chai – that's what he had last time and he said he liked it. I hate the stuff, so it was lurking at the back of my cupboard.

I'm a straight peppermint or camomile girl, when I'm not tanking up on caffeine. I've just poured the water on the bag when he knocks. He's wearing the same clothes as this afternoon and gives me a warm hug on the doorstep.

En route to the kitchen, I reach in to switch on the living-room light. He stops my hand with his own.

'Where were you when I called?'

I hand him his tea and lead him to my room, which admittedly looks very cosy with the little bedside lamp and the plumped duvet.

'Can I be really cheeky and sit on the other side of the bed? Then you can go straight back to where you were before and, when I let myself out, you can just fall asleep like you were going to?'

I'm suspicious. It sounds sensible but also dangerous, considering what went on last time Pat was here. Seeing as I've already let him in without my war-paint and in my checked pyjamas, though, I've already broken several of my own golden rules. So I shrug.

'Okay. But behave. I have to be up for the shop.'

'Sure thing.'

He slips off his shoes and climbs up next to me. I'm inside the bed and he's on the duvet.

'Do you realize you have broken my sister? She is basically a jelly in jeans.'

'I'm sorry about that, Pat. She's obviously a bit fragile.'

He looks knackered, I notice.

'That's one word for it. I'm pleased, to be honest. She really needed to hear something and, boy, did you deliver. That song . . . I have no idea how you did it, but getting that song – it sent Caitlin into another dimension. Unless you are the best guesser on the planet, your powers really hit the jackpot.'

'I looked on psychic Google; it told me everything about her.'

He laughs. I don't. Something has been niggling me.

'Pat, I've been thinking. This "getting messages" thing. I'm wondering if it's maybe just telepathy? Picking up on what people need to hear and on the memories of departed loved ones, then feeding the information back to them, to give them what they need? Does that sound feasible? That it's nothing to do with "spirit" at all?'

'Jeez – deep. Yes, it sounds feasible, but either way it would be a miracle, wouldn't it?'

'I suppose so. But it could just as easily have been telepathy that gave me the Joe Dolce song, couldn't it?'

'Why do you want to believe it's telepathy?'

'Well, it's a bit more scientific than talking to dead people, isn't it?'

'Actually no, not really. Reading minds isn't yet a science, is it? And it's only if you're regarding the "dead" in a horror-movie kind of way that it sounds weird. If people are simply people, and they move on in pure electric form when they die, why can't they sometimes slip back and present themselves in electrical non-solid form, to give a bit of comfort to those they loved?'

God, Pat's far too mature for his age. He thinks about things most people wouldn't even approach. All of that and a cracking arse!

'There's no reason why not. I just don't have any

answers for what's going on, and I'm looking for something that doesn't make me sound like a madwoman.'

'It's a bit late for that, isn't it? You tell people stuff you shouldn't know about them. *Plus*, you help ghosts leave houses. You already are a total and utter madwoman. And all the better for it.'

I'm glad he's here.

'You're right. That's kind of the conclusion I was coming to anyway. It doesn't matter where the messages come from, if I'm helping. How was Caitlin before you went to work?'

'Still crying. But she put a film on and got a bar of fruit-and-nut out of the fridge as I was leaving, so she wasn't exactly dying from grief. Plus, I got a text from her earlier and she'd called Brian. That's the guy she's been holding at arm's length. I'd have chucked her by now, but he's got the patience of a saint. He's over there tonight.'

Pat was so gentle with Caitlin this afternoon. It didn't occur to me how much he probably has to play 'big brother' to his elder sister.

'You're a really nice person, aren't you?'

He wrinkles his nose.

'I'm just a normal lad getting on with shit.'

He kisses me. It's not the urgent, passionate, crazy kissing from the other night. It's slower and deeper than that. And he doesn't make a move to do anything else. I try to do the same, but I'm afraid I can't help myself. Without breaking the kiss for a second, I pull the duvet from under him so that he's next to me properly and then cover him again, so that we're both underneath it. But even with our

169

arms wrapped around each other and our legs entwined, I still can't get close enough to him. I want every bit of me that can touch him to do so. But not with these stupid bloody clothes between us. He stops the kiss for a moment.

'Aren't I supposed to go, so you can get your rest?'

'I don't want you to go. I want you to take your clothes off.'

He kisses me again, then begins to push off his sweater. 'Music to my ears.'

Afterwards we both collapse into sweaty sleep, which suits me down to the ground. I wake up before Pat does and lie against his back, marvelling at the fact that I slept a full night. In the old, old days, before Blake, I was no good at having sex with new people because I couldn't sleep beside someone I hardly knew. Once finished, I'd always make excuses and run off. You'd think men would like this, but they're not as pleased as you'd think when the shoe is on the other foot. I actually think it's much more trusting to be asleep next to someone than to have sex with them. This may be linked to me constantly reading about murderers. I mean, you could wake up in some garage, suspended from the ceiling by winches with an apple shoved up your arse, and who would know? It doesn't bear thinking about. And because I only have an hour before I have to get up, I stop thinking about it and snuggle in.

HOUSE OF THE
CD TERRORIST

When Sheila and I reach the cottage it is just before noon. It is one of a bunch of rundown little council bungalows that protrude strangely into a field, the last one being surrounded on three sides by scrubby grass. This is the one we're aiming for. It's not horrible or anything, but it's strangely situated.

We set out from London an hour and fifteen minutes ago, armed with takeaway cappuccinos and a skinny muffin each. Sheila says the sugar is good to have before a ghost-bust, and afterwards as well, so we also bought Skittles and bottles of water for the journey home.

The woman who answers the door looks haggard. She is rotund with straggly hair, straggly slippers and a straggly tent-dress that envelops her breasts and belly and hangs to her knees. Her eyes are tired and her breathing is thick and laboured. She looks so wiped out, I feel like giving her a cuddle. She is called Ann. When we get inside the hallway, it is dimly lit and the air is heavy. Also the carpets are aggressively patterned and the walls are a dusty yellow. We follow her to the living room where another younger, slightly less rotund woman sits at a rickety dining table looking rather nervous. We are directed to a small, patterned green sofa and offered a cup of tea, which both of us decline.

'This is my daughter by the way – Sue. She doesn't like coming here, do you, Sue? The whole family hate it here, don't they?'

'I wouldn't stay here overnight, I'll tell you that for nothing.'

Sheila grimaces. 'Now that's no good, is it? We'll have to see if we can change that. Ann, love, can you take us through why you brought us here, so we can get a feel for what's been going on?'

I'm not saying much at this point, because I'm putting the feelers out as I listen to them talk. I can tell there's someone else in the bungalow, some heavy presence, but I can't properly pinpoint 'him'. I'm pretty sure I can feel a 'he', though.

'Well, it all started just after my Raymond – Sue's dad – died.'

As Ann wheezes into an inhaler, she points up at a picture on the wall of her hugging a man with dark hair and a widow's peak. He looks sweet. She looks much, much younger.

'When was that?'

'That was five years ago. My health's gone up the Swanee through all of this . . . I'm telling you, that nasty man is killing me.'

'*Mum!*'

172

Sue is evidently horrified by such talk, but Ann certainly doesn't look too healthy.

'Two weeks after the funeral I was sitting in front of the telly and it was my bedtime, but I couldn't face it, because I still wasn't used to sleeping without Raymond. So I put a film on and tried to get some rest in the chair. Anyway, this banging started over my head and kept going all the way round the room, like someone hitting the walls with a toffee-hammer. I was terrified. I didn't know what to do because I was on my own, so I started shouting at it to stop. Eventually it did, but from that moment I felt like I was being watched. And every night, if I didn't go to bed at my normal time, the banging would start.'

'Bloody hell, Ann, I'd have made a run for it.'

And I would have done, too. She's braver than me.

She shakes her head. 'Where would I have run to? My next-door neighbour is older than me – she's eighty and she's almost deaf. I didn't want to go bothering her. Two of the other houses are empty, and I don't have a car.'

As she speaks I begin to feel a pressure on my left-hand side.

'Thing is, I stopped wanting to go to bed, because you don't want to get undressed if you're being watched – and I definitely was. If that wasn't bad enough, when I did get into bed, the noises would start. They're still going on most nights. I don't know how to describe it, but the closest thing I could compare it to is bottles being rolled in a concrete yard. I'll be falling asleep and suddenly there'll be this noise. It can go on for more than an hour.'

I'm getting a headache on the left-hand side of my head. I look at Sheila, who glances back at me and indicates my left-hand side with a quick bob of the head and a sideways glance. Boy, he's a strong one.

'Mum. Tell them about the music.'

Ann sighs.

'Yes, that's his latest trick. I can't play my Shania Twain any more, or my Celine Dion. As soon as I put them in the player, the thing jams. I was beginning to wonder if the stereo was broken, until the first time the CD drawer opened itself back up and Celine Dion flew across the room. He's done that three times.'

'Sorry, Ann, but in this case I think he has a point.'

We all laugh at my joke, but it's becoming more and more uncomfortable in the room. Ann is the first to acknowledge it out loud.

'The bugger's in here now, isn't he?'

I look around me, feel him coming in even closer.

'Yep. Can you feel that, Sheila?'

'He's not pleased we're here, is he?'

Sue shivers.

'He pushed me over once – that's why I don't come here unless I have to. I've asked Mum if she wants to stay with us for a few weeks, but you don't want to go, do you, Mum?'

'No. This was where me and Ray were going to live out our retirement. *I'm not being pushed out by you, you bugger!*'

The air is palpably shaking, then he's gone. There's a

crash from the kitchen. I jump out of my flippin' skin. Ann emits a little rasp and tuts.

'It's my sweeping brush. He pushes it over when he's angry. He sometimes knocks plates off the bench, 'n' all. I wish I knew what he bloody wanted. He wasn't here when we moved in and now he rules this place. He doesn't like visitors, he won't let me sleep, he knocks on the wall when I'm trying to read. He's a bleedin' nuisance, and I'm going to end up in hospital if he doesn't leave me alone. I just want him to go away.'

I'm excited by all of this (and, of course, scared) because he can mess with physical things. I thought that kind of thing only happened in fairy stories, but obviously not. I look to Sheila again, who gives me the proper nod. Time to go in.

'Right, Ann, love, what we need to do is have a look around – just Tanz and me – and we can hopefully find out a bit about him. Maybe work out what he wants? If you two stay here, we'll report back to you soon.'

Seeing as a lot of the disturbance is going on in Ann's bedroom, it's the obvious place to go first. We look in on the kitchen en route and see the broom lying on the floor. His energy doesn't seem to be concentrated in there right now, so we pile into her bedroom and perch on her double duvet. The room is dingy, but not messy. This only adds to my impression that he's a strong energy, and so is Ann. She is battling to keep her life ordered, and he is battling to break her down.

We sit quietly and centre ourselves, waiting for the surge of energy that will signal his presence. Sure enough, it comes. And, to my amazement, I feel him trying to push me back on the bed. I'm so surprised that I almost laugh – not because it's funny, but because he is so brazenly sexual.

'He's here, love, do you feel it?'

'Feel it? He just tried to push me backwards on the bed, the cheeky sod.'

'Bloody hell.'

'Get out!'

It's unmistakable. The voice of an angry man. It immediately strikes me that being scared is pointless and will only give him power. Obviously I'm being helped. I imagine my protection around me.

'He's telling us to get out, Sheils.'

'I thought he might be. Tell me anything else you hear. I can see him pointing to the door. He's a big bloke.'

I'm glad I can't see his face properly. He sounds very mean.

'Get out. And get away from my wife.'

'Oh God, Sheils – he's saying Ann's his wife.'

'Ohh. He's claimed her, has he? Explains why he turned up after her Raymond died. Still . . . where did he come from?'

'Who are you? Do you know this isn't your house? And Ann isn't your wife?'

We're both speaking out loud, as it makes it easier for both of us to synchronize.

'This is my field, this is where I do my horses . . . I saw this house and decided to get married and live here. It's on my field! YOU SHOULDN'T BE HERE, I DIDN'T INVITE YOU.'

'He's saying this is his field. He's saying something about horses?'

'Aw, yes. I'm getting horseshoes and hot metal. He's a farrier. I wonder when he worked here?'

'This is MY field.'

His name comes to me suddenly. He's called Thomas. The picture of him in my head puts him straight into a Catherine Cookson drama.

'I think he's from a long time ago, Sheila. He's called Thomas.'

Sheila speaks up authoritatively.

'What year is this, Thomas?'

He snickers unpleasantly.

'Is she stupid? It's 1904. Stupid bitch. Are you both stupid?'

'God, he's abusive. He reckons it's 1904. It's not, Thomas, you know – it's not 1904. I think you died then, in 1904. It's 2012 now, and this field doesn't belong to you any more.'

'It's 1904, and this is my field and that's my wife, and you two better go before I wring your necks!'

He is one furious bloke. Sheila gets the gist without me having to tell her. His energy suddenly sucks out of the room. He's sensing danger probably. I don't suppose nasty, stuck spooks like him want to be faced with the truth. I suddenly feel sure that he did something terribly wrong in his life and he's afraid.

Sheila has gone a little pale. She whispers, 'I think he mistreated his wife. She died after years of misery. It was natural causes, but she had a horrible time of it. That's why he's still here. Guilt, and fear of going to hell. Thomas must have been stuck in this field, then they built the houses and, when Ray died and Ann was at her weakest psychically, Thomas jumped in and claimed her for his own. Ruling her life like he ruled his other wife. If we don't get rid of him, he will finish her off, I'm sure of it. She won't have a lot of time left. He's a bloodsucker.'

If anyone knows about abusive husbands, it's Sheila. No wonder she's picked up on it.

I stand up.

'Right, we know his weakness now. Let's get him.'

We straighten the duvet like good, polite girls and go out to the hallway. Thomas is not letting us feel his energy. I go to the kitchen and the bathroom, I look back into the living room, where Sue and Ann glance back at me curiously. I wave a jaunty hand, then return to the hallway. Sheila shrugs. Then all at once I know. I open the tiny airing cupboard. I get closer, I empty my mind. Then I laugh. I make myself laugh more. Bully the bully: isn't that the way to defeat them?

'Sheila – Thomas, the great big coward, is hiding in a cupboard. Hiding in a little cupboard from two women like a *girl*.'

'*I WAS NOT HIDING, YOU STUPID FOOL.*'

Do ghosts have a habit of calling people stupid? It's the second time that's happened. A furious whoosh through the air and Thomas has vacated the cupboard and is back in the bedroom. I feel him go. Sheila winks at me.

'Brilliant.'

We head back into the bedroom and stop in our tracks.

We straightened that bed a few minutes ago. Now there's an indentation, like someone is sitting there. I feel a mixture of fear and admiration. This is one powerful spook. On instinct, I take Sheila's hand. We step forward. It's time to change tone.

'Thomas?'

He doesn't answer.

'Thomas, we haven't come to cause you trouble. We've come to tell you something.'

'*You have nothing I want to hear.*'

Sheila introduces a deep calm into her voice.

'Thomas, your wife didn't die because of you. You didn't give her the best time, but she died naturally. You will not go to hell; you will go to her and apologize, and she will forgive you because she is peaceful and happy now.'

'*My wife is in that room next door!*'

He doesn't sound so convinced now.

'Sheils, he's saying *Ann*'s his wife.'

Sheila takes a deep breath. This must be hard for her, but she's keeping her cool.

'No, she isn't. She is someone else's wife, and she will die as surely as yours did if you don't leave her alone. This isn't your home, and you have an apology to make. You have got to make your peace or you will be miserable forever.'

All at once I get a picture in my head of this big man with a mean face falling to the ground in a muddy field clutching at his chest. I keep my voice calm and low.

'You died in this field, Thomas. Do you remember? A heart attack in this field, in 1904. You have to go and talk to your wife – you have to find peace.'

As I hold Sheila's hand, I see something in my mind's eye. It looks like a treasure chest: the top opens and it has a toy drum inside it . . . and I see this big mean-faced man, and he shrinks and shrinks until he is a sweet little boy. He looks into the chest and sees the drum. He climbs into the chest and closes the lid on himself. The vision fades. And suddenly the room feels empty.

Sheila lets go of my hand.

I am shell-shocked and very moved.

'He was a beautiful child.'

'Probably the last time he felt happy.'

'Jesus, Sheila. Was that it? Has he gone?'

'What do you think?'

I put out 'feelers'; I don't 'reach' exactly, as I don't want to pull any energy back. I just tentatively feel around with my senses. Nothing.

We migrate to the hallway and it's the strangest thing. The sunlight is now reaching through the windowed door panel. There is much more light in here, I'm sure of it. As we walk towards the living room, Ann emerges. She looks at us, one and then the other, then nods.

'He's gone, hasn't he? I feel it.'

If anyone would know, it's Ann. She's been tuned into this bloke for a long time. When she smiles, I suddenly see the attractive woman she was before. I only hope she can get her health back and be that again. As we go to the living room to explain what just happened, I already know that we won't be charging. Sheila is as soft as me really. And I can't imagine that Ann has a penny. I only hope Thomas finds his peace, and that everything gets better for this poor woman.

I know one thing, though. Ann should repaint this place and change the hallway carpet. It is horrible! I don't want to say that exactly, so I tell her that if she changes the decor, it will help her move on. She is grateful for my advice. Sometimes I'm the gift that keeps on giving.

THE WRATH OF
THE WEASEL

S o it all kicked off in the shop today.
I came in this morning and did a bit of dusting, as usual. Sheila came with me, gloriously clad in a bottle-green velvet jacket and aventurine jewellery, but sauntered off for a coffee as it was still early. At ten o'clock she reappeared, closely followed by Maggie, who was looking mighty fucked off. She informed us that she had sacked Martin the weasel the day before. I asked why and she told me there had been a complaint.

Turns out that midget Rose West's husband was not happy. Martin had told Rose that her husband was gay and that she needed to escape. Apparently Rose West was completely traumatized – no wonder she looked so weird when she left the shop. Next day her husband called to say he would press charges unless Martin was sacked. Which he has been. Now there's a vacancy.

Maggie is quite determined that I should fill the gap. She is so pushy, like a Yorkshire terrier, apart from the fact that you can throw a Yorkshire terrier in the bin and you can't throw Maggie in the bin. Worst luck. Actually I wouldn't be in this predicament if Juliette hadn't called the shop within half an hour of the angry non-gay husband, to request that I become a reader. She told Maggie that I was the best medium she had ever met. Bless her, she laid it on thick, so now Maggie is determined. She says she doesn't care if I'm a reader, a psychometrist or a hands-on medium – I'm taking Martin's place.

I am given a couple of hours to 'think about it'. I'm not sure what Maggie's going to do if, after those two hours, I say no. Before I can ask Sheila about it, a very laid-back young Jamaican lad walks in off the street and asks for a reading.

Sheila has just closed the door behind him when, horror of horrors, an irate Martin scoots into the shop, cardigan flapping, half-mast trousers billowing and all guns blazing. Despite which, if I'm brutally honest, he still manages to make fury look a little limp. He accuses me of getting the job on the till in order to depose him. Hustler that I am. I mean, really, I plotted his downfall, did I? Sometimes I forget that not everyone wants to be a show-off for a living, and his job was probably important to Martin. But now I'm mad, so I inform him that I got the job in the shop because I was skint, and I'm being kept on now because I'm nice to customers and they like me. As for the tarot-reading post, I remind him that I'd never even owned a deck of tarot cards until yesterday.

Martin calls me a 'total cowbag', bursts into tears and leaves.

For all my mouthiness, I'm actually terrified of confrontation and I feel ashamed that he's in such distress. Saying that, I'm also very relieved that he didn't murder me; though I'll wait a few days before I truly believe he isn't going to return with a Taser.

As I sit pondering, thumbing through my Scapini deck, I get the strangest feeling of dizziness, like I'm whizzing backwards on some God-awful funfair ride. It's accompanied by a sudden jab of nausea and it's all I can do not to fall off my chair. Holding onto the counter for balance, I take a sip of water from my half-finished bottle and attempt to steady myself, closing my eyes and breathing out for ten. As I open them again, I glance towards the coffee shop across the road and see a man at a table in the window directly opposite, looking like he's watching me. But he can't be, because he has no face.

'Oh Christ, he has no face – it's just a blank oval. FRANKKK, it's a man with no face!'

But Frank doesn't answer and I rub my hands over my eyes. My heart is going like the clappers. When I eventually force myself to look back, I see that it's actually a man with dark, droopy-looking eyes; he does have a face after all and he's getting up out of his seat. The light's bouncing off the cafe window, so it's hard to see much more. Then a lorry stops at the lights outside Mystery Pot and blocks my view. When it moves again, the man has gone. I'm so shaken up that I rush over to turn the door sign to 'Closed' and put the lock on. Then I go through to the kitchen at the back to make myself a camomile tea. As the kettle boils, I decide ten minutes is a fair amount of time to hide, in case the scary man decides to pop in for some impromptu shape-shifting.

When Sheila emerges, she is looking very stern and the laid-back Jamaican lad is distinctly less laid-back. As he pays, his eyes keep darting to Sheila, like she might put a spell on him. There is wonder mingled with fear in those pretty eyes. Before he leaves he almost genuflects. Sheila gives him a stern look.

'You remember what I've said. Otherwise you are letting down your mother. Make things right, love, or you'll regret it. I'm warning you.'

I can't believe it. I've not seen this side of Sheila before. He all but runs out of the place. Suddenly the fact that I imagined a bloke had no face becomes yesterday's news.

'Sheila? What the . . . ?'

She sighs, takes a bottle of water out of her bag and sits in the seat next to me at the till.

'He's over from Kingston on a catering course. He's twenty-two and talented, and his mother worked very hard to make sure he had a bright future. She sent him here to study and escape the violence at home. Within minutes of him sitting down, I saw a gun in his cards. A bloody gun.'

'Oo-er.'

'Exactly. Some distant cousin of his who lives in Tottenham offered him a different option to working hard at college. He came here because he's going to court soon, and he wanted me to tell him it would be all right. He hid a gun for his cousin and it won't be bloody all right at all – he's an idiot. I told him that, plus things about his mum and his life that a stranger shouldn't know, and it's put the fear of

God in him. I hope it's scared him enough to make this the last thing he does for this 'cousin'. There's every chance he'll be going down. I told him he's made a terrible choice and now he has to put it right. I hope he will. I don't like seeing guns in the cards; it scares the hell out of me. I'm going out for a fag.'

She exits through the kitchen to the back door. I feel unsafe suddenly. Martin and his outburst, then a gun-toting criminal. Well, he isn't exactly a gun-toting criminal, but it sure sounds like his cousin is. I wonder if this is one of the 'dark energy' days that Sheila was talking about? I take a can of cherry Diet Coke from my bag and unplug it. I pull out a card. Death. I know about the Death card. It's all about change and a new way of life coming in. I wonder if the card is about me, because everything in my life seems to be changing right now.

I pull out another. The Falling Tower? Oo-er. There's no good way to look at that card, not when it's next to Death. No, thank you. I shove them both back into the deck and try to think about something else as the shop door pings.

MUNCH'S *SCREAM*
AND THE SCARY CREEP

As if I'm not freaked out enough, the faceless man has just come through the door with the most hard-faced woman in England.

My stomach hits the floor.

There's something weird about both of them; the atmosphere in the shop is immediately thick and treacly. But, in better news, the tiniest shaft of rationality begins to creep over me. Closer up, the bloke is definitely made of solid flesh; he's small enough to bash over the head with a lampstand, if I have to, and his eyes, nose and mouth are in roughly the right place. I'm now sure that the light on the cafe window caused an optical illusion. Without staring too hard, I manage to ascertain that he's around fifty, with thick, dark hair and round, slightly droopy, basset-hound eyes. I remember a cartoon with a character who looked like him. What was it now? Deputy Dawg – that's it. He's shortish, stocky and fit-looking in a well-cut suit.

As for her, she's taller than him and younger. She's wearing a red jacket with a black pencil skirt and patent court shoes. She has long, wavy auburn hair and extremely mani-cured eyebrows. She looks like she might be part Filipino, but obviously not a massive part, as Filipino women are not generally known for their height. Also the make-up and the expensive haircut cannot begin to hide the fact that she's a granite-faced cow and her energy's as cold as a witch's nipple.

I force a smile as she approaches me.

'I have a reading here in two minutes.'

Obviously better things to do than say 'hello' or 'excuse me' then? Her voice is a bit Essex, although she's trying to hide it. Being an actress, I'm quite good with accents. I check in the book.

'Mrs Beck?'

'Yes.'

The husband looks uncomfortable. Books about angel healing and little pottery fairies on branches don't appeal to everyone. Sheila reappears and I introduce them.

'All right, Mrs Beck, if you'd like to come through.'

She turns to her husband.

'Dan, pay now. I don't want to have to hang around after.'

Charming!

'Right.'

'Go and get a coffee or something till half-past.'

'Right.'

She follows Sheila, and I'm left with him. As soon as the door closes, he looks at me and smiles. He smiles like a fucking snake. What an odd couple – a pair of lizards. He pays in cash and I feel a wave of discomfort when his hand brushes mine. When I've given him his receipt, he goes over to the bookstand and pretends to study the titles. I sit sipping my drink, feeling more and more uncomfortable. His energy scares me. The shop actually feels darker now; maybe the sun went behind a cloud or something, but I wish another customer would come in.

'Nice little shop.'

His voice is deep. He has a Somerset burr, I'm surprised to note. I try to look him right in the eye so that he doesn't think I'm scared of him.

'Thank you. It's not mine, I just help out.'

He breaks my gaze. Ha, one to me!

'Not really my sort of thing, I have to admit. Would make a good little bar, though. Nice size. Carmen would do the interior, my boys would sort out the cracks in the ceiling.'

I look up. It is a bit dusty and cracked up there.

'Sorry. Carmen? Is that your wife?'

He's closed – that's what it is. Everything he says covers up what he really thinks.

'Sort of.'

I want him to go away, as these attempts at small talk are weirding me out.

'If you do fancy a coffee, there's a lovely little place over the road. They do a mean cappuccino.'

'Thank you, that's very helpful.'

Then, thank fuck, he takes the hint and exits. There is something wrong with that man. He scares me with his absolute wrongness. I want to talk to Frank. But I don't have time to ask what's going on with Deputy Dawg before I hear a woman's voice inside my skull.

'*Oh God, oh God, oh God . . . Help me, please help me. Oh God . . .*'

There's a desperation to the voice that is sickening to hear. I have no idea who she is. I try to ask, but I can't break through. I just hear the same lament over and over again.

'*Please . . . Help me, Oh God, oh God, oh God . . .*'

It is an eerie and lonely cry. I try to 'see' her. All I can picture is dark, thick hair and terrified eyes. She's about ten years older than me and attractive. But she's completely in shadow. I want to talk to her, but I can't smash through the train of horror careering through her brain. What the hell happened?

My hands have started to shake. This is not fun. She is now weeping copiously. I do the only thing I can.

'FRANK!'

To an outside observer, I'm sitting behind the till in a hippy shop staring into space. In reality, inside my brain, I am screaming for my friend's help.

'FRANNNKKKK?'

His voice is calm when he speaks. Like he was just waiting for me to ask.

'*Hey there, cheeky. What's up?*'

'Can't you hear her?'

'*Of course I can. The poor woman's demented.*'

'Calm her down!'

'*I can't. You and Sheila will have to sit down together. It's very hard to talk to someone who's as panic-stricken as this one.*'

'She sounds alive. Is this a living person, trapped some-where? Crying out for help?'

'*No.*'

'For God's sake, who is she then?'

'*She's been murdered. She needs someone to talk to about it. She's a bit upset.*'

'WHAT THE FUCK?'

I always swear too much when I'm scared.

'*You and Sheila have to work together to calm her down and get it out of her. Go somewhere quiet, the two of you, and sort this out. She needs to be released.*'

It's funny how I have spent the whole of my life inter-ested in the psychology of murder, but the minute I come across the spirit of someone who seems to have been killed horribly, I am absolutely crapping it.

'Oh God, Frank, she sounds agonized.'

Suddenly the door swings open and the weirdo's wife comes storming out, followed by a troubled Sheila.

'I'm really sorry, it sometimes happens . . .'

'Well, it isn't good enough. I drive all the way from St Albans for this? You can't take people's money, then tell them you can't read for them. What the hell happened?'

'I'm really sorry, I don't know. Please, of course, have your money back. Tanz?'

I open the till and take out the cash that her husband handed me not ten minutes ago. She grabs it from me.

'I think you'll find your husband is at Dino's across the road.'

'I *think* I know how to find my own husband, thank you.'

Oh, so now she learns how to say thank you? The granite-faced harridan.

As soon as she's gone, slamming the door behind her, I turn to Sheila, who looks ghastly.

'Are you okay? What happened?'

'I need a bloody fag – right now. I've had enough of today.'

I put the 'Back in ten minutes' sign up at the door, turn the latch and follow Sheila through the kitchen to the yard. There's a parking space out here for Maggie's car, and then a back lane that leads out onto a side road. Sheila's hands are shaking as she lights her Regal. I reach into my bag and take out one of my emergency menthols, and spark it up next to her. *What a pair!*

'What happened in there, Sheils?'

'A bloody nightmare happened in there.'

She takes a long drag on her cigarette. Clocks my panicked face.

'What happened to you?'

'You first.'

She takes another puff.

'I need a bloody vodka. As soon as I saw that woman I knew I didn't want to read for her.'

'I don't blame you. Aggressive cow.'

'Exactly, love. Face like a slapped arse. Anyway I started and I told her there had been some trouble in her past. Difficulties with her mother and all that. She stopped me, said she hadn't come to hear about her mother, she wanted to know about her business. He isn't her husband, by the way. She wants him to be, but it hasn't happened. I couldn't get any further than that because she told me she wasn't here about her relationship, either. Basically she wanted to know about money.

'Anyway I then asked her about her house . . . But as soon as I mentioned it, I started seeing this face. It was a woman; she was in shadow and in agony, and she was screaming so much she looked like an Edvard Munch painting. It was really traumatic. I could hear her – not loud, but I could – and I could see her pain.'

Sheila takes another drag, closing her eyes for a second. I am gobsmacked.

'I heard it.'

'You what?'

'She was crying in my head, Sheils, it was horrible. My friend Frank says she was murdered.'

'I thought as much. It's tied into her – the hard one.'

'She's called Carmen, that's what her fella said. And he's Dan. Speaking of which, he is one terrifying creep. I didn't like being on my own with him. Frank said we should sit down together later on and try to communicate with the murdered lady properly. She's too panicked to actually speak right now. He said if we combined forces, we'd probably have more success.'

'I like the sound of your Frank. Sensible.'

I feel pride on his behalf. Ever since the dream on the aeroplane I have been speaking to Frank a little more each day. Sometimes I still wonder if I'm making it all up, but really I know I'm not.

We make our way back into the shop and I almost have a coronary when I look towards the window and Dan Beck is standing there with his nose pressed against the glass like a pint-sized Joe Bugner. Sheila jumps when I yelp. I quickly smooth down my fear, as I don't want him to see it. I take off the door latch and smile.

'Sorry, Mr Beck, cigarette break. Is everything okay?'

'Filthy habit that. You'll ruin your looks.'

I try to laugh. Bill Hicks, he ain't.

'Erm . . . Can I help you?'

He steps forward, so I have to move and let him into the shop. He is drenched in Issey Miyake. I can tell that after-shave from a mile off anyway, but in this case I think he's bathed in the stuff. He wanders in with his hands in his pockets and looks at Sheila.

'I wanted to apologize for my . . . wife. She gets a bit stressed sometimes and I think she was upset that you couldn't read your cards for her.'

Sheila nods.

'Actually, I meet a few people I can't read for.'

'Really?'

He stares.

'What usually causes it?'

'There . . . there's not really one cause, Mr Beck, it's just that some people have their defences up and I can't get past them. Others . . . others don't want to hear what I have to say; they only want to hear what they want to hear.'

He laughs at this. His sense of humour is whacko.

He suddenly swivels his dark tunnel-eyes towards me.

'That's Carmen all over. Anyway just to say, to both of you, that I'm very sorry if she caused any offence. I don't know why she wanted to come here at all – superstitious, I suppose. You women. Always needing someone to tell you you'll get everything you want. But that's not always possible, is it, girls?'

I don't like his tone, and I can't help replying, 'Some people get what they want. Others get what life gives them.'

That laugh again. It's high and unnerving.

'Too true. Right, ladies, I'll leave you to it. Don't work too hard. And stop turning customers away or you'll make no money. Just tell them what they want to hear. Nice to meet you, Sheila, and . . . erm?'

I don't want to tell him.

'Tanz.'

'Tanz. Nice.'

I don't breathe again until he leaves.

Sheila sits and massages her temples. I run and lock the door.

'That is the scariest man I have ever met. I want to go home.'

'I think we should, love.'

'What? Really?'

'I think they bumped off that poor lady and for some reason they've got away with it, Tanz. I don't know what his problem is. Probably wants someone to figure it out. Jesus!'

I don't like that kind of talk. You see, it makes sense. From years of exhaustive reading, I know that loads of murderers have got themselves caught, when if they'd just kept shtum they would have got away with it. It's their ego.

'Sheils, what are we going to do? This is insane.'

'Well, I can't read for anyone else today, I know that

much. They've left evil in this shop. I'll get the smudge-sticks out when I'm next in. But right now we need to go home and work out who that poor woman is and how we can help her. Let's cancel everyone today.'

We always take a number from clients and put it with their name in the appointments book. Fortunately the three customers this afternoon are local and regulars. They are quickly informed of Sheila's horrid 'sickness bug' and we shut up shop and leave. We're both looking over our shoulder.

I like my murderers to be safely locked up in prison or already executed. This is fucking petrifying. As we speed towards Sheila's house, with Sheila clutching her keys as a makeshift knife, and me gripping my can of hairspray like a poor man's tin of Mace, I realize that we can't even tell a policeman if we see Dan Beck behind us . . .

'Excuse me. Sheila here was about to tell the fortune of a woman called Carmen when we realized that she and her husband had killed a woman. The woman's ghost won't stop screaming, and my dead friend says we've got to help her. Can you please arrest Carmen and her creepy husband for murder? That's him following us!'

We are all alone in this. Well, in the land of the living, we are.

THE MAGIC
CARPET

I buy us a bottle of red. A good Merlot. We're both shaken up, but once we reach Crouch End Broadway we feel less intimidated as there are lots of ladies pushing uber-expensive Bugaboos and tons of coffee-shop hoppers popping into Waitrose. Saying that, neither of us is completely comfortable until we're in Sheila's flat with the door locked. I open the wine immediately and pour a large one each into purple goblets, whilst Sheila opens up the French doors and lets in the smell of greenery and road-dust.

After half a glass, a fag for Sheila and a few wasabi peas for me, we both feel a lot better. A pig-headed part of me always refuses to be intimidated by bad people. Sheila doesn't 'do' bullies. But we're both frightened.

'What now?'

Sheila takes another mouthful of red.

'We chat to that poor girl. Call your Frank. He'll tell us what to do.'

Frank arrives when I say his name – I feel him like a

glow in my chest. I nod to Sheila. She sits still and closes her eyes.

'*Hello. She's called Monique. Calm her down and ask her direct questions.*'

'Frank, slow down. Why doesn't she stop crying?'

'*All right, moody-chops! Thing is, she's traumatized by what happened to her and, right now, time has absolutely no meaning. It might as well be the same moment that she died . . . You'll just have to get her to speak to you. I can't do it. Oh – her nickname might help. Everyone called her Mona.*'

'Thank you.'

'*No bother.*'

I relay this to Sheila.

We sit at the table with topped-up glasses of wine and ask for 'Mona'.

Eventually we both hear her cries, as pitiful as they were before. I decide to speak to her first.

'Mona . . . Mona, we want to help you and make you feel better. But to do that, we need to know where you are.'

Her sobs carry on as if she can't hear.

'Mona. Come on, we want to know what happened to you. Where do you live?'

She stammers out a reply.

'*Just outside . . . St Albans. We built it together; it's my dream – our dream.*'

I get a picture in my head. A large property on plenty of land. There are stables and at least one horse. I tell Sheila, but she's already seeing it.

'Mona, your house is stunning . . .'

'Thank you.'

This calms her a little.

'How long did you live there with Dan?'

I'm taking a risk here, but I'm betting Mona was married to Dan Beck.

'Twelve years.'

I tell Sheila, who's pretty much getting this anyway. Neither of us is surprised.

'So, Mona, what changed?'

She sobs again.

'Our business. He went into the office and I stayed at home with the horses. I love animals. There was a girl there. His secretary—'

Neither of us, Sheila or me, has had the easiest time with other women. There have been wonderful ones of course, but there have also been jealous, cruel-mouthed, snide, bitchy and needy fuckwits littering both of our lives for years. We both seem to attract them. So both of us are appalled, but not completely surprised, by the secretary that Mona shows us. She resembles Mona in hair colour and figure, but is younger, tougher, angrier and ready to take what she wants. Carmen.

As Mona gasps out her story, we learn that she knew Carmen was after Dan and, more precisely, his money, but she didn't believe for one minute that Dan would bite. Dan could be a shit when he was stressed, but Mona saw this as part and parcel of marriage, after experiencing her own father's fury when she was a little girl.

When I ask exactly when things went wrong, she shows us a calendar in the office of Dan's workplace. Apparently

Carmen came into Dan's life about two years ago. Mona whispers that she thought they might be 'dabbling', but she hoped Dan would get bored of her, like he had of the 'others'.

But he became obsessed and, as far as Carmen saw it, Mona was in the way.

When I ask Mona what happened when she was attacked, there is a long pause. Sheila tells her not to worry and to take as long as she wants. The sobbing starts again as Mona shows us a night on her own in front of the TV, with a cup of tea. Then Dan comes into the living room. We see her jumping up to kiss him, and Dan pulling back. We see his right hand emerging from behind his back, holding a large wrench. She can't quite comprehend what he is doing until the wrench connects with her head.

Suddenly I'm there. And it is the single most shocking moment of my life, when I feel the reverberation of a giant spanner smashing me over the head, wielded by the man I love. And, make no mistake, I feel it. I'm in the room. I look into Dan's eyes to find an answer. I see blankness. I see a stranger in those empty eyes. And as I fall to the floor, bleeding and screaming, I see another woman entering. The hard-faced usurper of my husband's affections, looking triumphant.

God, it's nasty.

Carmen's hatred of Mona is overwhelming. It's coming over me in waves. When I try to 'link in' with Carmen's energy at that time, I just get a wall of malice. Mind-boggling, when you think that Mona's only crime was existing. Carmen and Dan were poisonously 'in love', and

Mona had to go. I try not to think about it, but it occurs to me that Dan and Carmen's sex life must be bloody terrifying.

I speak to Mona as calmly and lovingly as I can, trying to keep her fear from exploding into panic again.

'Mona, listen. You have been brilliant at telling us your story. Amazing. But you have to tell us what happened to you next? Where are you now? Do you know where your . . . body is?'

Now I hear her screaming again. I know Sheila is experiencing this as some kind of film show. Sheila, being clairvoyant, sees everything as a kind of mime. She hears little snippets, but mostly she 'sees' pictures of what's going on. And whatever she's seeing is making her wince.

'Mona, listen to me, love, stop screaming . . . Tanz is telling the truth. It's all right now. We're going to help you, but . . . show me. You don't have to tell, just show. After he hit you, what happened next?'

That wine is disappearing fast. This is as intense as it gets. My head is spinning from Mona's distress and from that smack on the head with a wrench. Mona wants to help us, I know she does, but she's still so shocked and horrified by what happened, still reliving it every second of every hour, that she is finding it difficult to think straight.

Suddenly she bursts out, *'The rug! The rug.'*

Sheila gives a little gasp.

'They rolled her in the carpet!'

And now I can see it: rolling the living-room rug around Mona like she's a tortilla wrap. She is semi-conscious and trying to struggle. She is calling Dan's name. When she is completely bound tight in the carpet, with a rope securing it around the middle, it is my turn to jump, as Carmen picks up the heavy wrench and begins to rain blows down on the material, where Mona's head would be. She keeps swinging and hitting like she's trying to obliterate her. I can almost hear the crunching of bone. I am completely aghast.

Sheila grabs her wine.

'Oh God.'

'Stop. Stop, Mona. Don't keep replaying that. You don't deserve still to be living this nightmare. Let's find a way to make it stop.'

'*Pleaaase . . . pleaase help me, make it stop – help me.*'

'Sweetheart, we will. Promise. Won't we, Sheila?'

'Of course we will, darlin'.'

'Just think. Calm down and think, Mona. When was it? When did it happen? That night. Can you show us?'

I can feel her confusion. It was such a terrible time that maybe she's lost some of the detail because of it?

But then I hear the TV. Mona had the TV on. I hear the theme tune to some shitty soap. I hate soaps. That could be any week night; that could be a Sunday afternoon. But it isn't because it was night-time, I know it. The curtains are drawn, the lamps are on . . . Mona can't remember. I try to jog her memory.

'Mona, did you buy a magazine or a newspaper that day? That month? Can you remember?'

'*I don't know . . . Oh God, I don't . . . Oh, wait.*'

I can see a magazine: *Grazia* or something. She's holding it in her hand.

'Look at the date! Look at it, Mona. What does it say?'

Her reply is quiet but distinct.

'*It's November. NOVEMBER.*'

As she speaks, I hear a bang. Then there's a crash and another bang, from the past. Was there a storm? Was it gunfire?

'Sheila, it was November last year. Mona's been dead less than a year. And there are fireworks going off.'

'Oh. Well, that narrows it down, doesn't it? Brilliant, Mona. Brilliant work. Now, darlin', stay calm and think hard. What happened to you afterwards? What happened to the carpet?'

Mona's voice is diminishing now. I wonder if she's had enough. I'm not feeling her presence so strongly; she's becoming less and less distinct. I pick up one last snippet before she disappears completely.

'They put me in the ground. I was still alive.'

RUN FOR HOME

There's something so fantastic about driving at five o'clock in the morning. *Yeah, baby, you heard right: 5 a.m.* Hardly a car on the M1 (still plenty of lorries, though, the massive, murderous metal fuckers), sun still not up and a whole new day dawning on the righteous. And the wrongteous. If I ever feel out-of-control I drive up north. It's my default direction.

Sheila and I were not at our most comfortable after that performance last night. Sheila said she'd rarely come across such a distressed spirit. She said we should try to tune into Mona another time and find out where they buried her.

Sod that for a game of soldiers! I wasn't feeling like tuning into anything ever again. In fact I left in a taxi. Usually I'd walk, but *no way, José*. I, for one, was bricking it about that Dan. Carmen seemed too young and arrogant to believe that two strange, dippy-hippy females would sniff out her secret. Deputy Dawg Dan, on the other hand? The fact that he came back into the shop; the fact that he was being incredibly weird – I find random weirdness like that

204

very threatening. Which is why I double-locked my front door, closed all the blinds and checked under my bed when I got in.

I was jumpy as hell. If I'd not already had that half-bottle of wine I'd have jumped in the car there and then. I didn't feel drunk, but I knew I'd get sleepy an hour into the journey and have to drive another three hours in the dark. I was discomfited, not suicidal. So I put on a film, some schmaltzy Sky movie that turned out to be funny and took the edge off. I had a strong vod and ate a whole packet of seafood sticks with hummus. (Do not knock these unless you've tried them. Some may argue that I eat too much fish. I would counter that seafood sticks are so processed they contain *no* fish whatsoever. But they're lovely and comforting, and they don't make me fat.)

Near the end of the movie, about nine-ish, my phone went off. For a minute I just looked at it, as if it might bite me, then I checked and a strange number was flashing up. Not strange as in a numerical alphabet that I didn't recognize, but a number that wasn't logged into my phone.

Deputy Dawg found out my number?

That was my first thought. But it was impossible. I couldn't keep freaking out like this. So I picked it up. It was a girl's voice.

'Tanz?'

I didn't know who it was.

'Yes?'

'It's me – it's Ruth!'

'Sorry? It's who?'

'Ruth. Ruth from Spain!'

Spain's shenanigans had escaped my mind in all the palaver of the last day or two. Suddenly it came pinging back, like a frog on a stick.

'RUTH! How are you, lass? Recovered all right?'

'Yes. Yes, I'm fine. How are you?'

On our flight back, Rog and I had found ourselves sitting an aisle apart at the front and, mercifully, Ruth and her new beau had been many seats behind us, nursing hellish hangovers. I'd pointedly taken out my novel, forcing Rog to amuse himself with his iPod and several large Jack Daniel's. Unfortunately I couldn't, in any polite way, refuse to give him my mobile number just before we landed, though I was tempted to change a digit. Anyway I didn't mind hearing from Ruth; she was very magnanimous about the bruised scab on her ankle and she was touchingly grateful about our 'little talk'.

'I'm okay, thank you. Could do with more money, but couldn't we all?'

She laughed at this, like a little bell.

'That's kind of what I'm calling you about. Where are you?'

'Erm, I'm in Crouch End, top bit.'

'I'm in East Finchley tonight – that's really close! Do you want to hook up? I've got something to tell you.'

'Erm, if I'm honest, I'm not really in a position to come out. I'm not like you young 'uns; once I've nested, I don't put my face back on – not at this time of night.'

That's not necessarily true. I will come out, if it's pre-planned, but I certainly couldn't be arsed to put proper clothes back on then. Plus, of course, I was sort of in hiding.

Ruth gave that laugh again.

'Fair enough. I like to get my early nights in too, keep the skin looking good. I'm dog-sitting tonight, that's why I'm here. But, listen, you know you said I had a job coming in the next six months? You remember?'

I did, vaguely, though I do spout this stuff without really thinking about it.

'Well, it was even better than you said. After we landed, I slept for a day and a night. I woke up feeling like a different person. All that stuff about Rog, it had eased. I felt better. And that's when I got the phone call. My agent had put me up for this big telly drama – *The Siren*, it's called. I've done virtually no TV, so I usually only get seen for bit parts. Anyway I auditioned, and today I found out I got the part of the daughter. *It's a lead!'*

Actor's jealousy aside, this is fab.

'You're kidding me! Oh, Ruth, that's great.'

'It is, and what's hilarious is that it starts shooting in a month, for five months. Your six-month prediction was spot-on. You are a genius and I love you, and I want to take you out to celebrate.'

Actors are always telling people they don't know very well that they love them. Still, it was kind of heart-warming.

'So are they making you rich?'

I couldn't help asking. How could I help it?

'Compared to how I've been living since my accident, they are making me a millionaire. My agent says it's shit money for telly, but I don't care. I'm just over the moon that someone wants to employ me and I can have a rest from cleaning pubs for a living.'

'I am so pleased for you, Ruth, and I would love to see you. But tonight's a bit—'

'*No!* Honest, that's fine. I'm back next week for two nights. We can do it then. I want to take you for a tasty dinner and drinks. I'm now hopelessly addicted to Żubrówka, you know. Better than hopelessly addicted to Rog, though, eh?'

Ruth really did sound better. A bit of affirmation, a bit of success. We've all been there.

'That's a date. Speaking of which, how's the new fella?'

'Who? Oh. No. That's not . . . He told me he loved me when we landed in London. I'm afraid that's a bit much after a day, even for me, so I told him I was still upset over someone else and couldn't commit the way someone as wonderful as him would need. He started sobbing, and I sped off in a cab before he could fall to the ground and grab me by the knees. I mean, who can be bothered?'

Our call ended so amiably, I felt cheered. I still felt cheered as I crawled into bed and Inka got up beside me and curled up on the pillow, purring and touching my face with her pink paw-pads. Cheerily I drifted off to the strains of my bedtime compilation and a tree whispering out the back.

Less cheerily, I woke up with a silent scream on my face, having had a very realistic dream that Dan Beck was knocking on my bedroom window. Oh, how much less cheery was I to find a bat on the pillow next to me, in my confused,

half-awake state. A pointy black bat? A bat that was actually Inka's tiny head, the rest of her being under the duvet
as she attempted to emulate my own sleeping position. Still
less cheery was the realization that someone really was
knocking at my window. A terrified peek through the
blinds revealed a crow banging a snail off the corner of
the windowpane like something out of *The* bloody *Omen*.

That was enough to catapult me out of bed and into the
shower at 4 a.m. I chucked everything I needed into a bag,
opened the cat flap and filled up Inka's feeder. A quick note
through nice old Steve's door and I was away at 4.35 a.m.
A new world record, I reckon.

Now, safely at the beginning of the M1 with Aretha
Franklin lulling my ears, I feel I'm leaving that dark stuff
behind me and am barrelling towards safer territory. Or I
hope so.

SCARY MAMMY

When I arrive at 9 a.m. my parents are already pottering. Dad's in his shed. Probably having a fag and listening to his little radio. He must be on a late today. When I get through the door, my mam comes in from the kitchen and stops dead. She hasn't combed her hair yet and she's all in apricot. She looks like a baby chick.

'Eee, hello. What are you doing here?'

'*Welcome home, Tanz!*'

She gives me an awkward clutch.

'Eee, I didn't mean it like that. Are you not working today?'

'No. I'm, er, I wasn't feeling very well.'

'What's wrong?'

'Nothing! I couldn't sleep – think I wanted to see you two nutters.'

She's looking extra-anxious this morning. What on earth is going on here? She hasn't even offered me an unwanted cup of tea yet.

'Right.'

'Mam, you're being shifty. What's going on?'

'Nothing. I just . . .'

'What?'

She gives a dramatic pause. Sometimes I think my mam should have been the actress, as she's a master of the dramatic eye-blink and the martyr's sigh. That'll probably be me, in fifteen years.

'If you must know, I've been very worried. What's going on?'

'Eh?'

'With that psychic stuff you've been messing with?'

'*What?* Mam, I'm not messing with it. It's messing with me!'

'Well, whatever it's doing, you've got to stop.'

'Why?'

'I had a dream.'

'What kind of dream?'

'I had it the night before last. It wasn't a very nice dream. I've been fretting ever since.'

I'm now officially intrigued.

'Go on . . .'

'Are you sure?'

She's the master, this one.

'*Yes*, I'm sure – of course I'm sure. I'm very interested in this stuff, you know that.'

'All right. If you're sure . . .'

'Mam!'

'All right.'

She sits on the concrete two-seater and clears her throat, like a regular Hans Christian Andersen.

'I dreamed . . . that I was in some woods. It was night-time and there was a big hole, and then this woman sat up in it. I got the fright of my friggin' life. She had long brown hair and she was holding the sides of her face and scream-ing. She wouldn't stop. And she was bleeding, Tania. *Bleeding* everywhere. Then it was daytime and I was still in the woods. There was a fallen tree, like a big hollow stump, and there were flowers. Bluebells. You were sitting on a rug next to the bluebells and the stump. It was sunny and the birds were singing. I thought you were on a picnic blanket, then I saw it was one of them Indian-looking rugs and it was covered in blood. You were on this blood-soaked carpet, and the sun went dark and I looked over your head and there was this black angel floating over you. I started screaming at it to go away, but it just hovered over your head like the angel of death. I was sweating when I woke up. I didn't ring you straight away because I didn't want to scare you.'

I can't believe this. Yowzers! Mam saw Mona. Either Mona is the most powerful ghost ever, or my mam's one fuck of a good spook-detector. It's probably a bit of both.

'Is there anything you need to tell me, Tania?'

If I tell her what's going on, she'll be beside herself. She looks so freaked-out already.

'Not really, no. Do you think maybe you're worried about me being involved in spiritualism, after what your mam said about your nanna – with the ghosts and everything?'

Her face changes. She doesn't like being patronized, my little mam.

'No, I don't. It felt *very* real, and I don't dream wrong.'

She is indignant and earnest when she says this. What the hell else has she dreamed?

Just then my dad enters, with Zorro following at his heels like a love-struck shadow. Dad's wearing his overalls, so DIY must be on the cards.

'Tell her, Bob!'

'What are you doing here?'

Mam jumps in. 'She didn't feel well. Didn't I tell you? There's something going on!'

'Mam!'

Dad crosses his arms and looks me up and down.

'We've been talking and we're worried. What's happening?'

'Erm, how about "Hello, Tanz"?'

He remembers himself and opens his arms.

'Hello, come here.'

So I jump up and Dad gives me a big hug. I want it to go on for ages. That familiar smell always makes me feel better. But if I cling on for too long he'll know I'm out of sorts.

'Now. What's been happening?'

'Nothing. What do you mean?'

'Well . . . it's just, if you're not in any trouble, then I don't want you to get in any trouble. You're our daughter, all right? You don't usually come home out of the blue. Would you tell us oldies if you were in trouble, or scared or worried?'

'Of course I would.'

Wouldn't.

'Because if you're ever up the proverbial without a paddle, come straight home – we'll look after you. We'll pay for the petrol. Or the train.'

'Dad, that's lovely. But honestly there's nothing wrong.'

He's making me feel like I may be in trouble. They both are. So much for the safety of Gateshead.

'Okay. But no woods, all right? She's never wrong, your mam.'

Whoa, he's serious. I really, really love him for trying to support my mam in her spookiness. I had no idea he had such faith in her. Once in a while I get a glimpse of a part of their relationship that I don't know much about.

Mam looks at him and nods. Dad goes back out. That's the most words I've heard him speak at once in years.

'Did you hear him?'

My mam's hilarious.

'Yes, of course I heard him.'

'Well, just be careful – it's got me worried, this.'

'I promise I'll be careful, Mam.'

'Good.'

I spring up and put my jacket back on.

'Where are you going?'

'Costa. I'm going to get the biggest cappuccino in the world with a vanilla shot. Then I'm going to see Milo.'

'All right. If you pass Marks's, will you get me some crinkle-cut beetroot?'

'Yup.'

The only food she'll buy from a posh shop. She loves it like I love my seafood sticks and hummus.

'Erm, Mam. Lots of love, right?'

'Uh-huh.'

Back in the car, Van Morrison is crooning 'Sweet Thing' and I'm a bit shocked. We don't go in for 'I love you' in my house. We also don't usually go in for conversations about deadly portents in dreams, either. Especially not ones in which my dad gets involved. This is dark stuff. Not only did my mam dream about Mona, but she dreamed about the carpet. The black angel is a bit of a shocker, but that could easily be the spectre of those two who killed her being free and out there, and me knowing about it. Or something. That's what I hope anyway. But she saw Mona in a hole in the ground! Just like Mona said . . .

I call Milo – it's 10 a.m. None of my other friends would be around, even if I wanted to see them; they've all got day-jobs, even the ones with kids. They put me to shame, the lot of them. But it's Milo I need anyway. He doesn't answer the first time. He does the second.

'What the fuck's happening, Tanz, it's the middle of the night? Did your mam die or something? She better have, or you're finished in this town.'

'*Milo!* Don't wish death on my little mam!'

He laughs a groggy laugh.

'Sorry. Are you all right, sweet-cheeks? I was up till the wee hours. I've been writing a play about a family of dwarves who live in a cave on Whitley Bay beach and kidnap unsuspecting American tourists to turn them into sexual zombies, and send them off to rob the Esso garage. It's called *Yankee-Doodle Tanker-Wankers . . .*'

He's made this up on the spot, of course. Right now

Milo still happens to be slaving on that TV script, trying to become part of a stable of 'reliable' writers and earn some proper money. And it's driving him nuts. I sometimes wish he was an actor, because Bill and Joe, my agents, would lap him up. Gay, good-looking, clever, northern and warped like a 45-rpm vinyl left on the windowsill in summer. He would make a splendid thespian if he wasn't so crippled by his own introspective demons.

'I'm getting a gargantuan cappuccino, you want one?'

'Get in!'

'Muffin?'

'Ahhhh. *Marvellous*. Skinny lemon poppyseed, since you ask, you sassy bastard!'

That's my Milo.

DUVET DAZE

Two duvets on the floor in a pile. Settee cushions, pillows, blankets. We are lying there like Cleopatra and Mark Antony, both sipping coffees the size of Egypt, muffins already munched. Never has Milo been this quiet. He is simply too freaked-out to speak. Milo loves a bit of drama, but not if it's real, and especially not if it's about ghosts. He likes pretendy stuff. Twice, during my summing up of Mona, Dan and Carmen's tale, he grips my wrist so hard it causes actual pain.

Eventually, when I tell him about my mam's dream, he shrieks.

'Oh my God, Tanz, you have got to forget this ghost. I'm sorry she's upset and all that. Scary, spooky lasses are terrible things. But you can't have anything to do with it. Dark angels are *not* good. Do you not watch horror films?'

'I do, Milo. But I think Mam's dream was about the badness of the killers. Until I help Mona, that darkness is going to be hanging over me. So I'll have to go and help her. Then it'll clear. But that doesn't mean I'm not scared. I'm pooing myself.'

His eyes are like dinner plates.

'I think you're mental. You didn't know her, so why get involved? Why's she involving you? It's selfish. She's a self-ish spectre.'

'Mona needs someone to be there for her. She's lost.'

Milo puts his hand to his chest and clears his throat.

'Look, I'm no psychic medium, but I'll do what I can to help. Just don't leave any dark angels at my flat – it's hard enough keeping this place tidy.'

'I won't,' I promise.

'How long are you up for? You fancy a wee tipple across town tonight?'

'I can't. I'm working tomorrow in that bloody shop. I don't want to, but I promised. I really, really want to get out of it, though.'

'Are you telling me you're driving back the same day you came?'

'Yeah, but not straight away. I'll have a little sleep first at my mam's, then I'm off.'

'Why would you do that?'

'I just wanted to pop up. Wanted to see you.'

'Now I'm worried. You would never come up here without enough time to drink alcohol.'

'Hmm.'

'I can come back down with you, you know? I can bring my laptop and work at yours as easily as working here. We can listen to my new compilation and buy a massive bucket of sweets for the journey!'

That is so nice. For all his naughty banter, Milo is one of the kindest, gentlest souls I've ever met. And if I say I'm talking to ghosts, then I'm talking to ghosts – he would never doubt me. Despite the coffee, my eyes flicker as I snuggle into the duvet nest.

'That's lovely, Milo, but you've got a deadline and you've probably got a million things to do . . .'

I know he's having a nightmare with this script commission, and I don't think me distracting him will help. However, were he really writing a film about smaller-than-average zombie-makers living in caves, I'd be happy to load him straight in my car and take him to my place. He could describe ideas for plot twists and stay up all night writing, and I'd supply him with nice bottles of red wine and a bowl of gobstoppers. It still amazes me that two mates from a normal comprehensive became an actress and a writer. We are just *so* glamorous.

As my eyes flicker, I feel a blanket being lightly draped over me.

'Have your sleep here, why don't you? I'll make us some tasty pasta when you wake up.'

I'm asleep before I can reply. Milo makes fantastic spaghetti with spicy meatballs, so I nod off knowing that I'm in for a tongue-tingling treat.

THE ANGEL OF
THE NORTH

Of course I overstayed at Milo's. Two hours' kip, then the best, tastiest food. We decided I would drive back up north in the next fortnight, as soon as his script was finished and dispatched, and we would have one of our legendary all-nighters in the toon. We then giggled about nonsense, until I realized it was three o'clock and I'd have to go and see my parents for an hour. In the end I drove back to London at peak time. I'm an idiot. And I didn't even go to see my nanna, so I'm an idiot who's going to hell.

On top of all this, I got a call from Bill and Joe, which held me up a bit, before I left. Mostly it was Joe's call, but Bill piped up here and there, bellowing Scottish obscenities about the producer being 'a fucking bell-end'. They were very, very pissed off because they'd put me up for a job and it had been offered to some vacuous pretty girl whose Geordie twang was as convincing as my Martian accent. The first ep had aired and she sounded like she was Danish or something. I wasn't surprised; the acting world was never fair, but this was particularly galling.

'OMG, Tanz, the part was made for you. It said thirty-seven-year-old, gin-soaked, fast-talking Geordie! I mean, *come on*!'

'Are you calling me an alcoholic, Joe?'

'Of course not. I've never even seen you with a drink in your hand.'

I could hear Bill roaring with laughter behind him. *Pair of gits.*

'Anyway, I wouldn't usually call you about this stuff, but I wanted you to know how hard we're working for you, and how ridiculous it is out there at the moment. They gave it to Posy Potter. She's *twenty-six*, for the love of God. She's nowhere near as talented as you and she can't do accents. What are they *doing*?'

'They're doing what everyone else is doing. Promoting telly-faces and ignoring has-beens like me.'

'Fucking bollocks. We will have a great job for you soon. *Promise*.'

I felt very sorry for them actually. They really thought I had that job in the bag. I don't dare think things like that any more.

Fast-forward to my flat, ten o'clock at night, and I'm travel-weary, dreading work tomorrow and needing a shower. Inka comes and sits on my lap, purring like a freight train, which is usually a great comfort. At least she hasn't taken a dump on my duvet today. Bonus! Carefully I pick her up and lay her on her favourite fluffy cushion.

'Ten minutes, babba – I'll be back.'

The shower over my bath is surprisingly powerful. And it splooshes away the worst of the fear and weariness from the last twenty-four hours, especially when I douse myself in grapefruit shower gel and allow the water to get a teensy bit too hot. I emerge like a citrus lobster and return to my silky feline: scrubbed, moisturized and wrapped in a six-inch-thick bathrobe.

I light a nice white candle on the side table next to me. It smells of figs. I grab my phone charger and look for my phone. I eventually locate it in my coat pocket. Two texts. One from Elsa and one from Pat.

Elsa's says:

What you doing this weekend? Would love to take you out. Lots to tell xxx

She's probably got a bloke. That's when she usually says 'lots to tell'. It must be easier without an umbrella-wielding dead pensioner looming over her flat. I don't want to live through another of Elsa's doomed romances, though, so I ignore that one.

Pat's text says:

Help me! x

Both of these texts are cryptic, I notice. Pat's seems to be demanding an immediate response. He sent it half an hour ago. I'm sure he can wait a little longer. I actually can't be chewed with a night of shagging tonight, shocking though that is. I'm too worked-up about the shop tomorrow. I'm not a tarot reader. I don't know what I am. I quite like the word 'sensitive'. I'm that all right. Usually with the word 'over' preceding it. If anyone asks, I'm a 'sensitive'. Until I come up with something better.

With the candle casting a lovely, calming scent about the room and Inka reinstalled on my lap, warmly revving her engines as I tickle her ears, I close my eyes for a second and let the aroma envelop me.

Without thinking much about it, I ask for protection from my 'angels'. Immediately Frank says hello. Not quite an angel, but he'll do.

'*Hiya.*'

'Hey, Frank. How are you?'

'*Better than you. What's with the drivathon? Nearly six hundred miles in a day?*'

'I wanted to go home.'

'*You were scared, weren't you?*'

'Of course I was – after yesterday, who wouldn't be?'

'*We're looking after you, you know.*'

'Well, that's very nice, but there's not a lot you can do if that nutter Dan gets hold of me, is there?'

'*Fair point.*'

'Should I just drop it, Frank? The Mona thing? Should I let it lie?'

'*What do you think?*'

'I think Mona came to us for a reason. Milo wants me to drop it. My mam and dad want me to drop it – and they don't even know what's going on. I need to know more about the situation, though. Forewarned is forearmed, and all that. What can you tell me?'

'I can't help you with this, but I know someone who can. Do you want to meet her? She's here now.'

I'm scared. But always overriding 'scared' is 'nosy'.

'Only if she's nice.'

'She's very nice . . . Now, still your mind. Slow down all other thoughts and then ask questions. Direct, non-ambiguous ones, please. It can all get a bit literal over here. She'll help you, though. She's great.'

I do as I'm told. I pick up Inka and put her around my neck and sit on the floor on a cushion, with my back against the sofa, and put the lit candle on the floor in front of me. I don't know why I do that, but it feels right. I empty my mind and breathe, whilst watching the flame. Soon I feel a 'closeness'. Someone has stepped forward, so to speak. *Wow.* She is *blue*, flippin' sparkly *blue.* If I unfocus my eyes, I can 'see' her to the side and just behind me. She's bigger than any human I've ever met, and she tells me she's Jemimah. She is very tranquil.

'Ask me a question. I shall try to help.'

'Who are you, Jemimah?'

'I am a friend.'

'You're a very big friend!'

I don't know what else to say. She has a shimmer to her, or that's how it looks in my peripheral vision. I wonder why I can never see things square-on? But then, as Sheila says, it's probably because I'd flip out. Jemimah's voice is androgynous and soft, yet I can hear every syllable. I think of my questions.

'I want to ask you about Mona. If that's all right? I want to help her.'

'*What do you want to know?*'

'Why did Carmen and Dan kill her?'

'*Money. Divorce costs a lot of money. Carmen wanted the house. The lifestyle.*'

I'd guessed this, but I wanted to make sure.

'Why haven't Carmen and Dan married yet?'

'*Mona is dead. They have done many sneaky things to cover it up. But if he files for divorce, people will look for her and discover their lies.*'

'Why did Carmen come to Sheila yesterday?'

'*Carmen is desperate to be very rich. She thought Sheila could give her the answers she seeks.*'

'Why did Dan come back to the shop?'

'*You interest him very much.*'

Oh God.

'Would he hurt me?'

'*I don't know.*'

I don't like this bit. But I plough on.

'Will I be able to find Mona's body?'

'*If you so wish.*'

'I do so wish. I don't think the police will take us seriously unless we find where she is.'

'*Perhaps.*'

'So what should I do?'

'*You will be led.*'

'Thank you.'

Jemimah is utterly still. The whole room is silent. It's like being in a trance. Slowly I feel her fade into the background, but I know that if I ask her, she will come back immediately. Suddenly Frank pipes up.

'Jemimah's one of your guides.'

The spell breaks. Now I'm sitting on the floor of my ordinary room with a candle burning in front of me, and the TV on pause. Inka, who has been a statue until now, suddenly climbs down and approaches the candle. Two whiskers are on fire before I manage to pull her away and blow them out. What a doofus. I scoop her up and cuddle her. She now smells of scorched hair and is shaking her head about, trying to get rid of the stink.

'Frank, Jemimah's amazing.'

'Isn't she just! Toodle-pip.'

He's gone. I blow out the candle before Inka can burn off her whole head and I place it on the side table again. I pick up my phone and call Pat.

For a while I think he won't answer, then just as I reckon it's going to answerphone, he yelps, 'Hello!'

'Hi, Pat, what's with the SOS?'

There's noise behind him. He may be in a pub. He may be at work. When he speaks, his voice is lowered.

'I'm now outside the kitchen, at my sister's. A minute ago I was inside the kitchen. She's got some of her school-teacher friends round. She's not usually a major socializer, and talking about six-year-old children and Ofsted for three hours is not my favourite thing. Plus, most of them are usually stuck in the house with their own kids in the evenings and, now they're off the leash, I have become their pet for the night. I'm starting to feel sullied.'

'That's not great.'

'No, it isn't. Please tell me you're calling because you want me to come over? I don't care what we do. I will happily watch a documentary on the history of vacuum cleaners or help you paint a yak, as long as I can get out of here. *Plus*, you are probably the only excuse on the whole planet that my sister will accept, seeing as she thinks the sun shoots rainbow-lasers out of your arse.'

I groan a little, inwardly. I am such a fickle cow. I think Pat's gorgeous, but it's already late and I don't want to wake up tired tomorrow. I am always worried about this 'not getting enough sleep' thing. I am a monster when I'm tired. Conversely, he's asking a favour and I can't say no.

'Okay. I have a yak here waiting to be emulsioned – I shall allow you a sympathy visit. Just so you can escape your sister, of course.'

'Of course! Would you like me to bring you anything? Żubrówka?'

'No, thank you, I have plenty. But I can't be staying up. I need to sleep.'

Half an hour later I hear a tap on the door. Outside is a grinning Pat, wielding his bike and a backpack.

'Sorry it took so long to get here; trying to escape a bunch of wine-filled primary school teachers is not as easy as it sounds. Plus, I stopped to get you this . . .'

He delves into his backpack and presents me with a big box of truffles. He probably got them from the all-night Tesco, but it's still basically a box of chocolate heaven. Now I seriously have to let him off the fact that he's arrived at my bedtime.

'They look delicious. You're not getting any!'

'How kind. Should I make us a cuppa and we can dig in?'

When we're nicely ensconced on the sofa with an open box of chocolates, I relate the past couple of days' adventures in absolute skeleton-form; I make it sound less scary and I miss out anything about blue, sparkly angels or black, doom-mongering ones. There's such a thing as overkill, even with someone as open-minded as Pat. Then, very quickly, the day's driving catches hold of me and I'm nodding.

Pat has to literally carry me to bed. I hope he didn't come looking for a night of naughtiness; he's more likely to be painting a yak.

MYSTERY POT
MENTALISTS

I'm so reluctant to be in this bloody shop today. Especially as a 'reader', something I'm grossly under-qualified to do. Last night I slept like a rock, and I woke up thirty minutes before I was supposed to be here and had to abandon Pat with barely a kiss. It isn't very long before he leaves the country now, so I suppose it's good that we're not at it like rabbits every day. He is not and never will be my fella, so spending too much time together would be bloody stupid. *But still . . .*

My tiredness from too much driving has turned into a headache this morning, despite a good night's sleep, and I'm in a right strop. I hate doing things I don't want to do. Plus, because Maggie is on the till, I have to be on my best behaviour and not swear or take the piss. I feel very much like swearing. I've set up the room like I've seen Sheila do, but it doesn't feel the same. I'm basically a fraud.

I drag my moody arse in there and close the door to sulk. Ten minutes later Maggie pops her head in and, with jolly-hockey-sticks enthusiasm, tells me I have a walk-in customer.

I try to look professional and straighten my card-deck as a woman lumbers to the table. She's a big lass, not so much fat as well-built and clumsy. She's in black. Black trousers, black jumper and black trainers with greasy, mousy hair. I wonder if she always dresses like she's headed to a downmarket funeral. I know I shouldn't be nasty, but I'm so not into this.

'Hello.'

She speaks like a sack of potatoes.

The one thing in her favour is a pair of violet eyes – the trouble being that they are vacant, and set in a doughy face. She is watching life from a planet in her head. After she sits, she produces a twin pack of Jaffa Cakes and proceeds to shovel them into her face like there is definitely no tomorrow.

I smile.

'I'm Tanz, hello. I'm going to shuffle the cards, then I want you to do the same and hand them back to me.'

Probably covered in Jaffa Cake juice, for fuck's sake . . .

'If there's anything you'd especially like to know about, bear it in mind as you shuffle the cards.'

She shuffles, still chewing, and hands the cards back to me. I lay eight of them down in front of me, placing them carefully, hoping it looks like I know what I'm doing.

My first impression is that her dad is ill. I tell her, but she shakes her head.

'I'm not here for that. I have a love problem. I love a man and he loves me, but we have problems.'

I look at the cards, I rack my brain, but there's no man. I put the feelers out – I can't sense anything from this woman and I can't find a bloke. This is pitiful.

'So, I'm looking and I'm not sure who this man is. Is he your partner?'

'No. Not yet. But he cares for me, I know he does, and I just want to know when we will be together.'

She speaks slowly. I can't work out if she's thick or simply weird.

I'm now in big trouble, because there is no sign of a bloke in the cards or in my head. And my instincts are telling me that this woman is not well. Obviously bringing this up is not the best idea. So I go for plan B. Talk to her. Forget the bloody cards.

'When did you first meet him?'

'He's at my work.'

'And is he nice to you?'

She puts another cake in her mouth.

'We don't talk. We look at each other. I know that he wants to be with me, but it will take time. How long do I have to wait?'

I want to bang my head on the table.

'I'm so sorry, I don't want to upset you, but I don't think he feels the same as you do, this man at work. I think he has a family and a life. In the cards I don't see an involvement for you at this moment. I see other things. I can see that your dad hasn't been too well, and I can see your mum wasn't the most supportive . . . and I see that you get very down sometimes.'

Actually I can't 'see' these things in the cards so much,

but I can feel them, and it hits me that my first impression was bullshit. She's not just some thicko who dresses badly. She suffers from chronic depression and . . . what? Something else. She glances at me vacantly. I'm wondering about that glassy look now, I think it may be medication. Strong antidepressants or sedatives, or anti-psychotic drugs – maybe all of them? I don't know. There are things, big things, I could get from holding this lass's hand and concentrating. But I doubt she would be stable enough to talk about them. Or she might be too doped-up to care.

'What's your name?'

'I'm called Vella.'

'I've never heard that name before. Nice. You like Jaffa Cakes, I see?'

'It's my breakfast.'

I nod encouragingly. I don't know what I'm nodding at.

'Where do you live, Vella?'

She indicates vaguely with her head.

'Just a place. Up the road.'

I am well aware of open facilities in the area for people with mental issues. I wonder if any of her 'carers' know what she's spending her money on.

'Well, Vella. The thing is, I think you have to feel stronger in yourself before you get yourself a boyfriend. The man you like, even if he's looking at you, I think he's simply being friendly. It feels like he already has a wife. And you can't go taking other people's husbands, can you?'

'When will we be together? I know we will.'

'Vella, I'm sorry, but I can't see it.'

'Thank you.'

She stands up, clutching her Jaffa Cakes, now dwindling in number.

'Vella, you haven't had your full half-hour, you know?'

Sheila told me that when Maggie is on the till, people have to pay up-front for readings.

'You should get some of your money back.'

Vella isn't even listening; she is leaving the room. I follow her into the shop, but she doesn't look back.

'Thank you. Thank you.'

She lumbers off. My stomach is clenched with nerves. That poor lass. How could she even afford this?

'Maggie, she is mentally ill and drugged up to the eye-balls. I shouldn't have been reading for her.'

'Oh, don't worry, you probably perked her up!'

'I doubt it.'

There's no point arguing. Maggie is a businesswoman in her own topsy-turvy way, and a client is a client. I don't know how Sheila does it. I'm pretty sure that with a cus-tomer like that, you have to put down the cards, find out what they want and try to be understanding as you explain it's not going to happen. Or lie. Tell them what they want to hear. I doubt Vella will remember anything about this reading in a few hours. She may even imagine that I told her 'Yes, yes, he loves you, you'll get married soon.' This kind of stuff scares the hell out of me. This is the second time in a week I've been completely uncomfortable in this shop.

I go and sit back in the reading room. I remember Sheila saying the shop needed to be smudged after the other day's shenanigans. I wonder if she did it? Maybe not. perhaps that's why my first reading was such a disturbed one. I sit, hold my head in my hands and speak to Jemimah.

'I don't like doing readings like this, in a shop. The money would be a great help – it's not like I'm rich. But it doesn't sit well with me. How do I get out of it?'

I don't hear anything for a moment or two, and then comes a calm, androgynous voice, clear and succinct.

'All will be well.'

'All will be well' isn't exactly the same as 'the roof will cave in in five minutes and you'll be able to go home', but it will have to do.

MIDGET ROSE WEST,
PART DEUX

I decide to go to the coffee shop to escape this place. I'll pop to the one across the road, from where I can spy on who's coming in and out of the shop. I'm still freaked out about Dan Beck, but I can't tell Maggie about the murder scenario because her brain will reject it. There is no room for that kind of nonsense in her head. She'll tell me I'm being 'silly and dramatic'. This, ironically, from a woman who claims to be able to converse mentally with her stabled horse from her living room.

I slip out, waving my phone to show her that she can reach me if I'm needed. As I'm crossing the road, I spot a tiny, bespectacled figure coming towards me on the other side of the road. It is miniature Rose West, looking very anxious.

'Excuse me?'

Her voice is extraordinarily timid and accented. I stop walking.

'Is Martin working today?'

'Erm, I'm very sorry, Martin doesn't work at the shop any more.'

Her face caves in at the edges.

'Oh no. That's my fault – oh no. Who's reading instead?'

'It's me, supposedly, but I'm just off for a coffee.'

She bites her lip.

'Could I talk to you, for a minute, while you have your coffee?'

Oh, for fuck's sake. I can't even drink in peace without some Mystery Pot mentalist dogging my steps. She has an interesting accent, though. Very musical.

'Erm, okay. I'm just going in here.'

She follows me and I order my cappuccino. She gets a little bottle of orange juice and we sit at a table a foot or two from the window, with its wonderful view of the shops opposite and the constant, endless traffic.

She doesn't say anything for a minute or two. I'm not sitting having my 'escape' coffee next to a midget-mute, so I clear my throat.

'So, erm . . . ?'

'Nadia.'

'Nadia, I'm Tanz. What did you want to talk about?'

'The other day I had a reading with Martin.'

'I know, I was on the till.'

'Yes. Well, we had a chat. He was very understanding about things . . . I needed to talk.'

'Is that why you extended the reading to an hour?'

'Yes. He was helping me think things through. He is a good man, Martin. Very shy, I think, but kind.'

'When you left, you looked alarmed. I thought Martin had scared you.'

'No! Martin gets it right. I like to get a reading once a month, just to hear what he has to say. He was frustrated with me because I couldn't take his advice, even though he was completely accurate.'

Oops!

'Okay, so now I'm confused.'

'I don't want to ruin your coffee break, but I have to say something in Martin's defence, because my husband is a big bully. And I can't talk to that woman in there – what's her name?'

'Maggie.'

'Yes, her. She's another big bully. I don't like bullies.'

I'm warming to Nadia.

'The thing is, my husband is a very difficult man to live with. He is bossy and controls everything in my life. What I wear, how I have my hair, who I talk to . . .'

I look at her dowdy clothes and nondescript hair. She dresses like a fifty-year-old nun. I'd stab any man repeatedly who even suggested I walk the streets in sensible brown shoes like that. Nadia begins to chew at her thumbnail and sighs.

'He works from home twice a week, but three days a week he has to go into his workplace for four hours. He gives me lists of chores to do, so that I don't go out, but once a month I come and see Martin. My mother pays, because my husband doesn't let me have any money and she thinks it does me good. We moved here when I was a teenager and she thought I had met a good, hard-working man. Now she wants me to leave him. The problem has always been that I don't have a job. I'm not qualified to do anything . . .'

And I'll bet her husband likes Nadia to think she's useless. My blood boils for her. She's probably an A1-quality cleaner, the poor cow, with his lists of bloody chores. Half of North London employs cleaners. Even the women who don't work still employ cleaners – she could make a bomb.

'He only lets me have a front-door key if he needs me to get some groceries, so I have to see Martin on a grocery day.'

She smiles at me conspiratorially.

'Though sometimes I climb out of the kitchen window to visit my mother and climb back in before he gets home.'

Her tinkling laugh is such a surprise. Oh my God. I want to go round there in a mask with a baseball bat. This bloke sounds terrible.

'Anyway, when I came here last grocery day I was only meant to be here a half-hour, but I had a problem. My husband goes out on a Wednesday and Saturday night and leaves me without a key. Says it is business. I was tired of it, so I did something I am not supposed to do and switched on his computer. He thinks I don't know how. But knowledge is power! I learned how to go on the Internet at the library – he allows me to go once a fortnight for new books. I checked his emails. He has a woman. She has a wonderful life. They go to restaurants and the cinema. They are planning to go on holiday soon. He is a bastard!'

That word, out of nowhere, almost has me honking coffee on the table.

'When I first saw this, I was devastated. He had all of

my youth and now . . . this? So I came to Martin. Martin told me I should leave him, and I said I couldn't – I have no life away from him. But then Martin made me stay and talk to him some more. Said I didn't have to pay extra, but I said that wouldn't be fair! So I listened to Martin and he told me about the future I could have. He told me that money was coming shortly and I could change my life. He said I would find out within the next week.

'When I left, I was anxious because I knew I was late. When I got home, my husband was waiting for me. He shouted and screamed, until eventually I told him where I had been and he was very, very angry. He accused me of having an affair. He didn't hit me, because he tried that before and I knocked him on the head with a frying pan. Instead he said I was a slut. I told him that wasn't possible, as Martin is gay, and he got even more angry. He locked me in my room. I heard him on the phone and I know he lied to this Maggie. Everything he said was a lie. He is a coward and now I really want to talk to Martin. Do you have his number?'

'I'm sorry, I don't, but Maggie will. Do you want me to go and get it?'

Nadia looks at her watch. Takes out some paper.

'Please, I have to go now – could you write down your number and I will call you to get Martin's? He was right, you see! My uncle died and he has left me some money.'

I write down my number as she talks. It's phenomenal what goes on in the real world. Much madder than telly.

'I found out yesterday. Enough to rent a small place for a whole year! My husband doesn't know about the money, or that I can use his computer. And now I have a plan! I will phone you from a call box – I have no mobile. I want to thank Martin. I must go. Thank you for this.'

I grab Nadia's hand as she's about to run.

'You are amazing.'

'Thank you. I like your clothes. Soon I will stop dressing like my grandmother!'

And she's off.

It never ceases to amaze me how ridiculously judgemental I am of people I don't know. Midget Rose West just turned into the mighty Boadicea before my eyes. And she has a plan! That glint behind her specs was dangerous. She could take over the world. She is completely right. Knowledge *is* power.

The smell of mozzarella-and-tomato panini is starting to get to me. I order a cheesy treat and sit back at the table. There are magazines to read and I idly pick one up and look at the cover. It shows three 'celebrities' who are a little heavier than usual: 'Girls Celebrate Their Curves'. All of them are shown at unflattering angles, and all of them are supposed to make us think 'Jesus, look how big her arse has got.' We are a world obsessed with the superficial. Not only that, but it is women who are pillorying other women, like this. I'll bet if we all had proper problems, like my new mate Boadicea, then we wouldn't be flapping around calling other people fat bitches and complaining about things that are basically fuck-all in the grand scheme of things.

I've eaten precisely half of my panini while glowering over these nasty magazines, and I have overheard the whole gynaecological history of a woman with endometriosis in a 'private' phone call that is delivered as if through a loud-hailer, when I glance at Mystery Pot across the road and do a double-take. There's a man looking through the window over there. He's in an expensive sweater and slacks, not a suit, but I know his build and his hair. It's Dan Beck. And now he's entering the shop. Never has my appetite abandoned me so suddenly before the end of a meal. Not since I was five and was given tripe and onions. I jump up and my seat scrapes loudly. I grab my bag and jacket. I turn desperately to the waitress and hand her a tenner, even though I only owe her five.

'Keep the change.'

'Thank you!'

My breath is now speeding up. I look at her name-tag: Berta.

'Erm, listen, Berta, I know this sounds weird, but do you have a back exit to this place?'

'Oh yes, but it's not supposed to be for the public.'

I groan inwardly, panic mounting.

'Look, I . . . I saw my ex-boyfriend hanging around outside and I wondered: could you help me escape? Just this once? He can be a bit unpredictable.'

Berta looks at the tenner in her hand, then lowers her voice.

'Go through to the loo and take the door on the left that says "Emergency exit".'

'Thank you so-o-o much.'

I am off like a rocket. Once outside, I take every back-way I can, cutting through side paths and snickets that cars can't use. My phone has rung twice by the time I get to my flat, slam the door behind me and lean against it. I have two messages, both from Maggie, the second one sounding pretty furious. There is a man, it seems, waiting in the shop for a reading. *ARRGGHHH!* I can't believe he came back. Not only that, but Mona's back too. I can hear her crying and begging for help again. Fucking hell!

I try calling Sheila, but I know she has some home-readings today and might be working. She doesn't pick up. With no other choice, I call Maggie back.

'Maggie, it's me.'

'Where are you? A man has asked for you specifically, for a reading. He's having a cup of tea across the road, then coming back.'

The hairs on my arms prickle. Dan would have walked in on me if I'd stayed at the coffee shop.

'I'm so sorry. I was sick twice after my coffee – I've had to come home. I think I may have caught that bug from Sheila.'

Maggie's voice noticeably rises in pitch.

'You were fine this morning!'

'No, I wasn't, I was out of sorts this morning.'

'Well, you could have rung me instead of sloping off.'

'I'm so sorry, Maggie, but I think I'm going to be sick again . . .'

'Well, just so you know, he's asked for your number, but he's not getting it. If he met you here, you do the reading here – you're not poaching customers from my shop.'

'Oh my God, don't give him my number. Don't give anyone my number. I don't do readings from home.'

'Well . . . good. And I shall hope you're over this silly business asap. You're back in the day after tomorrow.'

'I know, I know. And I'm really sorry. Please don't hand my personal details to anyone.'

'I *won't*.'

The receiver goes down. Now I think I actually am going to be sick. This is too much.

I'm tempted to drive round to Sheila's and bang on her door, I'm so shaken up. I try Pat's number. Male protection is always nice when you're feeling threatened by a bloke. But he's not picking up, either. So I call Milo.

'You're making a habit of this.'

'Sorry, Milo, have I called too early again?'

'Why are you hyperventilating?'

'I'm not, I'm . . . well, actually I am. I just ran back from the shop – that bloke Dan turned up there, wanted me to do him a reading.'

'Dan who's Deputy Dawg? *The murderer?*'

Milo's voice has climbed several octaves.

'Yes, well, suspected murderer. It's not proven yet, is it? Anyway, don't worry, he didn't see me and he doesn't know where I live.'

'How do you know? He might be torturing your boss as we speak.'

'No. He's having a cup of tea at Dino's.'

'Oh. Well, I'd lock your doors anyway. Do you have lots of tins of beans and plenty of vodka? Stay in for the next four weeks. Resign from work and don't go out. Or come home. That's it – come back here right now. I just got the box-set of *Horrible Histories*. We can stay in together and sing folk songs to keep our spirits up!'

'Stop it, will you? This is serious.'

'I bloody know it is – I am serious. Why don't you call the police?'

'And say what? Any way you look at it, Dan showed up at the shop to buy a reading, which is what we sell there. He didn't do anything bad, and screaming ghosts calling him a murderer probably won't wash with policemen. By the way, I can hear her again: Mona. She defo follows him wherever he goes.'

'Tanz, this is *so* scary. What are you going to do?'

'I'm going to have to try to find her, Milo. If Mona's body's found, Dan will have bigger things on his mind than getting tarot readings from a mental Geordie.'

'*God*! Please be careful. Will you call me later? Take a weapon with you.'

'Eh? What weapon? Do you think I have an arsenal in my spare room?'

'A penknife will do. Come on, all Northerners have penknives.'

'Actually I do have a tiny Swiss Army knife. It's really pretty, with flowers on the handle. It has a nail file and a bottle-opener. It was one of my mam's bizarre stocking fillers a few Christmases ago.'

'Your mam is nuts.'

'Leave her alone. She was only trying to be original. Oh, wait, Milo. Sheila's ringing, I need to cut you off. I'll speak to you later.'

'Tanz, please be careful. You're like Jessica Fletcher and

that kid out of *The Sixth Sense* all rolled into one. You're my little Dan Aykroyd.'

'Thank you, Milo. Bye, bye-byeeeee . . . Sheila?'

'Hiya, love? You okay? Mona's shouting in my ear again. I was just cleaning the bathroom.'

'You can hear her too?'

'Yup. Started up half an hour ago. Are you okay?'

'Dan Beck showed up today, looking for me at the shop, and I took off like Usain Bolt. I think I broke three world records getting home.'

She whistles.

'He's keen. I didn't think he'd show his face again.'

'Have you got phone readings today?'

'I've done 'em. One at nine, one at nine-forty-five.'

'You fancy a drive?'

'You mean, to look for Mona?'

Sheila is uncharacteristically quiet for a bit.

'I'm not sure, Tanz. I just wish we could read for ourselves as well as for other people. I've got a bad feeling . . .'

That's not good.

'Okay. Well, I'm going to take a drive and I'll let you know what I find. I probably won't even get out of the car – I'm too much of a scaredy-cat – but I do feel like I'm being pushed to hurry up and sort this.'

There is another pause.

'Oh, sod it then. I'm in. Come and get me.'

I'm not going to lie. I'm pleased she's coming. We're a good team. Truth is, I want this all over with. And if this is one big flippin' delusion, then I can stamp it out and get on with my life.

WELL, THAT WAS A CLEVER IDEA, WASN'T IT?

I pick up an apprehensive middle-aged medium in a purple crushed-velvet jacket that I covet enormously, just after 1 p.m. Sheila clambers into the front seat and her eyes are so wide I almost change my mind. If she's nervous, then we have something to be nervous about. But she also seems as determined now as I am to see this through.

'She said St Albans, didn't she, love?'

'Yeah, baybee. Let's hit the M1.'

I slip on some calm music; heavy rock is not right today.

When we eventually reach the motorway, after a typical blip on the A406, we both fall silent. We need to tune into Mona. As we pass junction 5A, Sheila turns to me.

'We're coming off at the next one, aren't we, love?'

My heart is beating faster.

'Yup.'

We do exactly that and drive towards St Albans. The countryside is very lovely and the skies are a warm blue with soft cloud. In the distance there's a bank of grey coming though, and I wonder how long it will be before it rains. This lovely weather is not making me feel any less odd. Something is going to happen. Really, I know it. I don't know whether to ask for help from Jemimah or Frank. Frank pops into my head immediately.

'There's going to be a sign soon. You'll see it and know. So will Sheila. Follow it until you find the next right turn.'

I don't say anything to Sheila. Then we come to a sign for Mersham and Bancroft.

Her head whips round.

'Mersham? What do you think? Mersham?'

'Yup. definitely. The M hit me in the face like a shovel. Oops, sorry, no pun intended.'

She chortles, uncomfortably.

'You are *terrible.*'

We take the turn. The road is narrow and rendered into a tunnel by trees. Quite fitting, really. A scary tunnel leading to somewhere unknown.

We drive about two miles, then comes another sign for Mersham. We turn right. What now?

As we reach Mersham village I slow down. We pass cottages, then a school. All very picturesque. We're about to leave the village completely when a large pub looms into view: The Bluebell. Its brickwork has been painted white, the name is in bold black lettering and there's a large pub sign with bluebells on it. My heart does the fluttery thing it always does when I'm excited or nervous – the one that makes me think I'm having a heart attack.

'Fuck a duck!'

'What, love?'

'The Bluebell! We have to stop.'

We pull into the pub's car park. The lovely day contrasts completely with the pressure in my temples, the kind of tension I feel when a storm is brewing.

'My mam. She mentioned bluebells in her dream. It can't be a coincidence. Anyway, I can feel it – can't you?'

'I feel dreadful, Tanz. I'm scared. Feel that . . .'

She puts her hand on top of mine. It's cold and slightly clammy, which freaks me out because the car is warm. Sheila is not given to histrionics, as far as I know, so this winds me up more than the distant screaming that has flared up like tiny tinnitus.

'Mate, we need a drink.'

She concurs by grabbing her bag and reaching for the door handle.

The pub is enormous. It has swirly brown carpets, 'original' beams and three different areas. A snug with an open fire (unlit), a large bar area with a little stage and a great big restaurant area. We go to a bit of the snug overlooking the pub gardens. There's a huge expanse of lawn, and at the end is a tall wooden fence with trees behind it. That is where my eye is constantly drawn, as the bar girl places down two glasses of wine and a menu.

'Just in case you fancy a spot of lunch, ladies.'

She's in her late thirties with a bossy air of confidence. Her hair and make-up are perfect and she has a perm with red highlights. I could as much eat as juggle Fiat Puntos at the moment, but the drink is extremely welcome. I point down the garden.

'I love the greenery.'

'Oh, thank you. We host events, if you're ever interested? Weddings, birthdays . . .'

'I'll bet they're great. It's so tranquil here. What about
the end of the garden, what's down there?'

'Oh, that's our famous Bluebell Wood. That's why we're
called The Bluebell. This place was called The Woodsman
until we took over, but I think The Bluebell is prettier,
don't you?'

'Much prettier.'

Satisfied with this, she wanders off to another table
where two wiry old ladies are just finishing up their lasagne
and salad, which, to be fair, looks like a nice portion.

Sheila is staring out of the window.

'She's down there, isn't she?'

That fluttering in my heart again. Distant sobs in my
head. Dread and excitement combined. Does it make me a
pervert that I'm excited as well as terrified by all of this? We
could actually help to solve a murder – one that, so far, nobody seems to know about. It's very cold wine. I approve;
wine is never chilled enough in pubs.

'Yup. But now that we're here, I'm wondering about
going in. I mean, chasing a moody spook around a bungalow is one thing, but looking for a burial site? Plus, we
haven't brought a spade, and we can't go around digging up
the woods willy-nilly anyway. On top of which, are you
prepared to see a decomposed body? Worse, are you prepared to find out that this is all bullshit and we're a pair of
fantasists?'

'Tanz, stop talking so fast, you'll be sick . . .'

Sheila picks up her bag and pulls out a garden trowel.

I'm so shocked that I inhale my wine and my laughter is peppered with throaty coughs, like an injured seal.

'Stop laughing! You can't come to a burial site and not bring a trowel. There might be evidence – a ring, or something. I'm not proposing digging up a whole decomposing body with this, you nit. We could destroy evidence doing that; we're not in *Silent* bloody *Witness.*'

Sheila is so cool. She has no doubt that Mona is real and that she's buried nearby. That is the confidence I haven't quite developed yet. Now I'm beginning to understand that I need to believe wholeheartedly in what we're doing. Healthy doubt is always good, but not being a total doubting Thomasina, like me. Part of me really wishes we'd called the police by now. *But what if we're wrong?*

We look at each other. Next move: drink off our wine and visit the loo. It's business time.

DARKNESS DESCENDS

The strip of pavement at the side of the country lane that passes for the main road through Mersham is rather thin. I don't like those little pavements. Even when the sign says 30 mph, in my experience country people drive like they're steering Learjets. They seem to have cars that don't go slower than 70 mph. They are basically mad. That's why I don't live in the countryside – it sends people bonkers.

Just down from the pub, twenty feet after the end of the garden, we come across a small lay-by with a wooden turnstile that leads into Bluebell Wood.

'Are we really going to do this, Sheils?'

'Look, if we don't, we are not going to shake off Mona. This way we can at least show her we're trying to get to the bottom of this. If we don't find anything, we don't find anything. That's that.'

I look at my phone. Virtually no reception. I reckon once we get under the trees there'll be none at all. That's

B-movie stuff. Why don't they build better phone masts around here, the total Neanderthals?

Sheila uses the turnstile first, the damp wood offering a little resistance before it gives and allows her to pass. The accompanying creak would make Vincent Price proud – if he wasn't dead. I am not liking the feeling that I'm currently the star of my own shit film.

She stands a few feet along the path, where the canopy of trees has already made it darker and cooler. For all her conviction, there's a sheen of sweat on her top lip. She is obviously edgy and, as I step up to join her, the trepidation is hanging heavily on me too. I've tried to speak to Frank a few times since we got to the pub and he's not been more forthcoming than *'Be careful'*. I don't like him saying that; he should know that I'm going to be fine, surely? I link arms with my spooked mate as we begin to tread the foot-worn path.

'Help me, please . . . Oh God, oh God – why? Please, help me-e-e, someone . . .'

I can't see the sky now, only branches and leaves. I imagine the night it happened: Mona being lugged into these woods like a sausage roll in a blood-stained carpet. I know it wasn't just one person carrying that roll. I can hear the breathing, the footfalls. There were two of them, in the dark.

Sheila grips my arm harder.

Suddenly I can hear Jemimah, as calm and steady as always.

'It's to the left. Look for the hollowed-out trunk.'

'Sheila, I think it's through there . . .'

To the left there is a very faint, less-trodden path that seems to lead to nowhere but a thick bank of bushes and trees. Sheila takes a deep breath.

'I can see her, love. Mona. Her face is . . . Never mind. She is beckoning to us from that tree over there.'

Ooh! Now I feel faint. As I've said, the whole 'seeing ghosts' thing is terrifying to me. Hearing them is not the same. I look towards the tree that Sheila's pointing at, then approach it. It's actually an optical illusion that the bushes and trees are impassable. Once you reach them, there's quite a gap between the first tree and the one behind it.

I slip through and am surprised to find another little path. Sheila steps in behind me. I don't want to move. I can see a bit of sky and it's greyer than it was. I pull my jacket around me. I am now wishing I hadn't come here. Mona's crying has become a keening wail and I am overcome by the worst, most all-consuming sadness I've ever experienced. It is crushing. She is nearby, I know it, and my legs don't want to take me there. Sheila holds my arm again and gives me a firm little tug.

'We've come this far. Let's take a peek.'

There's a clearing just through the trees ahead. I hold my breath, count to five, then walk towards it. In a very few steps we are past the oaks and willows, and there it is: a patch of bracken and earth. The clearing's not that big, fifteen feet across maybe. It's dominated by a large, hollowed-out tree trunk lying on its side and has a small patch of bluebells growing on the periphery. I am no gardener, but even I know bluebells are spring flowers. There shouldn't be bluebells growing wild in June. And yet here they are. That freaks me out as much as the hollowed-out trunk that Jemimah told me to look for, and which my little mam saw in her dream.

The feeling here is horrendous.

Sheila has walked over to the trunk. All at once she squats down and starts pushing at it. What the bloody hell is she doing? Her shove rocks it. She motions me to join her. She whispers, even though there's no one else around.

'Look over there. That shape in the ground. It's faint, but it looks pretty much the size of this trunk. I think this has been moved. I think it was embedded over there and then a while ago someone moved it a couple of feet.'

'Kids?'

'Maybe.'

Neither of us is convinced. There's no litter or sign of human visitation and, apart from distant bird-song, this clearing is eerily quiet. All at once I'm dizzy.

'Here! Here! I'm here, all on my own.'

I hear Mona. I fall to the ground again, by the trunk. Sheila joins me.

'We have to move this.'

We both put our palms flat on the trunk and give it another shove. It moves without much complaint, once I put my shoulder into it, uncovering a mass of fleeing wood-lice, shrinking worms and agitated grubs, unappreciative of their sudden exposure to the air and light. Then Sheila takes the trowel from her bag. I'm not laughing now. My heart is hammering. There is a pulsating, throbbing black hole in the middle of my forehead, and my chest is constricted by the pressure of being in this place.

Sheila has arthritis in her hand. I hold out mine.

'Here. I'll do it.'

I dig a few inches down. It's loose-ish soil.

'How far should I dig?'

'I don't know, love. Mona's here, pointing a few inches to your right.'

So I dig where I'm told. The smell of damp soil reminds me of being a child in Saltwell Park, when they'd dig up the large flowerbeds and overturn the soil, ready for the new spring planting. About a foot down, I think: *Maybe I should stop now.* A fresh pressure on my forehead tells me I shouldn't. I take another large scoopful out and dig the trowel in again. I come against resistance. My heart stops hammering and skips.

'Sheils, there's something there.'

I put down the trowel and we pull more soil back with our hands. Carefully. It could be anything.

Then . . . there. Right in front of our eyes – in front of my sceptical, scathing, sarcastic subconscious – is the thing I never truly expected to find.

There, becoming more and more uncovered as we clear away dirt with our hands and that tiny little spade, is the corner and side of a rolled-up carpet.

Fuck!

It's all I can do not to burst into tears. The emotion (and fright) could be mine or it might be Mona's, but it's probably both. Sheila is suddenly a whiteish-green colour and I hope she's not about to puke; another two trowelfuls and the smell is already bad enough. We don't need to dig any more, or attempt to look inside the carpet, as that stench tells us everything we need to know. There's only one thing it can be. I step away from the hole. Sheila does the same.

We stand there quietly for a bit.

'Mona, you did very well. Now we know, love.'

Sheila takes my hand and instinctively we both close our eyes. We each attempt a prayer. Sheila starts.

'Mona, I hope, now that we have found you, you can find peace and remember the beauty in your life, and not just the horrible ending.'

'Mona, I'm sorry you suffered so badly, lass, but now I hope you can be the special person that you are, and not dwell on the hurt others caused you. Safe journey.'

This is really emotional – it feels like a ghost-bust. I reckon Mona was released as soon as we found the edge of that carpet, though, because the weeping in my head has stopped.

We both check our phones. No signal on either. My teeth are chattering.

'Do we need to do anything else, Sheils?'

'No. That's enough. We can perform a little ceremony for her after she's been given a proper burial, if you fancy? Right now I'd like to get back to your car and call the police. I don't like this at all.'

No. The feeling of peace that descends after a spirit has been 'helped' is being superseded by the unease at being in this place, on our own, with phones that don't work.

I let Sheila walk ahead, as she's slower than me and I don't want her to feel left behind. In reality I want to leg it out of here, and all the way down the M1 back to London without stopping.

I'm wondering how the hell we'll explain this to the police when a hand, followed by a whole body – like a cheesy trailer for a slasher movie – shoots out from behind the tree ahead. My emotions are already heightened because of what we just found, but suddenly seeing Dan Beck in his casual jumper and slacks, grabbing Sheila by the hair, is enough for me to disbelieve my own lying eyes while simultaneously spasming like I've stuck my hand in a live electrical socket.

And worse than him grabbing Sheila is the fact that his other arm, currently around her neck, has a sharp-looking blade in its hand. And when Sheila tries to struggle, the knife is brought quickly to her under-chin and draws blood. She goes as still as a statue and Dan looks straight at me.

'I'd stay still and be quiet, if I were you.'

That accent. Like being threatened murderously by one of the Wurzels. I look at the cut on Sheila's neck and I want to chop his liver out. *Fucking coward!*

THE HOUSE
OF DEATH

Before being in that situation where a crazy person might murder you in cold blood at any given moment, you think you'll do certain things to save your own life. You think you'll fight and scream, and kick and tear. You think you'll use your ingenuity and your wiles – you won't be a victim – and you'll *definitely* fling yourself out of a moving car rather than risk murder or rape, or both.

But when a weirdo man puts his knife against my friend's throat, most of my options are completely buggered; especially when Dan bundles us into the back of his blacked-out 4x4 and ties us together with a skipping rope from the boot. He could slit either or both of us from ear to ear in a few seconds, the mad twat. Plus, Sheila is too old to be jumping out of moving vehicles and, seeing as she's tied to me, if I jump, she jumps. So I'm staying put. Because I can't let Sheila be harmed today – not a flippin' chance. It's my fault she's here and I'm getting her home safely, and that's that.

Dan only speaks once and it's to me, just before he pulls the car out of the wood that he recently dragged us from.

'That cut on her neck was a small warning. If I'd meant to cut her properly, she'd be dead. So keep quiet, both of you.'

I look at the back of Dan's neck and wish I could give him a Vulcan death-grip or kick it, so that I damage his spinal cord and cripple him. That's how pissed off I am. And that's the problem with films and TV: they make us think we're all Hong Kong Phooey. In my head, I cry out to Frank.

'Frank, what the *fuck* do I do now?'

'Keep calm.'

'Is that it? Thanks for nothing, mate.'

We've only driven about four minutes when we reach security gates and find ourselves on the gravel frontage of what is presumably Dan's home. And with iron gates closing behind us, I have no idea what will happen next. It's the most bizarrely menacing predicament to be in.

He stops and exits the car. As he walks round to let us out, Sheila whispers to me that we're protected.

A tear rolls down her face. She's obviously not feeling *that* protected.

'I'm sorry, Sheila, for getting you into this—'

Just then Dan's hand shoots in and drags us out into the daylight.

'No conferring!'

He laughs that hyena-laugh that gets right on my fucking nerve endings.

He bundles us clumsily through his front door into his hallway. This house has high, beamed ceilings. Mona's dream home, the one she helped to build. The wife he killed. *Dan*. The man we're now trapped with . . . This line of thought is not helpful. He bolts the front door, then unties us and leads Sheila to another door. It is a big coat cupboard. It contains various bits and bobs, including a small wood-and-leather stool shoved in the corner, with a Barbour coat hanging down behind it. He pushes Sheila onto the stool.

'Sit down and behave yourself, and life will be very easy for you. Make a fuss and you'll have more than a little shaver's cut to contend with. Okay?'

Cool as a cucumber, he brandishes the knife again. Her eyes lock on mine. If Sheila can be that centred, then so can I. He closes the posh stripped-wood door on her and puts down the wooden latch. There's a lot of wood in here; it looks like they built a house from scratch and filled it with old, reclaimed stuff. Right now it's difficult to appreciate its beauty, terrified as I am, but I can feel there was love in these walls, and I draw whatever strength I can from that as Dan takes me by the elbow and leads me to another room.

It's a television room, with large comfy-looking (and expensive) sofas. The curtains are open, letting in huge amounts of light; the window looks out over fields and a rose garden, with what looks like a stable to the side. There is a table in the corner with four chairs, which I imagine to be the dine-while-you-watch-TV part of the room.

On the dark-wood coffee table in front of a sofa seem to be the remnants of last night's dinner – an Indian takeaway, by the smell of it. And several empty cans. Carmen must be away, as there's only one plate, and I cannot for the life of me imagine a money-hound like Carmen drinking cans of lager. Dan puts his arm around me and I try not to stiffen as he leads me to the table and sits me on one of the chairs.

'Do I need to tie you up or are you going to be a good girl? Maybe you like being tied up? Yee-ha-ha.'

Keep laughing, mate. Until I'm angry enough to smash a chair over your head.

'No. I don't like being tied up.'

'Shame! Well, I'll let you off for now. But one false move and I'll gut your mate like a rabbit.'

To illustrate his 'point' Dan brings his face to the same level as mine and waggles the glinty knife. If he tries to kiss me, I will vomit. But he doesn't. He just sniffs my hair like he's trying to work out what shampoo I use, an action that freezes my blood, then sits down and stares at me.

'How did you find out about Bluebell Wood? Did Carmen tell your friend out there?'

What do I say? What? I want to tell the truth, but how do you judge how to play it with someone like this? His hangdog eyes are pools of blankness. How do I work with that? But Frank is here. To my relief, I hear him, bold as brass.

'Be exactly like Jemimah. The truth – the literal truth. He'll feel it.'

This is a film. This is a movie, and I'm playing a massive blue androgynous being called Jemimah. A blue being that has suddenly acquired a Geordie accent. I assume an absolute calm that I don't feel.

'You know she didn't.'

Dan flinches slightly.

'I didn't think she would. Good at keeping secrets,

Carmen. Anyway, if she had, you'd have called the police, wouldn't you?'

'Maybe. People who come for readings can be complete nutters, so she might have been lying.'

This catches him off-guard and he laughs that high, inappropriate laugh.

'I bet you get some nutters! I expected everyone at that ridiculous shop to be a nutter, but I was pleasantly surprised . . . When your mate couldn't tell Carmen anything, there was no charge. Instead of making something up, she sent her away with her money in her hand. Why would a faker do that?'

'Sheila is an amazing woman.'

'She's not the only one. You looked into my soul.'

I swallow hard. The words of a true mentalist. *How am I supposed to respond to that?*

'You met my eye in that shop and, for a second there, I felt something I'd not felt in a while. I was scared.'

Talk about irony.

'That's a surprise,' I say.

'Oh?'

'I'm not usually classed as scary.'

'You know things. Like my mother did. It was as if my mother was looking straight through me. My mother wouldn't be very pleased with me at the minute, I'm afraid.'

He rubs a hand over his perma-tanned face. If his eyes weren't so weird, Dan would be a handsome bloke. I'm sure Carmen and her ilk think he's gorgeous – this silver fox with pots of money.

'Tell me what's wrong,' I continue.

He looks so troubled, it simply slips out. I mean, Jemimah would ask, wouldn't she? Anyway I'm improvising.

'You see, that's what my mother would do. She's dead now, but she would care about the other person. You ladies are up the creek without a paddle and you're asking what's wrong with me? Will you just tell me, be honest: how did you find that place in the woods? I need to know.'

'You might get mad at my reply.'

'I won't. I asked you.'

That is so easy for him to say, while he brandishes a cutlass at me. Actually it's nowhere near the size of a cutlass. But it's just as sharp-looking.

'Your wife, Mona, told us where she was buried. She was very upset.'

Dan blinks at me, then looks away. He believes; I see it plainly in those unguarded few seconds. This man has more complications than a quantum Rubik's Cube.

'What do you mean? My wife's not buried. How could she tell you she was upset if she was buried? She'd be dead. That makes no sense.'

I feel sick again. This honesty lark is a risky business.

'Mona was screaming in my head. Screaming and crying, when you and your second wife came into the shop.'

He lowers his head.

'Screaming, you say?'

Dan places his hands on the table, as though to compare finger sizes, then pulls himself together.

'Carmen is *not* my second wife.'

His lips tighten at the corners. He gets up from the table,

goes to a drawer and returns with a photograph in a frame. He shows it to me.

'*This* is my one-and-only wife.'

I bite my lip, so as not to gasp. That's Mona. But not screaming, and not in shadow. The two of them have their heads together in the picture, and her eyes sparkle with life. She has expensive, shiny hair, much like Carmen's, but her face is softer, older; she probably wasn't as toned and up-tight as Carmen, and she certainly looks prettier. And Dan? His smile seems real and happy. But then he's a freak, so God knows what he was thinking, even then.

He stands the frame up on the table where we can see it.

'A year ago, on holiday. Then Mona suddenly disap-peared last November. It was a terrible time. She found out I was having a stupid bloody affair and she went. Took a lot of money out of our account. Took some more in France. Sent me a postcard in January – haven't heard a word since.'

I have no idea what to say next. Because that is a crock of poop, and he knows it.

'What I want to know, Tanz, is what you found down that hole you were digging?'

'Nothing. Some old carpet.'

My eyes well up without warning. *Damn them.* I can't help it; that poor woman down a bloody hole.

Dan reaches into his pocket and produces a packet of paper tissues and offers me one. He then pats my hand.

'You are a very caring girl. Look at you. I don't function well around cold people.'

What's he talking about now?

264

'My wife disappearing wasn't good for me. Not good at all.'

I'm not sure what to do now. Humour him for a minute?

'So you were having an affair . . . with Carmen? And your wife found out?'

'She did.'

'And she just upped and disappeared?'

He covers his face with his hands.

'We used to walk in the woods. She said it was like fairyland. I don't believe in bloody fairies, but it made Mona happy. She found that little place where you were today. Took me to have a look. Put a rug down and we had some of her home-made bread with cheese and a bottle of Château Margaux.'

'She made bread?'

'Of course. And she could bake a good cake.'

'Could?'

'Before she left.'

I don't want to push this.

'So . . . why have you brought us here, to your house?'

His eyes are confused. Probably deciding on his next lie.

'What were you digging for? In Mona's special place?'

'She . . . appeared to me and Sheila. That's why Sheila couldn't read for Carmen. She kept seeing Mona.'

Dan shakes his head like there's a bee between his ears.

'Carmen and her ideas . . . You'd think a cold-hearted cow like her wouldn't be superstitious, but there you go. She wanted to hear that our new business was going to make millions – building houses just like this one. Her bloody mate suggested Sheila. Made me drive all the way with her, like her bloody chauffeur.'

'How come you moved Carmen in, if you don't really like her?'

He gives a laugh with no mirth.

'If you lose your wife over another woman, then you've got to try, haven't you? Or it was all for nothing.'

I can feel Jemimah at my shoulder. Fuck it, I'm going to go for gold.

'Mona said you wrapped her in a carpet and buried her. Did you know she was still alive when you put her in the ground?'

Dan is up and out of that seat like greased lightning. It scrapes noisily over the floorboards as he jumps back, brandishing his knife and breathing heavily. I push my seat back and jump up, ready to run, but he doesn't come closer, just starts screaming.

'Don't you dare! Don't you fucking *dare* say that! I'll slit your fucking throat for you. What kind of monster do you think I am? I wouldn't do that to Mona!'

He bursts into tears, but keeps waving that bloody knife.

'I didn't say you did it on purpose.'

He takes a step towards me and, as he does so, the most extraordinary thing happens – the photograph of him and Mona, with its heavy gilt frame and glass cover, flies off the table and lands on the wooden floor with a crash.

I've never seen anything like it. Evidently neither has Dan, as he lets out a loud shriek and jumps back several feet, looking at me, then wildly around the room.

'What the—'

After the initial shock, I want to laugh. That is the first time I've seen an object fly across the room like that. It has to be Mona. I shout encouragement in my head. *'Woohoo. Go, girl!'*

She must be one powerful bird, now that she's been released, to move that frame like that. Dan's Deputy Dawg eyes are now bigger than the rest of his face.

'Mona? *Mona?*'

I relax totally. A warm energy rushes through my body. I speak, and it's not me.

'I knew about the women, Dan-dan. I knew about them all. I forgave – I forgave you all of them. You could have left Carmen, and I would have forgiven . . . You could have left me, I would have forgiven . . .'

'Oh my God. Mona, is that Mona? Or are you just messing with me?'

The hand with the knife is shaking now. I keep talking. It's my voice, but not my speech patterns. I am intrigued.

'I loved you, Dan-dan, and I would have done anything for you. Why would you hurt me? I would not have made things hard for you. You know it.'

Now he's sobbing and holding out his hand in supplication.

'Mona, I got bored, that's all, but I didn't want to leave you. She was a dirty, dirty witch. Carmen put a spell on me. She tricked me. She got me addicted to her, then she said you'd make things hard and take all the money. She said she and I were soulmates and we couldn't be together with you about. She fucking messed with my head. She nagged and nagged and nagged, then one night I couldn't take it any more. I brought her here, and we did it. I knew it was a mistake when she was bashing your head over and over again; I knew it was wrong when we were burying you. I knew I'd done something terrible. And I missed you so much. For Carmen, it was all about money and going out, and holidays. I only wanted you and the horses, and dinner in front of the telly again . . . Why do you think I've been visiting the woods every single day?'

'You are not a good man. I always thought you were in pain and I could help you. But you were simply spoilt and arrogant, and now you've spread your badness again. You're doing it now. It has to stop. You have to make it right! Make everything right, Dan-dan, or you will have to deal with me. Do you hear me? *Make it right!*'

Suddenly the telly turns itself on. Dan's head whips round. It's some kind of afternoon drama: a young couple arguing. Then the radio comes on: 'Wake Me Up Before You Go-Go' by Wham! at full volume. I'm as impressed as I've ever been. Dan is screaming like a woman. The *pièce de résistance* is when a giant portrait of a horse – probably Mona's horse – mounted over the mantelpiece, falls with a dramatic crash to the floor. To my absolute astonishment, Dan takes a huge breath in, as if to scream, then promptly *faints*. He goes down like a sack of shit.

Without a second thought, I've vaulted him and I'm in the hallway. I grapple with the latch to the door, which Sheila is now banging frantically, and grab her arm as she tries to query the racket that she heard coming from the living room. As we reach the front door, I see a button panel.

'The red one and the keys.'

Thank goodness for Frank. The red button has 'Gate' printed on it. I press it and scoop up the keys that I saw Dan throw into a wooden bowl as we came in.

As we both run out, I am scared to look back, in case he's chasing us. I unlock the car doors and scramble into the driver's seat. Sheila opens the passenger door, but the shock of what's happened makes her clumsy as she tries to get in, so I reach over and yank her as hard as I can.

'Owww!'

'Sorry, Sheila.'

'Just *drive*!'

The car starts very quickly, but the first time I try to move it I spin the wheels. I pull the seat forward and check the rear-view mirror; suddenly there is Dan, emerging through the front door. I yelp when I see him, causing Sheila to swivel round in her seat and wail like a banshee. Without further ado, I find that bite point and roar off, straight through the electronic gates, as Dan begins to run down the drive after us. I have never stolen a car before. I have never been held at knife-point before. And I have never seen a spook give such a demonstration of power before. *What a day.* I don't want two of these things ever to happen again. But what a day!

My biggest thought, as I bomb down the lane like a 4x4 InterCity 125, is that Dan looked so scared. I don't think he was chasing after us to kill us; I think he was trying to come with us.

THERE'S A *WHAT*
BURIED IN THE WOODS?

It's strange how fate works. Sitting back in my flat at 2 a.m. with a giant mug of camomile tea and Milo at my side, curled up on the sofa like a three-year-old, I can't help musing on the absolute fluke that saw me speeding off down the road in Dan's big car and, while Sheila fought an impossible battle to call 999 on my phone, as she'd lost hers, the boys in blue emerged anyway from a leafy little parking spot and flagged us down, lights flashing, for doing 58 mph in a 40 mph zone.

When I say 'boys in blue', I actually mean *boy* in blue. PC Markus. Later, just Neil. Lovely, smiley, out-of-his-depth Neil. The poor lad probably thought he'd caught a middle-class boy racer getting a bit overenthusiastic in the country lane. Wrong!

His first surprise was us two, spilling out of the 4x4, hyperventilating and speaking in tongues, pushing our way into the back of his vehicle, basically begging him to take us to a police station. His next one, before he could even issue a ticket, was realizing that we were claiming we'd been kidnapped and held at knife-point. Biggest surprise of all was when he caught the tail end of what Sheila was bellowing at him as I tried to apologize for being in a stolen vehicle.

'I'm sorry, madam, could you repeat that? There's a *what* buried in the woods?'

It was Neil's second week as a traffic cop and suddenly he was looking at kidnap and murder on his patch. He seemed doubtful, to say the least. We weren't greatly concerned with his mistrust of our credibility at that moment, though; we just wanted to get to a police station and hide in it. Dan Beck could be anywhere, and neither of us wanted to meet him again.

PC Markus obliged, and soon we were drinking absolutely appalling coffee and giving our statements to him. It took a long time. Mostly because the statement-giving was peppered with questions like:

'And then you heard a screaming in your head, madam? Are you sure that's what you want to say?'
And:

'Then the TV and radio switched themselves on independently, after the picture flew across the room, you say?'

I was acutely aware of how crazy my story sounded and I kept wondering if Sheila was okay, telling her side of things in another room. I gave them a detailed description of where we had found Mona. I was sure Sheila must be doing the same. Two officers were dispatched to check it out, and another two were sent to call at Dan Beck's house.

All this, Neil told us as he drove me and Sheila back to London, his mate 'Spike' following behind in my car so that I wouldn't have to retrieve it tomorrow. Never have I been more relieved at getting a lift; I was too knackered and overwhelmed to drive my car by that point. Sheila and I held hands all the way. Neil told us plenty of other things after they released us a little after 11.30 p.m. to go home.

Sitting here now, car parked safely outside and doors securely locked, I try to arrange the information I have into bite-sized chunks, so it doesn't overwhelm me. The whole thing is so ugly and sad that I can only cope with it in bits. It seems to run like this:

1. The police originally thought Sheila and I were on drugs when Neil brought us in.

2. Mona was exactly where we said she'd be. The general consensus being that they'd probably find a dead dog, or some other pet, wrapped in that carpet. On the sly, Neil told us that an officer had vomited when they unwrapped her. Murder isn't that common a crime on the borders of St Albans, apparently.

3. While I was sitting on a chair in Dan Beck's TV room, trying to make reasonable conversation with a total psychopath, upstairs in a spare room Carmen was lying dead, and had been for at least twenty-four hours. Neil was not at liberty to say how she died, but the way his boyish, clean-scrubbed face crumpled disgustedly when he spoke of it made me suspect that gutting Sheila 'like a rabbit' was maybe not an idle threat of Dan's, but a modus operandi. This is something that will haunt me for a while.

4. Dan Beck was not in his house when the police found Carmen. They looked everywhere for him. Eventually

some bright spark thought to search the stables at ten o'clock at night and found him in there, hanging from a beam.

5. It turns out we won't be charged for speeding or car theft, as there were too many extenuating circumstances.

6. Without wishing to blow my own trumpet, I think Neil likes me a bit. I have no idea what it is with me and these young lads.

I stroke Milo's floppy fringe. He opens an eye, then sits up. I made him a cup of tea before he nodded off. He reaches for it.

'You all right, Tanz?'

'I am. Thanks to you.'

Inka has wedged herself between us and is lapping up our warmth. Milo yawns loudly and scratches his head.

'I feel like I just lived a day-long episode of *Tales of the Unexpected*.'

He gives my arm a clumsy stroke. He's a bit like my mam when it comes to too much physical contact, but today must have been terrifying for him.

'Milo, I want to thank you again for coming down. How much did the train cost? I'll get the money back to you. I'm worried that I've disturbed your work.'

'Don't be daft. Fuck the money! And I can work here, I can work on the train back home. It's fine.'

I kiss him on the forehead. He strokes my hand. I've obviously given him a fright.

Apparently he tried to call me until teatime, then started freaking out and jumped on a train. On the way to London he had the fabulous sense to think of calling police stations in the St Albans area. There's actually only one, so there weren't many calls to make, and fortunately the desk sergeant, Kenneth, told him I was there 'helping with enquiries'. I don't know if he should have done that, but his honesty meant that Milo elicited from Kenneth the promise of a phone call from me, as soon as it was possible. So *yay* for Kenneth! And yay for ninety-year-old Steve, who took Milo in and regaled him with stories of the war until I got home. I shall get him some whisky.

At this moment I love Milo like the truest brother. I feel blessed and shaken up and grateful and sad, all at once. Everyone should have a mate as good as him.

As for Pat the Cat, I found his phone, out of juice and in my bathroom, when I got home. Crazy life.

LOOK TO
THE SKIES

It's taken me five days before I'm ready to go into Mystery Pot again. It took Sheila no days. That woman is made of reinforced steel. Her only major comment about the whole nightmare was: 'Next time we go looking for a murder victim, I'm taking a gun with me. If I ever meet another Dan Beck in the woods, I'll blow his bloody face off.'

I think she's still mad at him for the indignity of being locked in a cupboard, even though he's dead now.

Neil the policeman called me on day three and asked how I was. Then he swore me to secrecy and said that Dan had left a note that was an admission of guilt and an explanation of how Carmen's mum withdrew funds, pretending to be Mona in France, and sent a forged postcard from abroad. After a few self-pitying sentences about his own awful childhood, Dan suddenly finished with an apology to me and Sheila, and the bequest, to me, of his car. Bloody nutter. Why would I want the car he kidnapped us in? The car that is currently evidence, because there are traces of blood and rug fibres in the boot? I mean, really? Dan wanted me to have his death-car? Bloody men.

Neil asked if I wanted to go for a drink. I said I'd think about it when I was feeling better. Me and a copper – there's a thought.

I saw Milo back onto the train this morning. He's been my total rock since the 'happening', but he doesn't like being out of his routine, and my flat will never be clean enough for him. It made him very twitchy. So I thanked him profusely, told him I needed my space and made him go home. As he boarded, I handed him a giant-size bag of retro sweeties and I swear I saw tears in his eyes. I also hugged him for ages, which he took quite gamely, then waved him off as he tried his best to hide the relief on his face. Milo is not a natural traveller, he likes to be at home, which only makes it even more spectacular that he jumped on the train to London in the first place.

I take a deep breath before I walk into the shop. Maggie has kept my position at the till open. She didn't really have a choice, as no one else seems to want the job. I'm not supposed to be here today, so she's a little confused when I enter.

'Hello, stranger.'

'Hiya, Maggie.'

'How are you feeling?'

This is a rhetorical question, as she doesn't have a lot of truck with human feelings and thinks I should be fine by now, I can tell.

'A bit better actually. Can I have a word, please?'

'Oh. Sounds ominous. What is it?'

'Martin.'

She turns her nose up.

'What about him?'

'He didn't do it. Martin didn't tell that lady she was married to a gay man. Her husband is nuts. She is actually very fond of Martin.'

'Well, that's as may be. But Martin doesn't do enough readings and he doesn't come to work on time.'

'What if he bucked up his ideas?'

'Well, I've sacked him now. And I'm not apologizing.'

'No, but he might apologize to you, if you give him a second chance.'

'Hmm. What about you?'

'What if I get another acting job? You could cover the till, but you can't cover the readings. You need someone more reliable than me . . . Anyway I'm not doing it. You can't make me, and I won't.'

Maggie takes honesty better than I'd expected.

'Well, I'm not talking to Martin, Tanz. If you're ducking out of your post, you can sort it out.'

'Ducking out of my post? I could have been killed the other day.'

'Well, you weren't and neither was Sheila, and she's in that room right now earning her bread and butter with a serial monogamist from Peckham.'

There's a sense of humour buried beneath that Margaret Thatcher exterior, I know it. Sometimes it clambers close to the surface, then it sinks again, into the murky depths. I smile at Maggie, just a little one.

The whole St Albans debacle has threatened to properly

mess me up, it has to be said. I'm going to miss Milo's presence at night more than I will ever let on. The only way to get through it is to climb back on the horse of life. Or, in this case, the Northern Line towards Morden.

The walk from the Tube station is a venture into alien territory. Grey buildings, no greenery, lots of cars. Depression on a stick. I doubt blue skies ever reach here; it was invented for steely-grey vistas. When I reach Martin's flat, it's three floors up and has a balcony that smacks of Mike Leigh films and drug-estate dramas. I have no idea if he'll be in, but I have to try, because I'm not doing this over the phone. The front door is black and the windows are small. There's no door knocker, so I ring the bell, then rap with my knuckles. I wait a good couple of minutes before the door opens.

There stands a tiny, frail woman in a frilly pink blouse and brown trousers. Her slippers are pink-and-beige tartan and her hair is like candy spiderwebs. She's one of the cutest things I've ever seen. When she sees me, she grins and holds out her hand.

'Come in. I'm building my nest! OO-oo, OO-oo . . .'

I have little choice other than to follow this tiny, cooing woman into her humble home. Everything in the living room is in a state of disrepair. The television is so big and square it looks like cavemen made it out of stones and chewed bark. The walls have peeling wallpaper and the carpet has black age-marks on it. It doesn't smell nasty in here, it's just unkempt. And it's too warm.

'Helloooo! Helloooo!'

She seems delighted to have a guest. I'm pretty convinced I'm at the wrong house, but she is so adorable that I sit on her rickety sofa and pat the space beside me. She flies over, flapping her arms, and sits by me. Roosting, so to speak.

'What's your name, sweetheart?'

She stares at me, friendly but confused. I take her hand.

'I'm Tanz.'

'Hello, Tams. I'm DeeDee. OO-oo, OO-oo.'

'Are you a bird, DeeDee?'

She is inordinately pleased at the question and giggles.

'Oh yes. That's me. I'm a birdie. My son won't let me open the windows because he thinks I'll fly away! He's probably right. I want to escape and not be trapped here in these ruins . . .'

Joyous to tearful in five seconds! She just beat my personal best.

I'm guessing Alzheimer's. It's not a particularly intelligent guess. I take her tiny bird-frame into my arms and hug her close. She begins to coo contentedly, her tears melting away. She smells of oldness and sweet, papery skin. She starts to hum a song in a tremulous soprano. Then I hear a key in the lock. Martin enters, with bags like rubbish sacks under his eyes, wearing a more moth-eaten cardigan than usual and carrying a two-litre carton of milk. He stops dead, confronted by the sight of his arch-nemesis cradling what I can only assume is his mother.

'What's going on?'

'I just met DeeDee. She's beautiful.'

She looks up at him and waves.

'Oh, Martin . . . I found a mermaid!'

'I'm sorry to bother you, Martin, but I really need a word.'

'Have you come to evict me from my flat as well as my job?'

DeeDee senses discord immediately and whimpers. I stroke her spiderweb hair and attempt the tune she's been humming. She joins in. I squeeze her bony hand gently. She continues to croon to herself. I follow Martin into his kitchen. There's a Formica table for two with foldaway chairs in there, green-checked lino and the cupboards that my mam and dad had twenty years ago. It's so old-fashioned it's almost cutting-edge. I sit down without being invited.

'I got in a bit of trouble last week,' I say.

'What?'

'I've been off work. It doesn't matter why. But it means I'm doing this now, when I should have done it already.'

'What are you talking about, Tanz?'

'I had coffee with a client of yours. Nadia. A couple of days after Maggie let you go.'

Martin's eyes moisten and the corners of his mouth begin to drag down. It occurs to me that he has been devastated by this job loss. I doubt he had much confidence to start with.

'She said that you are a wonderful reader.'

'Did she?'

'She said her husband lied, to get you sacked. He was jealous.'

'He's such a controlling idiot. I don't know how many times I've told her . . .'

'Well, everything you told her this time was right. She came into some money. She rang from a call box early this morning, sounding very pleased with herself. She poured bleach on every item of his clothing yesterday after he left for work, then climbed out of the kitchen window with her suitcase. She then jumped on a coach with her mum and has moved into a flat next to her cousins in Hove. She says if her husband comes looking for her, they will throw him into the sea!'

Martin can't help a chortle as he switches on the kettle.

'You did that, Martin. Nadia's desperate to thank you. She wondered if she could have your number?'

He looks a tad disappointed.

'So that's why you came?'

'No. That's only part of it. You need to come back to the shop.'

He takes mugs out of the cupboard. They look like heirlooms from the seventies.

'I got sacked, remember? Maggie wouldn't listen.'

The petulant look is back on his face.

'I know you did. But that wasn't solely because of a mad husband complaining, Martin, you must realize that?'

'No, it's because you came and stole my place.'

This gets my back up.

'That is bullshit. I don't want to be a tarot reader in that shop. I got the job to earn a few quid sitting behind the till. That's all.'

'You could have fooled me. Sitting there like Gypsy Rose Lee, getting bunches of flowers and making people weep.'

'I didn't say I couldn't do it. I said I don't *want* to do it for money. I happen to be *extremely* talented!'

My joke is rewarded with a laugh.

'Come on, Martin, the customers scare me. I don't know how you and Sheila do it.'

'Do you want a cup of tea?'

Oh God, if I turn him down he'll be offended.

'Just a little one, please, I already had a coffee.'

'Okay. Has Maggie said she wants me back?'

There's such hope in that voice. He actually looks up to Maggie. Bless him.

'Well, the thing is – she's not *averse* to you coming back. But she feels you've been . . . well, taking the piss a bit. You know, with your erratic business hours.'

'Taking the piss? You've met DeeDee. She's a full-time job.'

'She is so adorable.'

'Not when she's weeing in my yucca plant, she's not.'

This is not said without affection.

On cue, in clacks the woman herself, resplendent in a red kimono and silver high heels. She's put a scarlet cupid's bow on her lips and looks thoroughly proud of her ensemble. I start to laugh and give her a round of applause. She bows down low.

'Mum! What are you wearing? Off out, are we?'

'I decided to dress for tea!'

She's giddy from the attention. She bows again, then takes her tea and carefully carries it out of the room.

'Does she have a carer?'

'Yes, me. Plus, she goes to a place down the road three

days a week. It's got all of these activities – dancing and whatnot for the elderly. She loves it. It starts at ten and finishes at five. The lady next door picks her up for me sometimes and gives her a sandwich. But it's not easy juggling it all.'

'It sounds like having a child.'

'It is like having a child. But a child who used to be my mum.'

Martin looks so wistful suddenly.

'Why didn't you say?'

'It's nobody's business. I don't want sympathy. She's my mum.'

I see him in a slightly different light now.

'Martin, you are going to have to ring up Maggie and say sorry. Sorry that you show up at noon and leave at three.'

'But if I haven't got a reading . . . Sometimes I want a minute to myself when DeeDee goes to her day-centre.'

'I understand. But come to work at ten, say hello, then have your "minute" in a caf by the shop. Just so you look willing. And stop being so bloody miserable with the customers.'

'What? I'm not . . .'

'Nadia says she thinks you're shy, and that's why people take you as being unfriendly.'

'I'm *not* unfriendly.'

'Martin, you look like you're curling your lip all the time.'

'You haven't worked there five minutes – what do you know?'

'You have hardly any bookings. The proof is in the

pudding. I'll bet you could double your clientele if you smiled. You obviously know how to read. Or that's what Nadia says anyway! Why waste it? Call Maggie, make things right and try again.'

He pouts.

'Why are you doing this, Mrs Goody-Two-Shoes?'

'Because life's too short, and I'm trying to be nice. But don't push it.'

DENOUEMENT

The sun is shining as I wander back to the Tube station.

I smile to myself as I recall popping over to Sheila's yesterday evening, intending to knock and see if she was okay, only to notice a familiar-looking young Jamaican man, who recently narrowly escaped a jail sentence for possessing his cousin's gun, walking up her pathway with a bag of groceries. I flattened myself against the hedge and listened to her let him in. The greeting was rather warmer than I'd expected, and now I'm wondering if he's as fired up by witches as Pat is. Even Sheila has her saucy secrets, it seems.

I'm supposed to see Pat later, but he's going away very soon and I've not been myself recently. I think, after persuading Martin to reclaim his rightful place in Mystery Pot and get Maggie off my back, the least I can do is reward myself with a little drink before I catch the Tube. I'm suddenly so tired. I enter a nice, bright cafe-bar on the main high street and sit down, taking out my book. It's something light and fun – I'm avoiding murderers for the time being.

As the waitress approaches, I hear a familiar voice in my head.

'*Good work, Grasshopper.*'

'You're such a wanker, Frank.'

'*You are!*'

The waitress doesn't know why I'm laughing. Neither do I really. When it arrives I hold my chilly glass aloft and offer a silent toast before I drink. To Sheila, to Mona, to Nadia, to Sarah and her budgie, to Ann and her haunted cottage, to little DeeDee. To life.

It tastes delicious.

ACKNOWLEDGEMENTS

I can't tell you how much support I've had from friends and family as I strove to get my books published. Thank you to everyone who has encouraged my work, read my drafts and even donated money when I had a Kickstarter campaign. Thank you to my son who didn't mind when I locked myself away to slave at my laptop. Thank you to Philippa Shallcrass for being my real life Sheila. Thank you Mandasue Heller, my sister witch, for being beyond kind and generous and seeing what even I sometimes couldn't. Thank you to my amazing pals around Muswell Hill and the rest of the country who've kept me going through the hardest times. And last but not least, thank you Wayne Brookes for taking a chance on this spooky Geordie.